mAybE mAby

What Others Are Saying About

maybe maby

"Chaotic and passionate, *Maybe Maby* is an outstanding display of emotions. This book hurt in the best possible way, and I'm not sure I've ever rooted for a character more than Maby. She is such a beautiful soul haunted by her own demons, and watching her overcome them was nothing short of miraculous. And her champion…he is just the perfect kind of swoon. Their moments were hot, intense, and tender, making me fall for the two of them hard and fast. A romance that is so much more—touching…unique…unforgettable— *Maybe Maby* is a phenomenal read you can't miss."
– A.L. Jackson, New York Times Bestselling Author

"I have a new book boyfriend and he resides within the pages of this book. Sharp wit, swoon-worthy romantic gestures and the tackling of difficult, but very real, topics come together beautifully in *Maybe Maby*." – Melissa Brown, author of *Picturing Perfect*

"Quirky, funny, sexy, heartwarming, swoon-worthy perfection. I can think of a million words to describe this book and all of them make me smile. Maby is adorable. Saul makes my insides flutter. Dalton clouded my head. And Coen made me feel … so much. I love this story! I just finished it and I already want to go back and read it again!"
– Claire Contreras, author of *The Darkness Series*, *Catch Me*, and *The Contracts and Deceptions Series*

"*Maybe Maby* is a book I will pick up often, and fall in love with again and again. Well done, Ms. Aster. This is a masterpiece."
– Maggi Myers, *The Final Piece* and *Lily Love*

"Willow Aster knows how to tug at the heart strings. *Maybe Maby* is an adorably witty story that shows you love's strength and its grand vulnerability."
– MJ Abraham, author of *Happenstance* and *Resplendent*

"A brilliantly written romance of a beautifully dysfunctional mind."
– Leslie Fear, author of *Villere House*

"Loved it. It's Willow Aster's best work yet. Maby's pain is raw and real and, at times, hard to read because of how much of her I found in myself. Yet, still there is so much hope to be found in this story and the romance was touching, it was tender but with just the right amount of that urgency you feel when two people have to be together despite their flaws or their own perception of unworthiness. Perfection."
– Rebecca Espinoza, author of *Binds*

"Navigating the labyrinth of Maby's mind was an exercise in self-discovery—not just Maybe discovery. Maybe she's you. Maybe she's your best friend. No matter where you start, *Maybe Maby* will be there to hold you when you come out the other side."
– Andrea Randall, author of *In the Stillness*

"The writing is pure perfection, although that is not surprising since I loved her previous work, but it's this story...this quirky, unusual, totally out-of-the-box story that is holding me captive."
– Natasha is a Book Junkie

"*Maybe Maby* takes you on journey. This is a story about healing, letting the past go, learning to accept yourself, and learning to allow others to love you in return. From the first words in the prologue to the last words written in the epilogue, I loved it. I was in love with each character, the story line, the sexual tension and the perfect way each and every word flowed. There is a connection so strong with these characters you just can't help but feel."
– Jodie from Lustful Literature blog

"Do you ever feel like you can relate to a character a little too well? Maby Armstrong is that character. She's a mess. She embraces that mess. Her story is one that made me cry, it made me laugh (out loud at some points even) and it gave me a feeling of infinite happiness. A book that can pull all of those emotions out of me is definitely a worthy read." – Laura Wilson from Word

"The awesomeness that is Mabel Armstrong will rock your world."
– Randi from Always A Book Lover

maybe, maby

by
Willow Aster

Copyright © 2014 by Willow Aster
Cover Design by Blade
Formatting and interior design by JT Formatting

www.willowaster.com

Printed in the United States of America

First Edition: June 2014
Library of Congress Cataloging-in-Publication Data

Aster, Willow
    Maybe Maby / Willow Aster. – 1st ed
        ISBN-13: 978-1500127183
        ISBN-10-1500127183

1. Maybe Maby—Fiction.   2. Fiction—Coming-of-Age
3. Fiction—Contemporary Romance

To my sweet Mama,
who made a 'touch of OCD' look graceful and beautiful.
You are forever in my heart.

Prologue

I'M HAVING A meltdown. I don't think it is the put-her-in-the-loony-bin kind, but the rock-in-the-corner-so-I-can-breathe kind. Maybe they're one and the same and I really do need to be put away, but I think I just need a little air. I'm bone tired. My eyes look like I haven't slept in weeks. I'm eating my feelings and developing a pudge that isn't gonna go anywhere if I keep binging on chocolate, nachos, and wine.

I'm 28 and everyone has left me. I have no friends. My boyfriend left. My mom died, so technically she left me too. I hate my job. I never have enough money and am sick of trying to scrape by. I've been told I'm attractive, but I probably couldn't prove it now. I'm chalking my looks up to another thing that's gone.

The only way I find any relief is by counting … everything … repeatedly.

In some ways, for someone with the non-hoarder type of OCD like mine, being in a psych ward is probably one of the best places to be. Everything is orderly, stark, and sterilized. But in every other horrific way that greatly outweighs any good, it's the worst.

The constriction feels like a noose around my neck.

The realization that I CANNOT GET OUT OF HERE.

The feeling of constantly being watched.

Knowing that if I have to pull my clothes apart or go wash my hands X amount of times, it will be analyzed to death.

And then there is the fact that I'm surrounded by other people who are either equally or more tormented than me. It's terrifying.

I had a 5-7 day stint in one (I can't remember exactly) and I wish I could say it was enough to cure me for life, but sadly, it wasn't. It just made me look at death with a lot more affection.

For *myself.*

Not for anyone I love.

I can't lose another person I love.

But the thought is so enticing for *me.* I get this overwhelming *oh my God, is this what my life is gonna be?* feeling and I want to die.

Curl up and die.

And since I don't feel my heartbeat fading or my breathing getting even slightly faint, I panic that I'm gonna have to live.

I just don't think I can live like this anymore.

Not Just Blue

I BARELY MAKE it to the subway on an early Monday morning and sit beside a smelly old man. It is the only open seat. I can hold my breath. Maybe I'll die that way. My obituary will read: *She held her breath trying to avoid inhaling body odor.* It doesn't work. I have to keep sneaking quick breaths and the old man asks what my problem is. It kills me when people who haven't bathed in weeks have the audacity to think I'm weird.

I ignore him and when another open seat is available, I hop up and take it. Old smelly man shakes his head at me and I wave. I can be much friendlier from afar. I smooth down my corduroy skirt and try to subtly yank up my tights. It's December in New York and cold.

My stop comes and I rush to get off, along with dozens of other people. I count to 127 as the crowd pushes and nudges and smacks their gum around me. I will never get

1

used to all these people in my space, but the alternative is worse: the thought of driving in the city is terrifying. On the 128th step, I turn to the right and take the 17 steps to my destination. I rub my finger through the ribbing on my skirt with each step. *14, 15, 16, 17.* Unlock the store.

Whatnot Alley is a gifts and furnishings boutique owned by Anna Whitmore. She used to be a friend of mine, but ever since she had a baby—and became the owner of her flourishing shop—she doesn't have time for anything as quaint as friendship. I came to work for her as a favor and have now run the store for 3 years. She comes in at least once a week, and my skin is on edge the entire time. Whenever she engages in conversation, it's to moan about how she never has time for anything. But she would like to have one more child, just one more … as long as it's a boy. She's already run ragged, but let's throw another in the mix for good measure. That's what nannies are for!

I lock the door behind me. We won't be opening for a while yet. Unlock. Lock. Unlock. Lock. Okay, I can move on. Moving to the back of the store, I hang my coat on the hook to my right. My gloves go in my purse, which I lock away in the bottom drawer of my desk. Unlock. Lock. If I'm going to have a good day, it takes 28 steps to do all of the above before I start the coffee. If I'm going to have a bad day, it takes 29. It's a 44 steps kind of day. I have to go back and redo my first steps because it just didn't feel right.

My grandmother, Mabel, who I'm named after, also had OCD. Speaking of leaving, she sure left me behind with a couple of doozies. Between the disorder and the name, I feel like she should have stuck around longer than my 11th birthday to make sure I survived.

Before I do anything else, I put my earphones in and begin playing my ocean sounds mix. Music is too stimulating. I find it hard to concentrate on anything but the music. The crashing waves calm me. It feels nice to know that somewhere it is more tumultuous than in my mind. Once the store opens, I will have to take off my earphones, but when it's just me, I keep everything turned off. When Anna is in the store, she plays Top 40 radio. Some days it's bearable; other days I'm certain I will break every trinket within close range. I usually stay behind the counter on those days, where I can only do damage with the cash register.

I take a sip of the coffee I pour in my smoky blue Zojirushi stainless steel mug, rated highest on Amazon for quality. It doesn't leak, and it keeps the coffee hot for 6 hours. I've tested it and found it to be true. I chose smoky blue because it suits my moods more than the cheerful lilac or the completely soulless black. Smoky blue maintains mystery but still has the touch of melancholy. I wish I were a lilac person, but I'm not.

I made my list for today before I left on Friday and I take a look at it this morning. I can already check off 4 things, so I immediately do. I then add to the list all of the vendors I have to call today and check which shipments might be coming in. I tidy up the throw pillows on the few pieces of furniture we carry and straighten the pictures over and over again. Symmetry is a requirement. Anything else is … evil.

At 8:30, I set my phone alarm to go off at 8:53, so I will have plenty of time to gather my notes for the monthly meeting in the small side room. Anna and a couple of part-time employees come to the meetings before we open. I'm the only full-time employee, so Anna asks that I'm always ready to give input if she needs it.

But at 8:37, I begin to get the unbearable urge to wash my hands. The hand sanitizer behind the front counter doesn't get rid of the dirt. 1, 2, 3, 4 times. I have to wash with water and soap. I take off my headphones and rush to the bathroom, forgetting my phone. I lose track of time in the bathroom washing my hands over and over again. It's getting worse. I'm not sure what to do.

When I finally get back to my desk, I have just a few minutes left. I take a deep breath, pick up my phone, laptop, and coffee mug and make my way to the back. I'll be the first one there. It's hard working with other people who are slow, lazy … normal.

I haven't even started working yet and I'm already exhausted.

Maybe Maby

I GET BACK to the room for the meeting and no one is there.

"Hello? Anyone here?"

No one answers. My phone rings and it's Anna.

"I've changed the meeting to 9:30. Forgot to tell you," she says before I can even say hello.

I frown. "Okay. I will—" and the line goes dead. "Okay," I say to myself.

All of a sudden there's a loud banging above me. I look at the ceiling and my heart starts thumping out of control. I hold my phone and start shaking when it happens again.

"Hello?" I call out. Nothing.

The banging gets louder.

"Who's there?" my voice shakes.

Still no one answers.

"I have my phone and I'll ... call the police," I stutter.

"Watch out," a voice calls.

"I mean it!" I try to sound scary.

The ceiling tile opens up to the right of where I'm standing and out jumps a hard, solid wall of man. I crouch down and my cell phone goes flying. Long, thick fingers pick it up and hand it to me, and when I get brave enough to look up, I see Saul Mayes.

"Dropped your phone," he says, in that slow, lazy way that always drove me crazy. The kind of crazy that wells up in your chest in a good, comforting way, when you're not *terrified*. He starts laughing and can't catch his breath.

I stand straight and hold my hand up to show him how hard I'm shaking. "What ... the *hell*?" I subtly take out a wet wipe and clean my phone while glaring up at him. "How did you get in?"

"Anna gave me the key. Sorry to scare you." He bursts out laughing again. "That was hilarious. 'I'm gonna call the police'," he mimics. "Here you missed a spot." He points at my phone and hands me another wet wipe. He knows. "It's good to see you, Maby," he says with a grin.

At 6' 3", Saul towers over my 5' 3". My mom loved him and said he was brawny. She always wanted to know when I'd bring that lumberjack over again. He's been known to haul me over his shoulder to throw me in the pool or to lift me up where I can see Maroon 5 in Central Park. He's close friends with my ex-boyfriend, and for a while there *we* became a little too good of friends.

But I'll think about that later. Right now, I cannot be late to this meeting.

"It's good to see you, but you caught me off guard.

What are you doing here?" I repeat.

"Set some mouse traps up there and Anna asked me to work on the new shop in Soho. I've drawn up plans that I'll be showing today."

"Oh, I didn't realize you were doing the work—that's great!"

Anna comes in the back door and goes flying by us. She pokes her head back in the door. "You guys gonna stand there all day or what?" She scowls at us and then goes in the room.

"Why were we ever friends with her again?" Saul asks, laughing.

"Because of Joey," I whisper.

"Oh that's right … I never see him anymore though. Anna keeps the whip after him at home and he's working like a dog." He points to the door. "We're gonna get in so much trouble," he whispers as we walk into the meeting.

I smile as I sit down, feeling a little lighter from seeing Saul again. I've missed him. I have a hard time paying attention to Anna. Toward the end of the meeting, he shows the plans and everyone is really impressed with his ideas. The shop will be twice the size of this one and will have more room for offices too. It has unique alcoves and playful nooks that will make it stand apart from other shops. I get tired just looking at all of the space, but a bit inspired too. Maybe I can hold off on my job search for a little longer.

When the meeting is over, I'm shocked that I haven't taken a single note. This is so unlike me that I sit there stunned for a moment as everyone leaves the room.

"You okay, Maby?" Saul stands in front of me, looking amused.

I nod.

"Would you like to grab some lunch?" he asks.

"It's only 10:28," I tell him.

"Oh, wow. Well, I'm hungry. Breakfast?"

"You're always hungry." I laugh. "I have a lot to do here, but it was really good to see you, Saul."

"Come on, it's been such a long time. Just come grab coffee with me. Twenty minutes, across the street?"

I look at my clock again.

"You can set your timer and when it goes off, I will disappear," he promises. "C'mon, Maby."

I roll my eyes at him. "You're still the only one I allow to call me that."

His eyes get lost in his smile. I've always loved that about his eyes and his smile.

I want to go, but I don't want to get out of my routine and be weird. Still ... I really want to talk to him.

"Maybe. If I promise Anna a coffee cocktail, she'll be fine with it. Okay, but 20 minutes, that's it."

"Maby." He crosses his heart and pulls my chair out. I gather my things and take them to my desk. He doesn't say a word as I go through my little rituals.

He studies my fingers doing their thing with the ribbing on my skirt as we walk to the coffee shop.

"How many steps from this door to that corner?" He points to the closest intersection.

"Fifty-seven," I answer automatically.

"Have you stopped taking the meds?"

"Yeah," I say softly.

"Why, Maby?" He rubs my shoulders, getting right to the knots that are on either side of my shoulder blades.

"Dalton didn't want me on them." We step inside the

8

shop and I pick up a bottled water.

"That's all you're getting?" He gives me a look and I shrug.

"I'm not really hungry."

It might be the first time in a year that I've said that and meant it. I've wanted to eat everything in sight for a while now.

"Well, don't waste away on me."

"Oh please, I know you've seen my fluff. Don't act like you haven't noticed."

"You look great," he says. "Your boobs are a little bigger than I remembered, though." He frowns when he says it, so I'm not sure if he thinks that's a good thing or a bad thing.

I snort and turn all shades of lilac. Finally, a lilac girl.

We sit down with my water and his breakfast sandwich and grande coffee. I'll order Anna's coffee before we go.

"Have you seen Dalton lately?" he asks.

I shake my head. "How is he?"

"I haven't seen him either."

"Why? What happened?"

He shrugs. "We had a parting of the ways. It's been a while."

When I realize he isn't going to say more than that, I nod. "Okay. I'm surprised. You seemed determined to keep that friendship…" I trail off, remembering the guilt he'd had over kissing me.

"I was … and I just didn't want to do the wrong thing." He avoids looking at me.

My heart starts pounding and I get panicky when I realize my eyes are welling up with tears. *Please don't do*

9

this now, I think. The tears spill over onto my cheeks. Once again my body has betrayed my mind.

"Maby, what is it?" he asks, alarmed.

I shake my head, not willing to talk until I can do it without a warble. It takes a minute.

"I've just missed you. You were my friend. We talked every day. And then *nothing…*" My voice gets shakier and shakier, so I stop.

He puts his elbows on the table and his hands on the top of his head.

"I've missed you too. I just … I couldn't do that to Dalton. And you were vulnerable. I knew it was not … I had to just step back. You were with him."

I bite my lip and try to bite down the bitterness too.

"Your 20 minutes are up," I tell him and walk out without remembering Anna's coffee.

Of course, I have to go back after he's gone and buy it.

Caught

THINGS GO FROM bad to worse when I get back to work. I hold it together long enough to get there and then crumble when I get behind the counter. I weigh out what will affect me more: stay here and have a full-fledged panic attack, or try to breathe through it and get work done so I won't have another worse one tomorrow when I come in to extra work.

My hands tremble and I don't analyze any longer. I find Anna. She's at her desk with spreadsheets out and starts talking before she looks up.

"Our numbers are great this month, Mabel. I think these are gonna be huge." She holds up the new line of burlap accessories. "Don't you think?" She looks up when I don't answer.

"I'm not feeling well." My hands shake and my eyes fill with tears.

"Oh, okay. Well, I can work the floor. Want to go through the orders for this company?" She holds up the catalog and waves it.

"I need to go home, Anna. I'm gonna be sick." When I say it, it's as if the words confirm my lie. My stomach twists and I turn around and run to the restroom. I don't throw up, but wish I could as sweat drips from every pore. When I get a little relief, I go get my coat and purse and give Anna a little wave. She's with a customer and barely acknowledges me, but I know she saw me. She's been fairly understanding with me, although I always work overtime and do extra to make up for times like this. I don't know why I think I could ever get another job anywhere else.

This time on the subway, I find two empty seats and hope that no one will sit by me. At my stop, I get off and instead of walking home, I walk to the hospital that's not far from my apartment. I get stuck on a certain part of the sidewalk and have to circle back and walk it again. And again. And again. And the fourth time, I hear my name called.

"Mabel? Is that you?"

I groan inside, not wanting to see anyone I know when I'm like this … which is why I haven't seen anyone in a long time.

I look up and my ex-boyfriend, Dalton, is looking at me with a tight smile and a little bit of concern.

Shit.

"I thought that was you," he says. "You coming to visit me?" He laughs and gives me a big hug, holding me just a touch too long.

Dalton is the last person I wanted to run into today.

12

Or really, ever. I have avoided coming near the hospital because of him, but my therapist also works closeby.

"I wasn't thinking about it. Are you still working a ton?"

He rubs his eyes and I notice how exhausted he looks.

"I can't keep the hours straight anymore. I don't know whether I'm going or coming. You okay?" he asks.

"I'm having a … rough stretch."

"I wish I could help you. How can I help?"

He looks so sad, I almost feel sorry for him. I quickly remember all the hurt and try to squash it down while I'm standing in front of him.

"You look so tired," I say. "Are you done with your shift? You need to go to bed."

He groans. "You didn't answer my question. What's going on with you?"

"It's nothing. I'm fine. Go home and go to bed."

"Okay, pretty girl. Come here." He holds his hands out and hugs me again. "You look so good," he says, skimming his hands down the side of my skirt. "We need to get together soon. It's been forever."

"It has! Take care." I wave and walk away, feeling even more unsettled. There's no way in hell I'm getting sucked in by him again.

❤ ❤ ❤

IT TAKES WAY longer to get inside my apartment than it should. I mentally berate myself for not just going into the office while I was right there and making an appointment with Dr. Still. It's possible she would have given me a prescription right then, before even having an appointment. She would want to know why it's been so long since I've been there and I don't have a good answer.

I can't tell her I've been doing good just to leave the house to go to work.

Dalton left a year ago. He wanted me to stop being this way. Just stop already. Don't do it. Quit. Don't be so silly, Mabel, you can stop this whenever you want.

At that point I hadn't started the hand-washing thing, secretly proud and relieved of the fact that I wasn't that bad off. A little harmless counting never hurt anyone. The problem was I couldn't *stop* counting.

He made me start seeing Dr. Still and she actually helped me. The medicine helped and talking to her helped, but Dalton had the power to undo it all.

❦ ❦ ❦

A COUPLE OF hours and a half bottle of wine later, I have a perfectly arranged closet. It was already in good shape, but now it's much better. As soon as I'm able, I'll take the giveaway bags to Goodwill and throw away the garbage, but first I have to do the kitchen cabinets.

I'm shocked when I look at the clock again and it's midnight.

I check my phone and have 3 texts from Dalton. It's been a while since he's texted me.

Dalton: It was great 2 see u. Let's have lunch sometime and catch up more. Were u ok?

A couple hours later…

Dalton: In case no one told u today, u looked really hot.

And a couple hours after that…

Dalton: I can't do this, Mabel. We're working non-stop. Both me and Courtney. We never have sex anymore. She's mad all the time. I never sleep. I can't do it.

I can't help myself and type back: **I wish I could say I give a shit, but I don't. You have some nerve, asshole.**

I hate it when people don't spell things out for the actual word. What's so hard about typing a couple extra letters? I used to love Dalton so much that I ignored my inner eye roll over this issue. But not now. Moron.

He's always been complimentary, so it amuses me more than concerns me that he told me I'm hot. He's prettier than most women, so it gives me a little boost that he thinks I looked nice today. The thought of Courtney finding out that he just shared that little tidbit gives me a little charge, I'm not gonna lie.

I think about how much he's changed since all the stress. I barely recognize the Dalton I used to know. It's hard to see. I wonder if he feels that way about me.

I fall asleep reading and have an intense dream about him. He's doing crazy things to my body and I wake up feeling very satisfied. You know the kind of dream where *it* actually happens? Yeah, that happened.

However, I'm so mortified, I can hardly look at myself in the mirror.

Dreams Suck, if They're Done Right

I CALL ANNA the next morning and tell her I'm sick. She sounds skeptical but doesn't press the matter. I promise her that I'll make it up to her.

It was just a dream, I tell myself. Dalton never responded to my last text. Hopefully that took care of that. He'll just have to deal with this one on his own.

I work on the hall closet and then my desk. My apartment is so small, I can't believe I still find things to organize in here, but I do. More bags accumulate against the wall by the door.

Growing up, we lived with my grandmother. She was a hoarder. I don't know if that's why I'm the opposite—I'd rather have a bare house with nothing out, than piles of Time Magazines in every corner, or every single shoe I've ever owned. Some of my earliest memories are of organizing her things. She was embarrassed by the condition of her house and as long as I didn't throw anything away, she let me make it presentable. Or at least as presentable as possible with junk.

She was a seamstress and could never, *ever* find her scissors. My mom teased her about it and laughed it off, but I was the one usually sent to find them. I determined in my young, naive brain that I would always have a particular place for everything, and everything would stay in its place. Scissors are the one thing I make an exception for semi-hoarding—I have 2 pairs in every room.

My phone starts buzzing.

Dalton: You have every right to be angry with me. Just let me know u r ok.

I text him back. **I'm fine. Hope you start sleeping soon.**

Dalton: Are u sure? I care about u and haven't shown it enough.

I'll be fine.

Dalton: I just wish I'd kissed u.

Where did that come from?

Dalton: Haven't you ever wondered what it would have been like if we'd stayed together?

I don't answer that one.

Dalton: It would have been a good kiss.

You can't talk to me like this. I had a dream about you last night and I am not up for this right now.

Dalton: You dreamed about me??? Tell me everything! I want you so bad...

No! Why did I ever open my mouth? I stare at my phone and turn the sound off. I try to wipe the dream from my mind, but it keeps replaying and my body grows warm all over. I haven't had sex in a year and the year before that I was on antidepressants. Enough said. I'm ashamed to say that my hormones are peeking out from their long stint of hiding and rearing their ugly head.

Fortunately, my brain kicks in and I rein in my speeding heart. It's only the thrill of doing something naughty, nothing else.

I look down at the phone and there's another one from him.

Dalton: I shouldn't have said that. Sorry. But it's true.

No, you shouldn't have said that. How long have you ... felt that way?

Dalton: Always. I love Courtney. I do. But that doesn't mean I've forgotten you...

You chose Courtney.

Dalton: I just think about you a lot.

Hmm, well you should probably think about your girlfriend.

Dalton: You're right. I'm sorry.

My phone is quiet for a few minutes and then...

Dalton: I still remember the way your ass looked in that one red dress you used to wear. Damn perfection.

Oh my word. Stop!

Dalton: Just give me a peek. Let me see you. I miss you like crazy.

No way.

But I can't help it, I'm laughing. It's been a long time since I've really laughed. When I think about this being *Dalton* ... I can't believe he's doing this. Part of me feels wrong since he's in a relationship, and the other part feels justified—he was mine first. Instead of being completely angry with him, I can't stop laughing. What's wrong with me? I'm losing my mind.

Dalton: Just one. It will be fun.

No.

❦ ❦ ❦

AVOIDING STARING AT my phone is what finally forces me to go outside. First I make 3 trips to the garbage chute, and then I grab the Goodwill bags and start walking. I lose count around 457 and have to walk all the way back to my apartment building and start over. By the time I get to Goodwill—3,475 steps—I'm sweating and close to tears. My arms hurt from carrying the bags and I gladly hand them over to the guy who takes donations.

La Colombe coffee shop is close, so I stop in there, order coffee and sit down. My coat is sweltering. I take it off and carefully hang it over the seat next to me.

Have you ever noticed how the universe seems to have it out for you? Or maybe sometimes it's trying to help. I'm not sure. I do believe in God, but I also believe there are other spirits contributing, making the universe, as a whole, a very confusing place.

It's that weird phenomena of when you really need a pretty dress for something and there are none to be found, but when you absolutely can't afford one, there's a variety of fabulousness to choose from…

Or when I haven't had male attention in a solid year and in the last couple of days, there's suddenly Saul and Dalton handing out extra. Even Coen the cute barista at La Colombe gives me a little wink when he writes out my name on the cup.

"It's been a few days since you've been in here. You know the place isn't the same without you," he says.

"A lot more cheerful when I'm not, would be my guess," I try to joke, but it just sounds sad.

Do I have an *I am needy* sign hanging over my head?

Maybe my pheromones are exuding an I-haven't-had-sex-in-a-year vibe. I take a subtle whiff of my armpits and the inside of my wrists ... and even my breath. I'm not catching it. I pull out the wet wipes and use one on my nose and another on my hands. Once I've started that, I have to go to the restroom and use the feminine wipes as well. I've read somewhere that you shouldn't use those, but I can't be having my pheromones outing me. Or if I am going to be outed, could it please be with someone who is completely unattached to any part of my former life?

I shake my fist at the universe, careful to not anger God in the process. I'm pretty sure he knows I'm crazy, so it's probably okay.

❦ ❦ ❦

I MAKE IT home finally, all 77 colors of crazy fully intact. I pick up my phone and there are 3 messages from Dalton and 1 from Saul.

Dalton: Did I make you laugh?

Dalton: How about a picture of your smile?

Dalton: And then your tits ... just kidding! But really it would be ok.

I shake my head and start to ignore it, but then quickly type:

Reminder: YOU HAVE A GIRLFRIEND.

Feeling much better about myself, I delete the whole

thread and look at Saul's text.

Saul: Can we go eat Mexican food this Friday night, like old times?

I hover over the letters, not sure what to say. I mourned losing Saul's friendship more than my relationship with Dalton, so I'm not sure whether I can just go right back into old times for a night and be okay with that.

My desire to see him outweighs my concern, so I say yes.

Saul: Great. Hecho en Dumbo at 7?

I'll see you there.

I'm convinced there's been a massive shift in the universe.

Pervs Anonymous

I DON'T KNOW if it's because I finally have something to look forward to or what, but the days leading up to my dinner with Saul are better. I try not to overthink it, so I don't undo all the progress by slipping … but I haven't excessively washed my hands once.

I get a late night text from Dalton the night before I'm supposed to see Saul. He's been quiet all week, so I thought I'd heard the last from him for a while … maybe Courtney finally gave him some and he settled down.

Dalton: I can't stop thinking about you.

I type one word.

Girlfriend.

Dalton: I'm drunk. Are u feeling better? U sure have been quiet this week.

We haven't talked in ages and since you saw me earlier in the week, you've been acting like a perv. What's going on with YOU?

Dalton: No, this is a perv.

I can tell he's sent a picture and my curiosity gets the better of me.

I open up the picture and his perfect naked buns fill up my screen.

Nice. You're right. That is pervy, but I have to say I've always been jealous of your tight cheeks.

Dalton: Your turn.

No.

My phone buzzes again and I turn it off and go to bed. The next morning when I wake up, I see 2 missed texts from him. It takes everything in me not to open them—for a few reasons.

1. He's beyond attractive.
2. I miss naked men.
3. We've already established that I'm in a bad way.

I get so uptight thinking about what I'm going to do about Dalton that I have to wash my hands 10 times. And another 10 times when I get to work. I put lotion on them because they feel raw and then have to go through another round of washing and lotioning. Finally, it feels okay to leave the lotion on and I get out of the bathroom as fast as I can.

We have our small Christmas party in the afternoon. I've been ignoring Christmas, but it's just 5 days away. However, I do have my Secret Santa Christmas present for Peggy. She comes in every two weeks to do the books and has never said more to me than, "Have any new receipts for me?" I bought her a wallet that I found at TJ Maxx for less than $12. That was the only criterion: no gifts for more than $12. And since I know absolutely nothing about Peggy except that she deals with money, I thought a wallet was the most logical gift.

It turns out that Peggy has my name too, so we manage a pretty clumsy exchange. She gives me a small quilted polka dot bag.

"To keep receipts," she says. "I made it."

"Oh yes, great idea. Thank you!" I zip and unzip 6 times. "It's made very well," I add.

"Thank you," she says shyly.

I leave as soon as that's over, figuring I can't make much more progress than that in one day.

GETTING READY FOR the night is also fairly painless. I put on the only jeans I own that fit, surprised that they're a little looser than last week. I brush my hair until it shines, something I could stand to do a little more often. I wish I could say that I don't care how I look since I'm only seeing Saul, but that is so far from the truth. I try to avoid my favorite blue cardigan because I don't want it to start getting nubby, but I need it. It's the last thing my mom gave me and it's become a security blanket.

The restaurant is a 10-minute walk from my apartment, but I'm wearing my high heeled boots and it's freezing, so I decide to take a cab. I walk out the door at 6:30, so I can have a few minutes to breathe before he gets there. I didn't use to need time for 'breathing' around Saul because it was just Saul, but that all changed a little over a year ago.

I get a nice table for us and order a margarita while I'm waiting. Dalton never wanted me to drink in public. He thought I became a little too free with my thoughts and hands when I had even a little alcohol in me.

Cheers, Dalton, I think as I lift my glass.

I see Saul before he sees me. His height immediately commands attention in a room. He looks like a rugged football player and I watch the people around him take a second and third look to see if he's someone famous. Either that or they just wanted to admire him one more time. I think about how vastly different his looks are from short, pretty boy Dalton. Short guys have always gone for me because I'm short. There's like this little unwritten rule that says tall guys are off limits for short girls. Right before I met Dalton I'd decided I wasn't going to date another short man just because I was supposed to. His green eyes won out and I gave in.

Saul cuts short my Tall Man/Short Man deep thoughts when he approaches the table. He looks good enough to eat. Yep, hello, margarita.

27

He grabs my hand and pulls me up for a hug. My head lands on his muscled chest and I think yes, this is why. I'm small, let me feel small in the arms of a big man. I choke back a laugh that sounds more like a cough at my own stupidity.

Saul pulls back. "You okay? Need some water?"

"Nope, I'm fine. Oh, you smell good too," comes out of my mouth.

He chuckles. "Thanks. And you look really ho—nice. Different. Your hair?"

"Brushed it." I smooth it down. *Fifty-seven times*, I think.

He laughs again. "Well, it's definitely working."

We sit down and dig into the chips and salsa. Once we order, he gets right to it.

"Maby, what you said the other day about … there being nothing from me. I feel really bad. You're right. I'm so sorry."

I just look at him, not sure of what to say.

"I did abandon you, and probably when you needed a friend the most."

"Dammit, don't make me cry," I whisper.

"Oh God, I can't seem to say the right thing. This is part of why I've stayed away." He rubs the stubble on his chin. "How are you doing about your mom?"

I look down at my hands and try to keep them still. "Not very well."

"I know I can't even relate. My mom sucked. She was probably the worst mom ever and your mom was the best. It's not fair that my mom is out there alive, who knows where, and without any thought of her kids."

"I think that all the time," I lean in, "I know it's

wrong, but I do. Why do the nice ones die? There are so many mean, twisted sickos out there. Hell, I'm one of them! Why couldn't I go? Why did my kind, healthy mom have to die? And you know, I like old people fine, but why not somebody old and cranky? She was beautiful and … good." My face is heated. I take a big gulp of margarita so I will shut up.

"There's nothing right about your mom dying or the way she died. I think about that all the time."

"You do?" I take out a wet wipe and wipe the saltiness from the chips off of my hands. "Thank you." It feels nice to talk about her. No one else has been brave enough to mention her around me.

"It's true. I left you a message when they caught the bastard. You didn't call me back," he says softly. "I don't blame you if you don't want to talk about her. I just … I was so relieved they caught him and wanted you to know."

"No, I'm okay talking about her. I'm sorry I didn't call back. It was just too hard then, but I appreciated you reaching out. You're the only one who did out of our group of friends. Of course, they all disappeared with Dalton and Courtney."

"I really thought you were gonna marry Dalton."

The waitress brings our food and a pitcher of margaritas. This could get interesting fast.

"How long did you know he was cheating on me?" I get right to it.

"I *didn't* know. I told you that. I suspected he was and asked him about it and he lied to me. He told me he wanted to marry you and I believed him. Even when I found out he *was* with Courtney, I thought he'd go back to you. He always went back to you."

"Well, not this time." I give a bitter laugh.

"And I felt too guilty myself to ask him for details about Courtney. I didn't handle any of it well." He shakes his head and looks at the bar.

We're both quiet for a few minutes. When I can't take the tension any longer, I tap quietly on the table. He looks at me.

"We made out. It was the wrong thing to do, but shiiiiit, I can't feel guilty about it anymore. Dalton was angry with me all the time, we weren't having sex, and yes, I should have broken up with him before making out with you, but he'd been cheating on me for months by then! I think he was doing everything he could to make me break up with him and I was too afraid of change. Chalk it up to my crazies." I lean in closer, because the people at the next table have stopped eating and are listening. "At least we didn't have sex ... although we may as well have." I blush thinking about the way he kissed and how good he made me feel with just his fingers. Flustered, I stutter, "I-I mean, once you go that far..." I shake my head.

Saul clears his throat and makes a steeple with his fingers.

"But anyway, it's a good thing we didn't, I guess, because here we are a year later, and we're still talking about Dalton."

I know now would be a good time to bring up the fact that I ran into him, but I ignore my conscience. I'm tired of Dalton wrecking everything.

"It scared me, what I was willing to stoop to. If I could do that to my best friend ... I don't know. I'm not a cheat, Maby. I'm a lot of things, but not that. You just ...

we were so close."

"I didn't think I was a cheat either, but … it was you and…" I can't finish that sentence because it would be: Maybe I just liked you so much that I was willing to risk everything.

After all, I am the mean, twisted sicko.

Take A Left At Depraved

OUR CONVERSATION GOES up in intensity by several notches, the longer we sit.

He looks at me for a long time, studying me so hard I start fidgeting.

"Maby … I'm horrible with relationships," he says, taking a bite of the Tres Leches cake we're splitting.

I've heard him say this so many times before and I see red that he's using it on me now. I don't say anything.

"What?" he asks.

"What?" I shake my head sarcastically at him.

"I know you're mad by the look on your face."

"You're not around anymore—you don't get to 'read' my expressions. Maybe I've changed," I snap back.

"Your tone proves me right."

I roll my eyes. "Fine. I *am* annoyed by you. You've probably dated everyone in this city *but* me, and you try to use your 'I'm horrible with relationships' line on me the minute we talk about anything heartfelt … like I'm trying to get in your pants or something."

His eyes widen.

"Yeah, I said it," I continue. "And I wasn't. I was trying to have an honest conversation with you. I'm sure I'd probably like it in your pants, but realized a long time ago—like whenever the hell it was you *bailed on me*—that it wasn't gonna happen."

"I'm not sure what you want from me, Maby. You know I'm crazy about you, but I don't know what you really want. And I haven't wanted to ruin what we do have." He looks at me out of the corner of his eye and sucks in a breath. "I also don't want to do anything to make you worse."

Ah, there it is. The truth.

He starts to say something else and I lift my hand.

"Don't. Just … don't."

I throw down enough cash to cover my drinks and food, get up, and walk out. I hear him behind me, but I've already caught a taxi and tell the driver to hurry up. I don't bother looking back and feeling bad for Saul Mayes' sad eyes. I've already done that more times than I can count.

I HAVE A dream about my mother. We're in bed and I'm spooning her. I slept with her most of my life. I never knew my dad. It was just us. She turns over and I see her. It's so real and I think, *Oh, I'm having one of those experiences! I can't believe I'm seeing her face.* I've been waiting for this since she died and it's never happened. Even in my sleep, my expectation is so high that whatever she says will be profound.

She looks down at me sadly. Her hair is so much darker than mine and her eyes look especially light. She's beautiful.

"I wish you hadn't done that," she scolds me. "I'm worried you're gonna end up old and alone if you keep acting so crazy."

I wake up with a jump, my heart pounding out of my chest, and the tears already forming in my eyes. I can't believe that was my time with my mom. Scolding and guilt. Like I didn't have that enough on my own without her using her voice from the heavens, or wherever she may be right now, to drive the message home.

It's 3:23 AM, and I get in the shower, scrubbing and scrubbing and scrubbing. My skin hurts, but I can't stop. I cry so hard that I have to get out of the shower to vomit. I get back in the shower to get clean again.

Around 5:39, I crawl back in my bed and for a minute before I fall back asleep, I think about how that didn't sound like something my mother would say to me. But whoever it was did have a point.

❦ ❦ ❦

I DREAM ANOTHER dream where I go to hug my mom and she's as hard as a rock, the way she was when I touched her in the casket. I wake up in a sweat. 7:02 AM. I fade back into another dream and I'm having to identify her body in the morgue. I dream it exactly the way it happened. I said it was her and fell on her chest. They tried to pull me off of her, and I told them I wouldn't touch her, but I needed a minute. They gave me just that and then longer after they'd gotten all the evidence. I fixed her hair the way I knew she'd want it. The bastard had knifed her in the back, just to get a measly $57 and a credit card out of her purse. I looked at the wound and cried more tears than I ever thought possible.

I wake up crying. I can't get a grip. I can't eat. I don't try sleeping again, too afraid of where my dreams will take me. I turn off my phone and numbly watch TV all day. The next night is tormented with dreams again.

On Sunday afternoon, I start my hatred party of Dalton. He left soon after my mom died. It was like he'd been so close to getting out and knew if he stayed when something that terrible was actually happening, he'd *never* escape. It's just as well. I hated him by that time and I needed to mourn without anyone watching and judging.

I suspected he was with Courtney. Every time we went out as a group they would gravitate toward each other. I saw the way they looked at each other. I knew when Dalton wanted someone. It hadn't been me for a while.

I start a bottle of wine and finish it. It's late and I have a nice, solid buzz going on.

My phone buzzes.

Dalton: I'm hurt I haven't heard from you.

I ignore him because I'm drunk and hate him.

Dalton: I'm trying to be a good friend here.

Why now? Have you and Saul been talking about me?

Dalton: No, why? I haven't seen Saul in forever.

It's just weird. Mother Nature seems to be ganging up on me all of a sudden.

Dalton: I'm thinking of breaking up with Courtney.

Then do it. I'm surprised you've been with her this long.

Dalton: Really?

She'll kill you if she knows you're texting me.

Dalton: I'm tired of her controlling every part of my life. Can I tell you something?

I'm afraid you're gonna.

Dalton: When I go down on her, I imagine it's you.

WTF! < Look what you made me do! Seriously! If you feel that way, why are you with her?

Dalton: Look what you do to me.

No! Don't you dare!

He dares. He sends a picture of little Dalton and it's just like him. Pretty and sort of perfect. At least on an iPhone screenshot and when I'm already seeing things a little fuzzy. I *have* missed it a little bit.

I stare at it a few minutes and then die laughing. I laugh for five minutes straight, glad that I don't even have a pet who can see my manic flip.

I pull out another bottle of wine and can't say what happens next.

❦ ❦ ❦

A RAGING HEADACHE wakes me up before the alarm. The floor is wavy as I walk to the bathroom. I try to glide so my stomach doesn't feel any movement. My throat feels like it's been rubbed with sandpaper. I can't imagine going to work, but I agreed to go in today and will be off the rest of the week.

I pick up my phone to double-check the time. I just feel so off. Awful. I feel awful. My phone dings with a message.

Dalton: I'm still smiling about our night.

What does that mean? I scroll up to see all our messages and drop the phone. Oh, holy cripe, what have I done? There's a picture of him in various poses, all comical if it wasn't so horrifying. It's basically the evolution of his penis while looking at pictures of me on Facebook. By the last one, it's standing to full attention.

And then, oh God! There's a picture of my boobs. *I*

sent him a picture of my boobs.

And at 1:07 AM, there's a video of him showing me his happy ending.

Now I'm not only crazy and depressed, but I am one of *those* people. Any shred of decency I thought I had feels like it's disintegrated like cotton candy.

A Second Skin Of Shame

THE SHOP IS non-stop busy all day. Ibuprofen is my best friend. Walking home from the subway, I think back on the day and know that I've walked the inner walk of shame all day long. I can't wait to take a long bath and crawl into bed.

If it weren't for all the cheerful carolers I could forget tomorrow is Christmas Eve, but nope. They're everywhere, making me want to bang my head against a thousand walls. All that keeps me going is the fact that I have time off. I've covered every holiday all these years and we finally have extra help, so I snatched the days. Anna put up some fuss initially about Christmas Eve, but Liv, the perky girl working part-time chirped up that she was just *dying* for more hours.

I have 7 steps left before I reach the stairs to my apartment building when I see him. The sun is about to go down, but his smile takes over where the sun leaves off.

"Dalton. What are you doing here?" I slow down but really want to just keep walking.

He grabs my arm and pulls me into a hug. "Hey you. I thought you were off this week! I just wanted to see you." He gives me his goofy grin and I have a hard time staying mad.

Really, he's just so cute, it's *always* been incredibly hard to stay mad at him.

"I still had to work today." I give in to the hug. Hugging Dalton is like putting on my cozy socks when it's snowing. It's comfortable and a given that I would eventually welcome the warmth.

"I'm breaking up with Courtney."

"You mentioned you might." I pull away from him.

"Yeah. I've thought about you all day. I had to see you." He draws me back in and leans his head against my forehead. He has gum in his mouth and smells like peppermint.

He's only a couple of inches taller than me, which actually feels nice when we're standing like this. Everything just sort of fits. But what he said finally registers.

"We can't do this." I back far enough away that he can't reach me.

"This is so hard!" He steps forward and puts his fingers on my lips. "God, you were so hot last night."

He ventures a look down at my chest and I bop him on the head.

"Dalton! It's me. We *cannot* do this. I ... I didn't even remember last night when I woke up this morning. And when I saw the texts, I was mortified. And the video!" I squeak and put my hands over my eyes.

"I know. I've felt guilty about it too, but it was so fun, right?" He tries to see under my hand and gives me a huge grin.

I shake my head at him, but can't stop a tiny smile. "Looked like it for you!" A nervous laugh sneaks out and I put a hand over my mouth.

"Come here," he says, taking my hands and stepping toward me, "we've gone through a lot together. You are the first girl I ever loved. I've always regretted what happened between us."

"Why now? I don't understand why this is happening." I look up to the sky like it will bring a great revelation.

He leans over and kisses me. His soft lips feel sweet and I lean in, despite myself, longing for any human touch. He goes for it and puts his tongue in my mouth, and I think maybe because of the gum, the whole thing is just a little too … wet. And not in a good way.

I keep kissing him, now almost more of an experiment than anything, but no. It's not getting any better.

I lean back and look at him. Huh. I didn't expect that.

He takes my silence as consent for him to do it again and when he comes back in for another kiss, I break it off and run up the stairs.

I don't even say goodbye, I just run up all the stairs until I reach my door. Once I'm inside I lock the door and turn off my phone.

I didn't count the stairs. I didn't count the stairs. I didn't count the stairs.

I'm too afraid to go back and do it again, though, because he might still be out there.

I didn't count the stairs.

You know there are 36 stairs, I rationalize.

But I need to go back and be sure. I have to count them or my life is going to continue going to hell.

The burning in my chest is searing. The pain is acute. There is a weight threatening to bury me underground if I do not go back and count the stairs.

I pace my apartment. Back and forth. In a pattern. Counting. Faster and faster until I give up and run back down to the first level and walk back upstairs, counting out loud as I go.

THE REST OF my night is a series of prayers and curses. Whatever tangible grip on sensibleness I had has dissolved into minuscule pieces. Any hope of getting a good night's sleep is out the window. I know what the night holds for me.

It's just as well. I don't need to be thinking of all that I lack at Christmastime.

I stay up all night counting the whole apartment. Every variation I can think of. When I've exhausted myself counting, I organize the bathroom cabinet and work a little harder on the kitchen. When that's done I get stuck counting again. The sun is coming up the next morning when I pass out, completely spent.

I WAKE UP late in the afternoon. The aloneness is almost a physical character lying next to me. Anywhere I look, there it is. I feel like a buoy, bobbing out in the middle of the vast ocean with not another soul in sight. Tiny and insignificant compared to the water, I can't seem to let the water take me all the way under, no matter how hard I try. I don't want to do this anymore. I don't want to *be* anymore. I pray God will untether whatever is holding me afloat and just let me drift off into nothingness.

I fall back to sleep and I see her. She's smiling that smile that only she has for me. No one will ever love me like her. She had a way of making me feel like I was just fine. More than fine, really, I was special and beautiful in the ways that matter.

"Darling, remember that Christmas when you were little and you asked for a dad?" she says, with a sad smile.

I nod, not wanting to wreck the dream with my voice.

"There have always been some things I can't give you."

I open my mouth and she puts her hand on my arm. I look down at her hands because they're one of my favorite things about her.

"You're stronger than you think, baby girl."

I look into her eyes and open my mouth again to argue with her. She smiles and shakes her head.

"Use the same fight that makes you want to argue with me right now and get better."

She laughs and pulls me close to her. I nestle in her neck and hope that when I wake up I can remember exactly how wonderful this feels.

Traces Of Hatred
Or
23,947

I HAVEN'T ALWAYS been like this. I've always liked to count things, but I never *had* to count. There's a difference. The first time I became compulsive about it was 7 years ago. I'd just turned 21 and decided to find my dad. My mom was more than enough, and I made sure I let her know it, but she encouraged me to find him to answer any questions I had.

I hadn't really had a boyfriend and knew this was unusual for my age, to have so many reservations about letting a guy get close to me. I had always given my father a lot of thought and hoped if I actually met him, it would settle some of the fears I had about ... everything. There's something about knowing your dad wants nothing to do with you that does a number on a girl.

He was my mom's college boyfriend and broke her heart when she told him she was pregnant. I wanted to ask him what was so important that he didn't even have time to meet me. And once the shock wore off that he was having a baby, as an adult, why didn't he find me? How was he capable of that and what kind of person did that make me, having that in my genetic makeup?

That was the key—determining how much of him was in me. I saw how my mother was all the things I aspired to be, and wondered if my dad was all that I was capable of being.

She warned me that he might not be receptive. She told me then that she'd tried a few times early on, to get him to see me, and he'd never wanted to. Still, I was determined.

I started with the last town she knew he'd been and was able to find his number with no problem. I called on a Saturday and hoped he'd be the one to answer. He was.

"Douglas Jacobs?" I asked.

"It is," he said.

His voice sounded deep and hoarse, like maybe he smoked a pack or so every day. I don't know if he did, it just sounded that way.

"This is Mabel Armstrong, your daughter," I said, my voice wobbling with *daughter*.

He cleared his throat and said, "I wondered when I'd hear from you. I have a family. I don't need any trouble."

"I don't want to cause any trouble, I just want to meet you," I replied, my voice taking on an edge now.

"Look, I told your mother a long time ago that I

wanted nothing to do with her. I've moved on, have a good life, and I've wished you both well. I don't have any extra money to go around, believe me."

There was a second's pause where my heart felt like it was going to shake my chest open. "Well, isn't that convenient for you," I finally said. "I wish she'd told me what a complete bastard you really are, but she's too kind to do that. Now I know."

Before I could hang up on him, *he hung up on me*. And that did it. I lost it. How dare that motherfucker hang up on *me*. Red. Livid. Rage.

I got drunk and walked the city in circles. I counted steps to drive out the sound of the son of a bitch's voice. When I was cried out and wanted to start all over again, I jogged up and down the steps of the Metropolitan, up and down, again and again, until I was ragged. I counted to 23,947 and then couldn't move. I called my mom and she came and lifted me off the stairs, practically carrying me to the car.

It was bad for a few weeks. I know now it was adult onset OCD, but then it just felt like my brain had snapped and I'd been replaced by a lunatic. Some days—weeks and even months—were a nightmare. I failed a few classes, delaying my college degree by a year and a half.

My mom was able to reason with me and get me to focus on other things. When I got a little healthier, I started going out and had a couple of relationships that eventually fizzled out. And then I met Dalton and we clicked. My little quirks, he liked to call them, were almost a charming oddity to him in the beginning, but when we'd fight or if I was stressed, it didn't become so cute anymore. It was harder to hide when we moved in together. I'd stay up all night working on the apartment. Or he'd catch me up, counting the tiles in the kitchen over and over.

We had a huge fight because I couldn't use the same hand towel as him. He tried to force me to, and it did *not* go well.

In the beginning, he'd steer me back to bed and distract me there, but when that stopped working, there wasn't much hope left. That's when he said I had to get therapy or he was breaking up with me.

I should have just broken up with him right then, but I blamed myself for every problem we had. I didn't see how he belittled me all the time, even in front of our friends. I just felt the rejection and thought it was all my fault.

I started seeing Dr. Still and she was great. Very understanding and helpful. She gave me an antidepressant that was effective with anxiety disorders. We worked each week on revaluing each compulsive thought that came through my mind. She said to tell my mind when I was struggling that this was a symptom of OCD and I didn't really need to do x,y,z. It sounded simple but was so difficult. Eventually it did start to help.

Next week I will try to go see her, I tell myself.
Right after I have this massive shutdown.

CHRISTMAS COMES AND goes. And the day after that. And the day after that. I've ignored my phone. Dalton and Saul have called and so has Anna. I only listen to Anna's message in case it has anything to do with work. It does, so I work a bit from home, and then don't look at my phone again in case she wants me to do something else. Let the ones who are actually at the shop do the work for once.

I get desperate for La Colombe's coffee, so I force myself to get out of bed to go there.

Coen is working as usual.

"Hi Mabel," he says.

"Hey, Coen."

"You okay?" He immediately starts preparing my regular order.

"I-ugh. Don't ask."

"Okay." He chuckles, but looks concerned. "Sometimes it can be liberating to tell everything to an absolute stranger." He leans his chin on his hand and bats his eyelashes at me.

I smile in spite of myself. "You're not an absolute stranger."

"There's that smile," he grins, "now, come on, spill. Since we're friends and all…"

"You do make it tempting." I take my coffee and before I walk out, I thank him. "You know, the small kindnesses you show me do help make things just a little … better."

"I'd like to make it a whole lot better," he yells as I walk out the door.

I drink my coffee and crawl back into bed as soon as I get home. I know I need to get out more. I know I need to make friends. I just … can't. I'm going under.

Some Like it Hot

THE SUN SHINES through my window early Saturday morning, and when it hits my face, I don't turn away. I let it warm me through and through until I'm completely toasty. Then I think about what my mom would say about me wasting away the sunshine.

If you're gonna laze the day away, at least save it for a cloudy day, she'd say. *Otherwise, the sun will stop shining on you...*

I jump out of bed. I've laid around long enough that my hair feels like matted dreadlocks are forming in places. It's time to get up. It doesn't look like I'm going to be able to die today.

I have two more days off work. I'd planned to spend all of my time reading, embracing my hermitdom, but the familiar stirrings of guilt rise up. I take a shower and have a frank discussion with myself about at least reading at La

Colombe. Instead of staying there, I order a coffee to go.

"We have some new books in," Coen mentions.

When I don't answer, he says, "I just … noticed you like to read … a lot." He throws a cookie in the bag even though I didn't order one.

"Thanks for the cookie." I smile.

"Anything to make you smile," he says.

Gosh, he's cute.

From there, I walk to a salon that I've always thought was probably too expensive for me.

"Oh honey, come in," a tatted up guy says. "We will fit you in."

I haven't even said what I wanted, but he can see the desperate situation that is my hair.

"I just had a cancellation," he whispers. "Your timing could *not* have been more perfect."

Paschal leads me to a chair and sets me down like I'm his new toy, promptly throwing a cape over me. He fingers my dirty blonde hair and has the decency to keep his expression neutral, even though it's obvious to everyone with eyeballs that I'm way overdue.

"What did you have in mind today?" he asks, lifting up my mop.

I shrug my shoulders, studying myself in the mirror. "You know what? Cut it off, please. And I'd like to go blonder."

"When you say *off*, what do you mean exactly?"

"All of it. All the way … off. Longer on the top, but I don't even want it on my neck anymore. Maybe I could donate it?"

He brightens up. "Yes! A touch longer-on-top pixie," he whispers. "Love. It. You have the face for it … it's just hiding under all this hair!" He swivels me around in the chair. "And when you say *blonder*..."

"Marilyn Monroe blonde."

He gasps and puts his hand to his chest. "I love you. People who just want a trim are dead to me." He shakes his head and laughs at himself. "Okay, not *dead*, but ... yeah ... dead." He swirls me back around and points toward the sink. "Let's get your makeover started, little darlin'."

I smile at him, thinking I'd go anywhere Paschal wanted just for calling me *little darlin'*. When he washes my hair, my commitment to him is further confirmed. I hold back the moans that nearly escape my lips. Maybe I'm not cut out to be a hermit. I'm like an attention starved kitten who purrs as soon as they're stroked.

All too soon we go back to the chair. He dries my hair a little and puts it in a ponytail. And chop. It's off.

He takes my picture holding up the ponytail.

"I cut off 15 inches," Paschal says, excited.

I close my eyes and lean my head back. "I feel a thousand pounds lighter already."

"I like the sound of that!"

He bleaches my hair. He has nail polish on his counter and I ask if I can use it while we wait for my hair to process. I paint my nails with OPI Road House Blues and Paschal finishes the haircut.

"You know, you kind of *look* like Marilyn Monroe with those huge brown eyes and blonde hair. Girl, you look *sizzling*!" He can't stop smiling as he looks at me from every angle.

I'm doing a lot of smiling for me too. I do feel sort of vixen-esque. I wouldn't go so far as Marilyn Monroe, although something about this haircut does make me want to go buy red lipstick and black liquid liner.

"It's about time…" I say softly.

"What was that?" He leans in closer.

"Nothing," I whisper.

As I'm paying, Paschal says, "Hey, we've spent all this time together and I never caught your name."

"Maby."

He smiles. "Oh that's perfect."

IT'S JUST A haircut, but damn, it feels good. I do buy the makeup and a scarf and immediately put on both. There must be some magic to the whole transformation because I don't feel like hurrying home. While I'm feeling somewhat peaceful, I practice walking leisurely. No, I don't need to count. *There's no reason to count* flies around in my head and I just let it fly. I cannot count because I am walking like a normal person right now.

I decide to call Saul.

"Hello?" I say when he answers.

"Finally!" he says. "I've been worried about you. I've called all week! Why haven't you called me back?"

"I am. Right now. Merry weekend after Christmas!" I try to pull off a laugh, but it sounds so fake.

"Yeah, you too," he snaps. "What are you doing right now?"

"Doing a little shopping."

"Where?"

"Why do you wanna know?" I sass.

"Meet me for a drink."

"Ask me nice and maybe I will," I tell him.

"Please," he huffs.

"Okay! *Sheesh*, you don't have to beg." I genuinely laugh this time.

"I'm gonna spank you when I see you. It's on. Ear Inn?"

"How 'bout Pegu Club tonight..." I'm needing a little something different *and* it's closer.

"Okay! See you there in 30?"

"30."

❤ ❤ ❤

I DON'T MEAN to take my time, but I see a short navy dress in the window that catches my eye. I'm in a devil-may-care frame of mind, so I buy it and the tights that were displayed so I don't freeze. It's the shortest dress I've ever owned and looks like it was made for my ankle heel boots.

I spritz on the last of my L'eau D'issey sample and rush inside. He's at the bar and I go stand by him. I can tell he doesn't realize it's me and he's trying to studiously avoid the girl who is inching closer to him. When he finally looks my way, his eyes go wide and his mouth drops.

"What!" he yells. "What have you done with Maby?" He looks me over from head to toe and groans.

"What's the groan about?" I scowl at him, hands on hips.

"Oh good, you're still in there. The starlet in front of me scared me for a minute." He laughs and pulls me up to him, opening his legs so I can get closer. "You look beautiful, Maby." He tilts my head back. "Look at that face." He runs his fingers along my cheekbone and I shiver. "Chilly?" he asks.

I shake my head, tongue-tied.

His hands roam over my body and I don't want to move. For so long I've been floating in nothing, but right now, tonight, I just want to *feel* something. He stares at me, and I want to know what he's thinking, but I don't want to wreck the moment. Sparks are definitely in the air.

Since the night things changed between us, he's never been able to keep his hands off me. It's what has made everything so confusing. To hear him talk, we've just always been friends, but I know with the look in his eye, the only reason his hands aren't on my ass right now is because we're in public. His hands have a mind of their own. It's probably because I want his hands on me so bad I can taste it, that I don't think he's being a sleazebucket. It's also probably why he's stayed away all this time.

I shake my head.

"What's going on in that mind of yours?" he asks.

"I'm trying to figure you out," I tell him.

"I'm pretty simple."

"No, you're not. You're confusing."

His hands stop caressing my hips and when he pulls them away, I miss them. He gets the bartender's attention and I order a drink.

"How am I confusing?" he continues.

"When we're together, we … can't stop touching each other. I would normally think someone doing that wants me, but … then we go a year without talking. After being so close. You had become my best friend … my only friend, really. I know … I need more friends…"

He waits for me to say more.

"Is this just how you are with everyone?"

"Well, I wouldn't do this with a dude," he says.

I lean my head on his chest and groan.

"Now *you're* groaning!" He laughs. He touches the back of my neck and I stay put for as long as he's doing that. "I think it's just so … *comfortable* with me and you. It just naturally goes there when we're together. We have chemistry."

"That sounds so … dull." I pull my head back. "I think you said it the last time we were together—the real reason it never goes further. I just haven't wanted to believe it, I guess. I gotta go. I shouldn't have called you." I stand up to go.

"Wait—why? You're speaking in riddles. You haven't even had your drink yet," he says.

"I can't keep doing this, Saul. I would have risked everything to be with you. I thought you were being so careful with me because you were guilty, but after all this time, I think you're the one who doesn't know how to have a relationship. It's easy to blame it all on the girl who pulls her sweaters into little nubs, but maybe I'm not the only crazy one between us." I kiss his cheek. "Bottom line: you don't really want *me*."

Late Bloomer

I TAKE A taxi and when I get out, I hear a voice behind me saying, "I never claimed to be sane."

I turn around and Saul is standing in front of my apartment building.

"How'd you get here so fast?" I ask, walking toward him.

"I told my cab driver to step on it," he says, brushing my long bangs to the side. "You didn't need to rush off."

"I've waited for you to come around for a year. It's finally clicked." I make the motion with my fingers, clicking on my brain. "Sometimes it takes me a while. I'll never be what you want and I'm done sticking around to have that banged over my head." I turn around and go inside.

He opens the door behind me. "Wait! Why do you keep walking away from me?"

"You're not listening. I'm done with this."

"Why are you saying this? You are—we haven't even started!" He looks lost and finally more confused than me.

"We started when you called me every day for years to see how I was. When you checked on me every hour when I drove across the country to California. When you held me when I cried about Dalton and comforted me with your hands. When you screwed me with your fingers and when you made me laugh every single time we were together … we've already been, Saul." I start up the stairs and turn around once more. "Why did you wait so long to kiss me and then feel so guilty when we did that, compared to—oh, you know, making me come?"

He shuts his mouth and opens it up, then shuts it again.

"I've been late to grow up, but I'm getting there," I tell him. "Problem is, I need a man now."

I trudge up the rest of the stairs and feel relieved when all 36 are behind me.

❦ ❦ ❦

I CALL DR. STILL during work on Monday and schedule an appointment for the next night after work. My new look shocks everyone, but it seems to be a hit. I want to buy all new clothes to go with the hair, but think I've done enough damage to my credit card for a while.

Dalton calls when I get in from work. I know I can't avoid him forever, so I answer.

"Are you mad at me?" is the first thing he asks.

"Yes. I don't know what to think about you right now. Do you have a pornography problem that I need to know about?"

He nervously chuckles. "What?"

"Enough said. Listen. I've seen your balls, you've seen my tits. Old news. Let's just call it a day and leave it at that."

"Now that I've seen your tits again, I want more," he replies.

"If either of us uses 'tits' this many times in a conversation ever again, I'll never speak to you again. Deal?"

"Deal," he says, sounding resigned. "I'll probably break up with Courtney either way."

"Won't change the matter for me, so don't bother unless you're over her."

"Dammit, Mabel, why do you have to be so heartless?"

"I think I might finally be finding my heart again," I answer, "and it's tired of messing around."

"Well, I hope you find what you want."

"It's doubtful, but I will make sure that I don't send a picture of my tits to start it off," I say, laughing. "Sorry, had to just say it one more time. Tits. Okay, I'm done."

He finally laughs. "You're crazy, Mabel."

"So you've always been happy to remind me."

MY APPOINTMENT WITH Dr. Still gets right to the heart of the matter … as soon as I get in the door.

"It's been a long time since I've seen you," she says.

"Yes."

"Why is that?"

58

"My boyfriend insisted I stop seeing you."

"I thought he was the one who got you to come to me." She checks her notes to double-check herself.

"He was."

"So what changed?"

"I got on meds and got better, but … stopped wanting to have sex."

"Oh … you mean, from the meds? You stopped wanting sex because of the meds?" she reiterates.

"Yes. And … well, he stopped being able to make me have an orgasm. Nothing worked." I turn bright red.

"I see. Well, did he realize that was also a side effect of the medication?"

"He thought so and then started insisting I get off of it."

"And what happened?"

"Well, I started getting worse. And then my mother was killed and I lost it."

"Oh, I'm so sorry. I didn't realize." She rapidly writes on her chart.

"Thank you. She was stabbed by a mugger not far from home."

"That's horrible! That must have been devastating. And … did you notice your symptoms increasing during that time?"

"Yes, I got really bad. I was afraid of everything and couldn't stop. A few weeks after my mom was killed, Dalton broke up with me to be with our friend, Courtney."

"Oh, Mabel. You do realize this is a lot to take for anyone, but for someone with a disorder like yours, the stress just feeds it. I wish you'd come to me then. It would have still been really hard, but I would have tried to get all the help possible for you."

"I've just sort of been frozen in time," I say, tears rolling down my cheeks. "I lost my friends. They went with Dalton and Courtney ... even friends that I thought were just as much mine." I think of Saul and how I really have lost him for good now. "But my mom, she is the only one I really had in this world. I feel like my anchor is gone. My history. My hope." I can't speak, I'm crying too hard. I blow my nose to try to reel in the pain.

"I would like to see you a couple of times a week for now. It's completely understandable that you've had an extreme relapse, but I have full faith that we can get you feeling better. I'd like you to try a medicine that doesn't have sexual side effects," she lifts her eyebrows, "in fact, some even say it helps stimulate a sexual experience. Not for everyone, of course, but it will be better than the other. If, for some reason it doesn't work, we can try others. You just have to communicate with me," she says. "That's very important. Do you understand?"

"Yes, I do and I will try."

"Good, now let's work on some exercises for the next time you're feeling like the OCD is kicking in."

ON MY WAY home, I stop by the drugstore to fill my prescription. I miss Saul, regardless of how he feels about me. Just talking to him that little bit more the last week has gotten him back in my system. I have to be on a detox from him and cut him off just like I would if I were going off sugar. One bite, and I just want more. I have to occupy my mind, don't put myself in a situation where I'll want any, and if I do get near it, only take a small bite to get the taste, but not overdose.

But it's easier said than done. I think of his broad shoulders and the way he can lift me with barely any effort. His smile and the way his eyes light up when they see me. The sooner I can get over him, the sooner I might be able to move forward. Feeling the slightest bit hopeful the last few days has given me the smallest desire to start over. This is all new to me. I've realized I can't wish away my life. I seem to be stuck here for now and have to make the best of it.

I just wish he loved me the way I love him.

Finish, Peak, Satisfy

THERE WERE SEVERAL nights that involved question-able behavior with Saul. One weekend, Dalton and a bunch of our friends decided to go to Boston to see our friend Luke. It was all spur of the moment and Saul and I couldn't get off work. I had a second job at the time but probably could have met up with them late Saturday. It just sounded better to have a low-key weekend, maybe see Saul. Dalton never had a problem with me hanging out with Saul. I think he knew that I needed more care than he could give me. Dalton had been going out a lot without me, and either came to bed late or fell asleep on the couch. I was still taking the meds and it was a huge point of con-tention.

I took two pizzas and beer over to his apartment. Like mine, his space was tiny, and we ended up on the bed talk-ing. He knew Dalton and I were fighting and we talked about that.

"I think he's seeing someone," I told him. "Do you?"

"I don't know. When we go out, he doesn't talk to anyone outside our group."

"I don't know why I'm still staying. I need to get out."

"You said that a long time ago and then you guys worked it out. You always work it out," he said. "I don't even believe you anymore when you say you're leaving."

"He guilts me. He guilts me and I want to go and then he guilts me and I want to stay."

"No one can make you do anything you don't want to do, Maby."

He put his arm around me and pulled me as close as he could into his side. I felt like I could stay right there forever and be happy. I think I knew somewhere deep down that I was playing with fire, but tried to reason it away. I thought I was probably too attached to Saul but knew I was just his buddy. I didn't try to figure out if it was more. I just liked to be with him. It was easy and always nice.

"Come here." He moved me in front of him and hugged me from the back. "Lay down." I did and he massaged my shoulders and back. "Breathe," he demanded.

I forgot about everything else, closed my eyes and just felt his huge hands rubbing the stress away. For a long time, he worked out the knots in my shoulders. Gradually, his hands dipped lower and lower until they covered my ass and all the way down my legs. Back up, just gliding his hands over and massaging. My eyes opened and my breath came in quicker, but I didn't stop him. He did it a few more times and then stretched out beside me. We talked all night long. About everything and nothing. His hands made constant passages on my body, nothing naughty, just steadily on me.

I fell asleep around 6 the next morning with him spooning me and holding my hand. I didn't want to think about if this was wrong, I just wanted to soak it in.

All weekend there were hazy snapshots of us crossing boundaries. It felt too good to stop. We drank wine and laughed our heads off. I spent time on his lap saying nothing, just playing with the little scattering of hair on his chest. We went swimming and when we came back inside, still in our suits, he pulled me on top of him and just held me there as we talked.

There was one moment where he said, "What's going on here, Maby?"

And I said, "I don't know..."

But that was all the mention of anything being out of the ordinary.

I hated to leave him the next night. He set me on his coffee table, so I was just a little taller than him and hugged me hard. Then he picked me up, wrapping my legs around his waist. Neither of us said anything, we just held each other.

"Do you have to go?" he asked.

"I should," I whispered.

He nodded and let me go.

❧ ❧ ❧

DALTON CAME HOME from his weekend extra loving. He brought flowers and took me out to dinner. I felt bad that I hadn't stopped touching Saul's arm or hair or chest or any part of him that I could touch ... but I didn't want anything to do with touching Dalton. I had to clear my head. Dalton hadn't been like my other flighty short-lived romances. We'd looked at engagement rings together. I got off of the medicine that weekend and tried to work it out. Like Saul said, we always worked it out.

He had sex with me every night that week. By the third week, the excuse that it was the medicine's fault that I wasn't 'excited' didn't work anymore. It should have been out of my system enough by then, but it seemed Dalton was as well.

I was going to break up with him the night my mom died. I needed to know it wasn't for any reason other than I wasn't in love with him, and I felt sure of that. I made dinner for us and was starting to tell him, when we got the phone call.

❦ ❦ ❦

THE NEXT COUPLE of weeks were a blur, but I do know that I slipped into a deep state of depression. The OCD came raging out. I cried all the time about my mother, which I think is normal, but the pain made all my old symptoms plus new ones come out. Dalton tried to be understanding for about a minute and then got pissed when he saw me acting out my compulsions.

"Just stop! You're making yourself worse. Stop already! You're acting like a crazy person!" he yelled.

"What's it hurting you whether I do this or not? Just leave me alone! You wanted me off the medicine. This is me!"

He got out of the apartment, slamming the door behind him. Instead of crawling back into bed the way I had all 12 nights since my mom had died, I left the apartment too. I walked the 16 blocks to Saul. I'd picked at the fuzzies on my fleece sweatshirt all the way there and when he saw me, he held me and then looked at my hands.

"You're bleeding," he said, alarmed.

"It's nothing. My hands are just dry and I can't stop picking at my clothes."

He looked at me sadly. And then he threw me over his shoulder like a bag of potatoes and ran up the stairs with me. I laughed for the first time in 12 days. He led me to the sink and washed all the blood off.

"We need to get some kind of ointment or heavy cream or something," he muttered. "Would it work to put Band-Aids over your fingers? Would that help you stop?"

"I don't know. I never thought of that. I'll have to try it."

He didn't ask what I was doing there and I didn't say anything about Dalton.

"Wanna watch a movie?"

"Yeah, that sounds nice." I feel my shoulders relaxing just being near him.

We cuddled on the bed and I fell asleep. It was a couple of hours later when I woke up and looked at Saul. The room was dark except for a streetlight shining in the room. He was sleeping too. I touched his face softly, loving the way his eyelashes looked against his cheeks. His eyes popped open.

"Sorry, I didn't mean to wake you up."

He did a little chuckle that always made me smile.

I kept touching his face and he touched mine. He touched my lips and I kissed his finger. His eyes grew darker, but he didn't stop. His hand trailed down the front of my body, over my breasts, down my stomach, down my legs and feet.

He looked in my eyes and saw the answer he needed and pulled off my shirt. I pulled off his. He pushed my pants down and I pushed down his. Bra and underwear came off next and we just lay there, quietly, touching each other. Slowly. He pulled me on top of him and his fingers wandered down, down, down and with just a few strokes, he made me come. I shuddered and was so overcome— with feelings for him and that I had even been able to go there with him after so long without—that I leaned down and kissed him. He kissed me, but then went completely still. His body felt heavenly under mine, but I could tell something had shifted for him.

He grabbed my shirt and put it back on me, tugging my hair forward on each shoulder. Confused, I got off of him and put my underwear on under the covers.

He took my hand and tried to pull me back to his chest, but I sat up and put on my pants.

"I should go," I said quietly.

HE CALLED ME early the next morning. Dalton had already left for work.

"Hey. Are you okay?" he asked.

"Um, yeah. As good as I can be, I guess," I answered.

"I just … wanted to make sure … after last night.

67

I—"

"Yeah, yeah, I'm okay."

"We *kissed...*"

"That's not all we did," I said.

"I know, but ... I'm sorry, Maby."

I didn't know what to say to that. I hung up and bawled. I was sorry, too. Sorry that I'd cheated on Dalton, sorry that I was really alone, sorry that Saul regretted what we'd done, sorry that my mom was dead and I wasn't.

❧ ❧ ❧

INSTEAD OF SNAPPING out of it, I got worse. I kept walking miles every day and getting lost. One night I passed out after walking too long and woke up in the hospital. When I came to and they couldn't get me to talk, they put me in the psych ward. I wasn't there long, but it was a nightmare. Being in the mental hospital was the closest I ever came to losing my mind. Enough that I swore to myself that if I ever got even close to being put in there again, I would kill myself first.

Dalton broke up with me when I got out.

Guilt 101

"I THINK MY job isn't helping me get any better."

I'm sitting at therapy, holding a hot cup of tea. Dr. Still looks at me thoughtfully.

"What do you think it is about work that's a trigger for you?" she asks.

"My boss is high-strung and demanding. I think since she knows about my issues she makes allowances for me, but I feel bad about that and try to be sure that I make it up to her. I do most of the work she should be doing, so she'll know I'm still valuable. I've started doing all of the buying. She seems to trust my opinion and I work doubly hard to make sure she doesn't regret it."

"You know, Mabel, a common thread I'm seeing in our conversations is *guilt*. The things you've told me about Dalton and Saul, and now even with work. You seem to be carrying a lot of guilt around about everything you do, whether it's warranted or not. In some ways guilt propels OCD symptoms: you feel bad that you didn't get something right, you have to do it again and again until you make it right. I'm going to propose for the next week, take note of everything you say and think that has guilt as the driving force. I want *guilt* taken out of the equation."

It's a light bulb moment.

"You're right. I'm not sure I know how to live without some form of guilt or another." I study my hands. "Why do I have so much of it and where should I focus all of it now?"

"I don't know," she says truthfully. "I'm hoping we can get to the bottom of it, but I'm not sure why you've taken on so much. The good thing is I *know* you can start recognizing it and deflecting it. Your responsibility is to take care of you. What fills you with peace? What makes you happy? What do you enjoy doing?"

"I wish I were one of those people who had a passion, you know, something I absolutely love to do. I feel like the only thing I'm really good at is organizing closets and counting."

"If you're organizing closets for fun or it brings you peace, I don't see anything wrong with it. If you're doing it because you feel bad about the way you did something at work or it's in any way tied into guilt, don't do it. Put your energy into things that give you joy."

I think about that for a few moments. "Saul always brought me joy."

"And does he now?"

"Well, I think I'm still too mad at him."

"What makes you the maddest about Saul?"

"Two things. I still don't really know how he feels

and he never fought for our friendship, platonic or otherwise. Oh … three things. He abandoned me when I needed him most."

"And if Saul is never in the equation? What brings you joy?"

I'm quiet for a long time.

Dr. Still finally clears her throat. "Mabel?"

"Nothing."

❦ ❦ ❦

INSTEAD OF BEING depressed by my revelations in therapy, I'm driven. I have to find something that makes me happy, besides Saul. I walk by a storefront and see my reflection in the window. My haircut. It makes me happy. As inconsequential as it seems, it has given me a little bounce in my step. I decide to walk the extra blocks to the salon and say hello to Paschal. I could also use a trim. I smirk when I think about his thoughts on that.

The place is quiet when I get there. Paschal is at the front desk and there's only one client getting their hair cut by another stylist.

"Hey, Maby!" he says when he sees me.

"Hi, Paschal! Sure is quiet in here."

"Ugh. I know. Business is so slow right now."

"Have time to touch me up?"

"Absolutely." He doesn't even grimace. Business must be *really* slow.

When he washes my hair, I tell him his fingers have supernatural powers. He laughs.

"That's what he said."

"Mm-hmm. I bet," I moan.

Once I'm in the chair, we're talking like old girl-friends. I know it's what hair stylists and clients do, but there's a bond. I don't think I'm imagining it. When he mentions loving the salon but not being sure if he's going to be able to keep it at that location, a seed is planted in my head.

"I'll try to help you get more business—it's what I'm good at doing. The place looks great and you have magical fingers—so it's just a matter of spreading the word. We could put an ad in the paper and give coupons out at coffee shops and nail salons. Do you have a Facebook page or a website?"

He stares at me, getting more excited with every word I say. "I'm terrible at all of that. I would love help. I can't afford to pay you, is the only problem..." he trails off.

"I know. I'm not even asking you to pay me. I need a distraction."

He finishes up my hair.

"Thank you, Maby. Any amount of help would be huge to me."

I snap a picture of him in the front entrance ... it's the only place that has enough light for a decent shot. He approves the picture and I make a salon Facebook page for him.

He shares it with all his friends and within minutes has a dozen likes. *10% off cuts and color all week* is his first post.

The other stylist gets done with his client and Paschal asks them both to share the page with their friends. By the time I leave, they've got 56 likes and 4 new customers have called to make appointments.

"My job for the night is done." I put my hands together and bow.

"You are a little pixie genius," he says. "Come here, let me hug you." He gives me a quick squeeze and I leave happier than when I came.

❧ ❧ ❧

I'M IN BED before I realize that I didn't count anything on my way home. Not once. I know the medicine has kicked in, but I also think I might be getting a little better.

I get a text right before I go to sleep.

Dalton: Courtney's pregnant.

Congratulations! You had sex again!

Dalton: Shut up. I think we're gonna get married.

Double congratulations! So I guess that was a no on the breaking up...

Dalton: Why were we ever together?

I've been asking myself that same question.

What Do You Tink?

THE NEXT NIGHT, I take fliers to Paschal and then go to a few cafes, coffee shops, and boutiques in the area to pin the flier up anywhere that has a bulletin board. I talk to each store owner or manager and tell them about Paschal's business, offering special rates for any salon services. At La Colombe, Coen asks if that's where I got my haircut.

When I say yes, he says, "I liked it long too, but you look smokin' now."

"Oh! Um, thank you," I stutter, flattered and surprised.

"What are you, like, 22-23?" he asks.

"Ha, no," I laugh, "I'm 28."

"Wow, had no idea. Well, if you ever wanna go all Ashton and Demi with me, I'm game," he says.

"Thanks, I'll keep that in mind." I smile at him. "That would make you 13, by the way…"

"What?"

"They were 15 years apart … never mind." I awkwardly back away with my coffee.

He laughs. "Oh yeah, gotcha. Well, see? We're not that bad. How 'bout you go out with me?"

I'm tempted. He's adorable and funny.

"You know what, Coen? I'm not looking for a boyfriend, but I could use new friends."

"Got it. I'm cool with that. My sister's playing at The 55 tomorrow night—would you like to meet up with us?"

I take just a moment's pause. "Yeah, I'd love to."

"Maybe get there a little before 8. I'll save you a spot."

❧ ❧ ❧

PASCHAL CALLS ME at work the next morning. "I've gotten several calls from people you met last night."

"Great! Everyone was really nice. It seems like they'll help spread the word. They have your business card and a few places have your flier up. Been giving your flier to all my customers today, too…"

"Wow, that's huge. Thank you so much! Okay, I know you have to work. I'll see you later."

"Oh hey—I have a *non-date, let's be friends* later tonight. Wish me luck."

"You'll have to tell me everything while I do your nails or something…"

"I might be willing to let you do that," I say with a giggle. I surprise myself with that giggle. I look up and Anna is standing there, watching me. "Gotta go." I hang

75

up quickly. "Hi, Anna."

"Do you have a boyfriend?" She wrinkles her nose as if that's the most disgusting thing she can imagine.

"Nope. Still single," I tell her. "How's the baby making going?"

What? She can jab me about being single but I can't jab at her about her desire to just have a baby boy when she already has a beautiful baby girl she never sees? Okay, I know. I'm bitter.

"I'm pregnant, actually." She beams. "I was just coming in to tell you. I knew you'd be happy for me."

Ugh. Stab. Guilt. Wait, Dr. Still says I can't have guilt. Except this time it might be well-deserved.

"Congratulations!" I tell her. I get up and hug her and as soon as I turn around I can't even wait until she's gone to wet wipe my hands. I do wait to spray the Lysol until she's stepped away. Huh. Seems Dr. Still might be on to something.

"I need you to stay late tonight. We have that huge shipment coming in and I need you to stay and cover the paperwork when it comes through."

"It was supposed to come in tomorrow morning. I can't stay tonight, sorry."

"They called and said it's coming in tonight. What do you mean you can't stay?" She genuinely looks floored.

"I'm not able to stay late tonight. Sorry."

Her eyes narrow into penetrating spears, pricking into me by the second.

"I don't understand. This is really important. I need you to stay."

"I can't … not tonight."

"This is your *job*. Are you telling me you don't care

76

about your *job* anymore?"

"You know what? Not really." I shrug just to bug her. "I've put in countless overtime hours without the pay that would normally come with a *job*. Find someone else who can stay tonight. I have plans."

"You've got to be kidding me. After all I've done for you…" She enunciates each word so clearly.

"You really *haven't* done much for me, Anna," I say calmly. "Any time I've ever taken off has been without pay. I don't go on vacations. I make sure everything is in order here for you before I go home every night, typically long after closing. And I've never once, in *3 years*, gotten a raise. I used to think you were doing *me* a favor, knowing my issues, but … not anymore. I'm not going to allow you to hold *anything* over my head any longer." I grin at her. Damn, that felt good to say.

"What … the hell?" she sputters.

"I appreciate having a job, so thank you for that. And congratulations about the baby. I really am happy for you."

And I am. Now that I've said my piece, I feel light as a feather and genuinely wish the girl well.

"I have a few more things to get done before I leave, so I better get back to work." I turn around and get busy finishing up my projects for the night.

I don't hear her walk away, but when I get up to file one of the contracts I've just finalized, she's long gone.

❧ ❧ ❧

PASCHAL PUTS A strip of blue in one of the front longer pieces of my hair. I love it. We work on my nails. I could get into this pampering.

"Hey—you should come to The 55 when you're done here. Live music."

"I wouldn't mind seeing this non-date … but I don't want to intrude."

"No, please! Come. I might need backup."

"Maybe I will." He checks my nails. "You're ready, girl."

I flashback to the past year in my apartment when I couldn't go out the door, paralyzed by what a fool I'd make of myself once I went out there. It wasn't that my friends left me—I just stopped existing. I feel a pang of grief for that girl and a whisper of hope for the one I'm becoming.

IN THE TAXI to the bar, I look over the texts from Saul that I've ignored the last couple of weeks.

Saul: It's funny. A punk Tinkerbell has been ravaging my dreams. She's an angry little fairy.

And a couple of days later…

Saul: Not funny? I'll have you know Tink is hot. Especially when she's mad.

And a few days after that…

Saul: Come on, Maby. Don't be mad at me. I miss

you. Tell me what you want me to do.

That last one was just a few days ago.

I text him back.

You can't do what you don't feel. I can't be mad at you for that anymore.

He texts back right away.

Saul: I don't know what that means, but maybe you can tell me over dinner tonight.

Can't. I have a date.

He calls just as I get out of the cab.

"You've got a *date*?"

I can't tell if he's mad or nervous. He sounds ... contained, but just barely.

"Yeah."

"Who?"

"A guy I met at the coffee shop," I tell him nonchalantly. "Actually I've gotta go. I just got to the bar."

"He's taking you to a bar?" he asks, scoffing. "What kind of dinner is that?"

"We're gonna hear his sister play, if you must know," I snap. "What's with the third degree?"

"No third degree. You finally texted me. I hoped we could ... I don't know. Just call me later, okay?"

I agree to it and hang up before he gets to me any more.

Can't See The Forest For The Trees

COEN OPENS THE door when he sees me coming.

"For someone so young, you sure are a gentleman," I tease.

"For someone so old, you sure are a fox," he teases back.

"Hey, watch it. I mean … thanks." I grin.

He holds up my hand and kisses the back of it. He's definitely charming. We walk to the table and he's still holding my hand. Two girls and a guy are already sitting at the table right by the stage.

"This is Mabel," he says, holding up our hands and pointing at me with the other.

"Maby," I say.

He grins. "Hi, Maby."

I'm grateful it's dark because I have a severe case of nerves all of a sudden. I feel the need to wet wipe my entire body. I swallow and smile shakily.

Everyone starts introducing themselves. Katie and Todd seem to be a couple. They both wave and say *hi* at the exact same time. Melissa hugs me right away.

"Hi! Cute hair! Glad you came. Coen's told us a lot about you."

"He has?" I look at Coen and he shrugs. I don't know what he could have possibly told since we don't really know each other at all.

"Well, mostly how he's had his eye on you for the last year. We've had to hear the ongoing saga of how you don't know he exists," Melissa says.

I glance over at Coen and lift a brow. "I had no idea."

"Exactly," Coen says.

We all laugh and somehow move on from that potential awkwardness with ease.

Geez. I'm going to have to rethink every interaction I've had with Coen over the past year. I can't remember anything significant, just morning pleasantries when he handed me coffee. We sit down and Coen finally lets go of my hand. *I will not clean it. I will not clean it. Okay, I have to clean it.* I discreetly reach in my bag and wipe my hands in the bag.

"He makes sure he's always the one to make your coffee." Melissa leans forward. "There aren't many managers who would do that."

Coen groans.

"She still just *barely* knows I exist, so let's not scare her off, okay?" Coen says. He sounds gruff, but his smile completely negates it.

Just then, a gorgeous girl with long red hair comes out on the stage and quickly walks to our table.

"Hey guys! Thank you for coming! You must be Mabel." She beams at me. "I'm Jade, Coen's sister."

"Nice to meet you. I'm excited to hear your set."

The rest of her band does their tuning and she backs up. We order appetizers and drinks and the band starts playing. Jade's voice reminds me of P!nk. I'm in complete awe.

Midway through the show, I realize I'm having a great time. Everyone in the group is so easy to be around that I don't even think about my junk. If anything, I feel light and like I'm coming out of a deep fog. I offer to buy a round and go to the bar when the waitress disappears for a while.

The place is packed. While the bartender is working on our drinks, I turn around to watch Jade, and Dalton is right behind me. Now I know the universe is conspiring against me.

His eyes widen when he realizes it's me.

"Mabel! Hi." He smooths his hand over his hair. It's gotten so long it's barely in a ponytail. I hate it.

"Hi." We stand there and stare at each other.

"I like your hair a lot," he says. "Shit, you look amazing."

"Thanks." I don't say anything about his disaster of a hairdo.

I look him over and try to understand why I stayed so long with someone like him.

"This girl is great, right?" He nods toward Jade.

"Yeah, she is. Where's Courtney?"

His cheeks darken. "I needed to get out."

"Awww. Hmm. History has a way of repeating itself." A giggle pops out of my mouth. I bite my lip to try to stop the manic laugh that's just under the surface.

A little fire lights in Dalton's eyes. Knowing him, I know he wants to say something sarcastic back, but he holds his tongue.

The bartender gets my attention and points to the waitress holding a tray of our drinks.

"Well, that's for me. See ya, Dalton." I smile and follow the waitress.

I don't look back and I don't watch for him the rest of the night. I've mentally given him the finger, both hands. I engage in the people I'm with and it feels damn good.

During the intermission, Coen turns to me and says, "Are you glad you came?"

"So glad. I love the music!" I look around the table. "And your friends are pretty great too."

"I think so," he says. "We've been through a lot together."

I look at Melissa, who's laughing at something Katie is saying. "Why aren't you two together? She's great."

"We're cousins." He pulls a face. "Ew, Maby."

I laugh. "Fair enough."

"Anything else you wanna know?" he asks.

"How old are you anyway?"

"I'm 25. Got my MBA."

"Wow, nice. And you're older than I thought."

"How old did you think? And what—did you think I just want to work in a coffee shop for the rest of my life?"

"No … I guess I didn't think—"

He laughs. "I actually do want to work in a coffee shop for the rest of my life. I just want to run my own."

"I've always thought that would be fun," I admit.

"You don't have to answer this, but … I hope you will." He leans closer so he's talking softly in my ear.

"What has happened to make you happier lately? You definitely seem different."

I turn and his lips brush against my ear, causing me to shiver. His eyes are dark brown and I get lost in them for a second. They are so kind, my eyes fill.

"My mom died," I whisper.

He takes my hand and then catches the tear that drops.

"I am *so* sorry," he whispers. "So sorry. That's gotta be the worst kind of pain."

His concern nicks the bricks around my heart and the tears fall. He pulls me to him and wraps me up in the sweetest hug.

I sheepishly wipe my face when I lean back. I smile wobbly. "No one else has said that to me. I didn't realize how much I just needed to hear that."

He frowns. "No one?"

"No one."

"You need better friends."

It's weird—the people you expect to rally around you in a crisis. I apparently didn't have a great group of friends to begin with, but the fact that even the one I thought I was closest to didn't say much more than 'this sucks'. I know I haven't been around Coen long enough to know if he'd be a friend who would stick around, but I do know he's already shown more compassion in a couple of sentences than anyone else. I think about Paschal and the kindness he's shown me in such a short amount of time. Perhaps I'm finally attracting the right kind of people.

"You're right. I do. I'm finally making an effort to change it. I think that's part of why I'm happier."

"I know you don't really know me yet, but … I think

this is the start of something extraordinary." He kisses my cheek.

The room looks a little crisper; everything comes into focus just a bit more.

I don't say anything. I just notice the curve of his full lips when he smiles. The wave in his hair. His eyes that are so dark that all the light in the room seems to bounce off them.

❖ ❖ ❖

WE TRY TO close the place down with Jade and her band. Paschal comes by late and, of course, hits it off with everyone. At one point in the night, I laugh until my stomach hurts, and it takes me by surprise. I watch everyone for a moment and wish I'd known these people forever. It's just … invigorating.

A picture flashes through my mind. I see myself surrounded by piles of baggage. Dalton, Courtney, Saul, Anna. My dad. Losing my mom. The OCD that takes over my life a lot of the time. I look at the heap and wish I could walk away from it all.

Coen looks at me. "What's going on in that mind of yours, Maby?"

"I wish I'd really seen you a long time ago."

He touches my cheek. "It's not too late."

I close my eyes and lean into his hand. When I open them, he's staring at my mouth.

"Let's get out of here," he says.

We tell everyone good night and run out into the cold. He has my hand and I don't think twice. We run all the

85

way to Washington Square Park. The lights shining down on the snow give it a dreamy effect.

"Hurry! We have to get there fast!" he yells.

"Where? Where are we going?"

"Riiiiiiiight here." He stops abruptly under the arch.

The spotlights shine on our faces. We stand there, grinning at each other like fools. I'm not sure who leans in first, but our lips meet and it's like magic. Not a first kiss trying to figure out what the other one is doing kiss, but a perfectly in sync and combustible kiss. Even if we were to never see each other again, he's already moved up to the extraordinary category.

I don't know how long we stand there, oblivious to the cold. All I know is that I would be happy kissing him forever.

He's not as short as Dalton, and almost, but not quite as tall as Saul. He might be just right.

15

One Order Of Lips To Go

"I COULD DO this all night," Coen whispers on my lips. "But I just got you to notice me. I don't want to blow it." He kisses me again and I turn to putty.

He pulls away and I whimper.

"Let's get you home. You're freezing," he says.

"I am?"

He grabs my face and kisses me hard. "For someone so hot, you sure are cold."

"For someone so … yeah, I got nothing. You've rendered me speechless. And I did notice you. I just didn't think…"

"I hope you'll see me again?" he asks. "And that you'll think about me at least a few times before then…"

His voice is light, but his eyes are vulnerable.

"Oh you've got me thinking for sure," I tell him, eyes wide.

He holds my hands up to his chest and then leans down to blow on them. We start walking and find a taxi. Coen asks the driver to wait for him while he walks me to the door of my building.

"This night was even better than I expected ... and I had high expectations," he says. "I don't want to scare you off, but ... how about a real date tomorrow night? I mean, tonight. Since this was, you know, just a get together amongst friends." His eyes shine when he teases me.

"Bring the lips and you're on," I say with a smirk.

"Deal," he whispers and kisses me again.

The cab driver honks. Coen takes his time and backs away, watching me go up the stairs to the door.

"I'll pick you up at 7?"

I nod.

"Night, Maby."

❦ ❦ ❦

I SLEEP IN the next morning. The afternoon passes quickly and before I know it, it's time to get ready. I wish I had something colorful to wear, but stick to my new navy dress. I haven't worn it since the night I saw Saul. Speaking of Saul, I owe him a call back. He left a voicemail around 2 AM.

"You didn't call me. I hope you're okay. This guy better not have been a creeper. Call me when you get in. I'll be up a while."

Instead of calling him back, I texted: **I made it home fine.**

It's quiet from him all day and then he texts at 5 PM.

Saul: I'm in the mood for Speedy Romeo. How about it?

Pizza does sound good. I have plans tonight though. Sorry.

Saul: Coffee shop guy again?

I don't answer. I'm a little peeved that he's coming out of the woodwork lately. Why now?

While I'm looking for my eyeliner, I knock over my bottle of medicine and realize with a tiny jolt that I haven't taken it for a few days. I've been so busy and off of my schedule. I apply my makeup and figure I'll skip another day since I'm doing so well. I've never wanted to have to rely on medication anyway.

Besides, I like numbers. It's not all bad. As long as I can keep a handle on it.

❦ ❦ ❦

AT EXACTLY 6:59 PM, the intercom buzzes. I love it when people are on time.

I press the button and he says: "Coen Brady, here to see the lovely Maby Armstrong."

"Hi! I know right where she is. Come on up. 305."

I look in the mirror and carefully put on my dark red lipstick that won't budge, mess my hair up in just the right places, and take a deep breath. I've counted to 27 when he knocks on the door. I wait 10 full seconds before opening it, so he doesn't think I was just standing there waiting, even though I was.

"Wow," he whispers when he sees me.

He looks adorable. He has a fitted argyle sweater over an untucked button down shirt and his hair is begging for me to latch on to it. His dimple gets more pronounced the longer I look at him because his smile just keeps getting bigger. Finally I smell something wonderful and realize he's holding a small pot of flowers.

"Are those gardenias?" My voice gets more excited with each word. "I *love* gardenias."

"For you," he says, shyly handing me the flowers. "You look stunning."

"Thank you." I flush under the intensity in his eyes. "I can't believe you brought me gardenias. They're my mom's and my favorite flower."

"I thought you looked like a gardenia kind of girl." He looks around my apartment. "It would work well by that window ... and don't let water touch the flowers." He grins. "Nice place."

"Would you like a drink or anything before we go?"

"We should probably go now to make our reservation." He holds up my coat and helps me into it. "God, Maby, you smell freakishly good."

I laugh. "You just have the smell of gardenias stuck in your nose."

He opens the door and we start down the stairs.

"No, I have the smell of Maby in my nose."

34, 35, 36...

We take a cab to The Bourgeois Pig, a place I've only heard about. It looks quaint from the outside, but when we go inside I'm surprised by the plush couches and the deep red on the walls. We're seated at a table that's set in a little alcove by the window.

"This place is a weird mixture of swanky and gaudy, but I kind of love it." I look around at all the mismatched furniture. "What's good?"

"This is my first time here, but they're known for their wine and fondue. That sold me. The thought of you drinking wine and eating with your fingers…" His eyes twinkle as he smiles at me.

I gulp. "What if I want a steak?" I tease.

He nods and takes my hand. "As long as you share the dark chocolate and Baileys fondue with me for dessert…"

My heart skips a beat or two. "Done. So what made you think I was a gardenia girl?"

His dimple deepens. "Gardenias seem delicate—difficult to grow, but under the right conditions, they flourish. Stronger than they look…"

"And that reminded you of me?"

He nods. "Just need a little loving care…"

The waiter comes and takes our order and I smile at Coen as I order the lobster bisque fondue.

Coen quietly groans and holds up a hand. "I cannot be held responsible for what I might do."

I'm giggling again. I can hardly believe it.

"How do you know so much about … flowers?"

"Well, my parents own a nursery and gift shop about an hour away. Some of my earliest memories are of me and my sister working outside with my mom and dad."

"So why a coffee shop and not running the nursery?" I ask.

"Actually I probably will eventually, so I'm hoping to do my own thing for a while before that time comes. I loved working there growing up but got a little burned out. I needed to be here for school and I'm not ready to move back there yet. Ideally, one day I'll add a coffee shop onto the gift shop side of the nursery and have the best of both worlds. I needed the experience of managing the coffee shop here, though, before I try to pull that off."

"You're just full of surprises."

"Good ones, I hope?" he asks.

"Really, *really* good ones."

We smile at each other and I'm amazed by how content I feel. Just then my phone beeps.

"I'm sorry—I forgot to turn the sound off." I pick up my phone and start to adjust the settings when I see that it's Saul.

Saul: I need to see you. If not tonight, tomorrow. Please.

I ignore it so I'm not rude to Coen, but inside, it nags at me. I put my phone in my purse and try to file Saul away in a little compartment that I don't have to think about right now … the way he did me for so long.

It begins to work when our food comes. I might have history with Saul, but the chemistry I have with Coen is undeniable. In fact, at the moment I can hardly remember what it was that ever had me holding on to Saul so tight in the first place.

"This is the best thing I've ever tasted," I moan as I dip bread into the lobster bisque.

I open my eyes and Coen is staring at me, mid-bite.

He swallows hard and then shakes his head, knowing I've caught him.

"Don't mind me," he laughs, "I just want to ogle you while you eat." He sips his wine. His eyes linger on my mouth. "Your lips ... I haven't stopped thinking about them."

I blush, remembering our kisses in the moonlight.

He lifts his wine glass. "I kissed a girl I've wanted to know for a long time, and in a single moment, we were instantly in sync. The stars and planets aligned. I've never had a first kiss that was so ... perfect."

We clink glasses.

"Me either," I admit.

"Our very own harmonic convergence, if you will," he says, as he kisses me. A light kiss, but my heart drops to the ground just the same. With a soft groan, he stops. "I don't think it's possible for us to have a bad kiss."

"We can keep trying, if you'd like," I tease.

He traces my lips with his finger and then my eyebrow and down my cheek. "I want to know what makes you tick, Maby Armstrong. Those eyes—they're deep. Tell me something."

"What would you like to know?"

"Do you believe in love at first sight?"

"No," I scoff.

"No? I do. Why don't you?"

His face is completely guileless as he smiles at me.

My teeth pull at my lower lip as I think about it. "Well, I just know that I'm too much of a control freak to ever fall for someone just by looks alone."

"What if it isn't just looks that you fall for? What if it's a cosmic aligning of spirits ... or maybe even simply

pheromones? Or kindred souls that finally connect ...
whatever it is that makes someone know that they've
found the half of themselves that's been missing."

"You've had that before?" I ask, my brows crinkled.

"Yes—whenever I see you. I actually know when
you've walked in the room before I ever see you." He
holds up a strawberry covered with chocolate and Baileys
and feeds it to me.

It's good timing because I'm at a loss for words.

Pardon Me, I Needed That Emotion

COEN INVITES ME to his apartment after the restaurant. I'm a little nervous by what he might expect and not ready to confront that issue yet, so I decline.

"I have something to show you. I promise I won't clip off pieces of your hair to put in a glass vial ... or ... anything." He tries to give me an evil look.

"Well, when you put it that way..." I laugh.

He pulls a doe-eyed sad face.

"Oh, okay, I'll come by. You have the most trustworthy face. You can't even pull off a scowl. Nothing fazes you, does it?"

"If you mean, am I laid-back? Yes. If you mean that I don't take anything seriously ... no. I do. I just don't let the inconsequential become significant and vice versa." He shrugs. "I think it works well for me. *However*, whatever I love, I love *hard*."

We both blush when he says that.

"You'll see what I mean," he says softly.

I like him so much in that second that I'd probably stay the night if he asked, but inside I secretly hope he won't. I want to just enjoy this beginning rush of feelings.

A few minutes later, the cab pulls up to his place and I'm surprised. "You didn't tell me how close you live to my house!"

"Again … not wanting to scare you off," he says with a wink, "but it's only a five-minute walk. And that's counting after I scale your wall to get in your window."

"Okay, Spidey. I'd like to see that." I crinkle my nose at him. He's slaying me with his cuteness.

He hugs me into his side. "Next date."

He's on the second floor and it only takes 30 steps from the front entrance to get to his door. As he's about to open the door, he looks at me and whispers, "Are you ready?"

"Uh, I don't know," I whisper back.

He grins and unlocks the door.

I don't know what I was expecting, but I was most definitely not expecting *this*. There's the bachelor's leather couch—only in brown, instead of the typical black. A red leather chair with a huge stack of books sits next to it. But it's everything else that catches my eye. On shelves are little seedlings growing under lamps and on every table surface are the most incredible things I've ever seen.

Terrariums in every size and shape are filled with a variety of beautiful little plants. I stand, stunned, taking it all in, and then eventually move to look at each one. Finally I turn to him.

"I've never seen anything like this. You have 33 terrariums!"

He laughs and nods. "Yeah. Actually I have 34." He points to one in his kitchen. "Still working on that. This one needed a mate." He motions toward the lone terrarium on his coffee table. "Too weird?"

"*So* weird! I freakin' love it. Each one is so unique! I can't get over them. How do you take care of all of this?" I stop in front of one that has colorful rocks surrounding the plant and sits under a glass dome.

"Most of them are succulents and only need watering once a month. This is a favorite." He walks over to one that looks like an inch tall hobbit is going to crawl out at any moment. "I get them started and then sell them at my parents' store. Tomorrow, actually … they'll all be gone and I'll have to start over. But come here—this is what I'm passionate about." He walks over to the small green plants on the shelves. "Do you know what this is?"

I shake my head.

"Coffee." He grins excitedly. "I start it here and then once it reaches a certain maturity, I take it to our land and plant it there. I'm starting to roast the beans there too."

"I-wow. This is unbelievable."

He grabs my hand. "There's one more thing, but you have to go in my bathroom to see it."

"Lead the way."

He kisses my hand. "That's my most favorite thing you've ever said so far."

I roll my eyes but can't stop the smile that takes over my face.

On a shelf sit gardenias at different stages. "I have a weakness for gardenias." He smiles. "You'll see you got the best one. There's hope for this one yet, though." He holds up a tiny potted gardenia.

"They're so beautiful—why are you hiding them in here?"

"They like the humidity…"

I nod. "Do you ever put them in the terrariums?"

He looks at me with mock alarm. "Never! That would not go well."

I laugh. "I think you might be as loony as me. In a far healthier way, but … still. I do see some madness here."

He lifts an eyebrow. "I should take that as a compliment then?" he asks.

"Most definitely."

We walk into the cramped hall and he pulls me to him. At first it's a hug and then he takes my face in his hands and kisses me. It's like our lips were just made to be connected. If he'd kissed me the first time we ever saw each other, it would have instantly sealed the deal.

He lifts me up and wraps my legs around him. My short dress rides up and he keeps it where it just barely covers me. Walking slowly and never taking his mouth off mine, he carries me to the couch and lays me back. He looks at me then and the vulnerability in his eyes makes my heart hitch. There's something about him that cuts through my hardened heart and makes me believe in more—something more than shattered fragments of a life and the endless emptiness.

He leans down about an inch from my face. "Do you feel this, Maby? I could almost swear that you feel it too."

I stare at him and slowly nod. I don't trust myself to speak without crying, so I wrap my arms around his neck and kiss him like my last breath is depending on it.

I can't say how long we stay right there, simply doing just that. Of course, every cell in my body wants more of him, but it's so good, so sweet to just do this that neither of us makes a move to do more.

Eventually my phone vibrates on the counter and Coen leans back. "Do you need to get that?"

I shake my head. "I should probably get going though."

He kisses my forehead. "I hate to see you go. Are you sure you can't stay a while longer?"

"You make it hard to resist, but yeah, I should get home."

He stands up and grabs both of my hands. "I'll walk you home."

"You don't have to do that." I say, pulling down my dress.

"I do." He kisses each knuckle on one of my hands. "Hey, before we go … pick out 2 terrariums to take with you."

"Really? But you need to sell them, right?"

"I've sold plenty."

"I could just take one … I do love them so much." I can't hide my excitement.

"It has to be 2," he says.

"Why?" I ask, my eyebrows crinkled together.

"They need to be together," he answers. "Just a little condition I have."

"Hmm. Interesting. But something I will not argue with … I actually kind of get it."

His dimple deepens as he looks at me. "This has been the best 30 hours of my life."

He doesn't say a word as I look at each terrarium again.

"Aren't there some that should be for the store? Like

this big one? Or this one?" I point to one that, to me, is the most magical one of them all. The container looks like a small glass house with an open roof and inside is full of tiny colorful plants.

"Nope. I want to see what you pick."

I pick up my favorite and another one that is stark in comparison. The round dish has a small hole in the top and inside is sand, a couple of pebbles and a tiny tree that is all branches, no leaves or flowers.

Coen nods, his face completely serious. "Fascinating choices. I completely see your reasoning."

And with that, we leave his apartment. Two odd individuals who have plowed into each other and are still standing.

3-Way Stop

I SORT OF float into my apartment, still riding high on the kisses from Coen. I set the terrariums on my table and think about the possibilities. They'll need the perfect spot. I look at them for a long time, intrigued by their beauty.

Finally I get around to checking my messages. The one I missed is from Dalton.

Dalton: I miss you. Sorry things have been weird.

I feel nothing when I read his text and don't even bother texting back. Someone who doesn't even know his own mind doesn't warrant a response from me right now. I've decided that wusses are not worth my time. I look at Saul's text again and don't text him back either. I haven't decided yet if he's a wuss or just slow on the draw.

When I go to work on Monday morning, my mind is occupied with more than just counting the steps. I'm reliving Coen's kisses. They feel just as magical in my mind as they did in real time.

I've barely counted the steps inside when I have a rude awakening. There, behind the counter and on my stool, sits Saul.

"What the hell?" is my response.

He quirks an eyebrow at me, daring me to say anything else. "I'm tired of you avoiding me. I have a meeting with Anna today and I'd really like it if we could go to lunch and talk about things."

"What is there to talk about? And a simple invitation to lunch would have done the trick."

"Would you have gotten out of it?" he asks, frowning at me.

"Number one: you ask me to do things at the last minute and think when I say no it's because I'm avoiding you. Maybe I am, but, number two: I do have a life."

His face flushes slightly and he stands up from my chair. "Sorry. I do realize you have a life and maybe I'm used to the days when you just always said yes to me."

I nod. "You sort of lost that privilege, so give me a little warning the next time you get a whim."

I look at my schedule and wish that I had something at lunchtime so I could tell him no, but my schedule is pretty open. Instead of saying that, I say, "I might be able to switch some things around, I'll let you know. How long are you going to be around?"

"I'm always around, Maby," he says.

I roll my eyes. "Right. Okay. Can I get to work, please?"

He moves closer and looms over me. "I'm ready to move forward in my life, Maby. I hope you are too."

I cross my arms. "Good for you," I say with an edge of sarcasm. "Good for you."

I can tell my response aggravates him, but I don't really care.

"I'll come back by around 11:45 and see if your schedule has opened up," he says.

I nod but turn away and effectively dismiss him.

WHEN 11:40 ROLLS around, I'm no more prepared to answer Saul than I was in the hours previous. At 11:44, I decide to just say yes. I don't want to, but maybe it would be good to hear him out. He comes up to the counter at promptly 11:45 and I sit up on my stool a little straighter.

"Got time for a bite?" he asks.

"Yep," I answer.

"Good, let's do this," he says.

We go to a deli on the corner by my office and after we order our sandwiches, the conversation gets a little awkward.

"So how did your date go?"

I can tell he's trying not to sneer when he says 'date' but it's not working out so well.

My insides are gushing, *"Wonderful. Best date ever."* But I only say, "Good."

"So you're gonna see him again then?" he asks.

"Yeah," I say.

He nods and we both look away. When we look at

each other again, his eyes are dark. "I've never gotten over that you went back to Dalton after that night we were together. I thought you'd leave and be with me and when you didn't, it shook up my whole world."

"Really." I chew the inside of my mouth, staring at him. "I didn't know you even wanted to be with me. It seemed like you immediately regretted what we did and wanted me out of there." I'm shocked that he's saying any of this outright.

"I did regret that we did that while you were still with Dalton, but I still hoped you'd end it with him and be with me."

"So why didn't you tell me this when I did end it with him?" I stare him down without blinking.

"Everything was so messed up ... your mom. I was ... confused. But I'm not anymore. I *know* that I want to be with you." He reaches out and takes my hand.

I hold it for a moment and then pull away. "If you'd said this a year ago or even a month ago, it would have been a different story, but now ... I don't know. I used to think we were easy, Saul. Our friendship didn't take work, it seemed effortless. But the truth of the matter is, the moment any sign of feelings came into the picture, you got cold feet. Since then it's felt like work every time we're together."

"It doesn't have to. Now that I'm being honest with you and myself ... it doesn't have to be difficult. We can be us again, only better." His eyes light up as he smiles. "We've had some good times, right?"

The way he looks at me, my face heats up. "Yes, lots of good times," I admit. "It also hurt more than anything when you disappeared."

"I won't disappear on you again, Maby. I promise."

"I have to get back to work." I look at my watch and jump up. "Thanks for lunch."

"I'll walk you back."

WORK IS CHAOTIC during the afternoon. Every employee is in the shop, so I work in the back at my desk, trying to secure advertising for the shop in a few new venues. I can't seem to get anyone to agree to it. My paperwork doesn't get done. I still have a huge stack to finish as everyone is going home. Overwhelmed, I do something I never do: I leave it there for the next day.

My discussion with Saul plays over and over in my head. It sits in my gut and churns there. How could something I wanted for so long feel like such a lump now? I can't even define this feeling. I'm ticked at him for putting my euphoria about Coen on the back burner for even a minute. I would rather still be basking in that, but instead, I'm pondering what Saul said. He does know me, after all. This thing with Coen is new and he doesn't have a clue about all my weirdness. He'd probably run if he did. Saul knows it all and still says he wants me.

I have to recount my steps right before I get home and instead of it alarming me, I find comfort in it. I put it on like an old sweater and keep it on the rest of the night, organizing until I'm too sore to stand up.

I STOP BY La Colombe the next morning. Coen is the only person I see, even though the coffee shop is full. His smile makes my heart pound.

"I was hoping you'd stop in today," he says. "I've been missing you."

"Miss you too," I tell him. And when I say it, I realize how true it really is. I went two days without seeing him or talking to him, but just seeing his smile makes me feel a thousand pounds lighter.

"I've wanted to call," he says.

"So, why haven't you?" I lean against the counter and watch him work.

"I get the feeling you could run if I go too quickly," he says, looking up for a minute to read my reaction.

I nod and shrug. "You could be right." I move in closer to him. "But I could also run if you don't have the balls to just do what you feel."

His eyes grow wide and he stands up tall. "Okay!" He starts nodding. "*Okay!* Message received." He comes around the counter and gives me a quick peck on the lips. "I've definitely got the balls," he whispers.

I laugh. "All right then."

"How are my babies?" he asks.

"You need to come visit them," I say with a grin.

"I get off at 4."

"I'll try to leave work by 5," I tell him. "Probably can't get off any earlier than that."

"How 'bout I bring takeout over at 6? Does that give you enough time to get home and hide any skeletons you might have?"

"Ha-ha. Yes, it does." I can't even do sarcasm with him. As much as I try to hide it, he gets to me, and I end

106

up smiling like a five-year-old.

"My balls and I will be there then." He gives me a longer kiss this time and then steps back, biting his lip as he smiles

Doubt Without the Benefits

I RUSH OUT of work. When I get inside my building, I pull off my jacket and cardigan as I run up the stairs. I quickly run bath water and take the fastest bath ever, getting rid of every hair I have ever owned. I know better than to shave when I'm having a guy over that I'm so attracted to—being overgrown is my best method of putting off sex. But I'm feeling a little reckless.

Fricken-frack!

I nick my knee. Crap. It's deep too. After I get out of the bath, I jump on one foot until I can get to a Band-Aid. When I finally have my knee covered with a cute mustache Band-Aid, I try to figure out what to wear. It's still chilly, so I go for a cozy long shirt and leggings. It's just a few minutes before 6, when I hear the buzzer to the outside door of my building go off. I say, "Hi!" and buzz him up before he even says a word.

Two minutes later there's a rap on my door. I open it and see Saul standing there. The buzzer goes off again and in a daze, I push to let Coen up too.

"What are you doing here?" I lean against the door.

He holds up pizza. "Thought maybe we could do the pizza tonight … continue our conversation."

Coen comes around the corner and stops when he sees us in my doorway.

"Hey…" he says, with a tentative smile.

"Coen, this is my friend, Saul. Saul, this is Coen." I wave my arm between the two of them. "Saul was just stopping by."

"So you're the coffee shop guy," Saul says.

Coen nods. "Yep, that's me." He has a bottle of wine tucked under his arm and two bags of food from MD Kitchen. "Looks like we're on the same wavelength." He motions to the pizza. "I brought shrimp parmigiana and spaghetti with meatballs." He looks at me with a grin. "I wasn't positive how you felt about shrimp, so…"

"I love it. Sounds wonderful." I take the bags from him and we both look at Saul.

He shifts uncomfortably on both feet and is about to say something when Coen speaks up.

"I brought plenty of food—should we open this bottle of wine and get after it?"

"I should get going," Saul mutters. "Unless—do you want to add some pizza in the mix?"

There's a beat of quiet.

Coen looks at me and smiles. "Okay by me."

I sigh and give Coen's arm a squeeze.

"All right. Come on in," I tell them both, opening my door wide. "I guess my diet will have to start tomorrow." I take the bags from Coen.

"Oh please, you don't need to go on a diet," Coen says.

I grin at Coen and lift an eyebrow at Saul. He lifts his right back. His eyes look a little more mischievous than I'm comfortable with.

"You look good with a little extra meat on your bones," Saul says, nodding.

I glare at him. "I *knew* you were just waiting to throw in that I'm heavier," I snap at him under my breath.

There is one thing I know about the women Saul favors. Twigs. He likes twigs. Preferably twigs with booty … more like what I was about 25 pounds ago. Being short, there are only so many places it can go.

"Your ass *is* looking pretty damn good from here," he whispers in my ear.

I look to see if Coen heard him. He didn't, thank God. He's opening the bottle of wine.

I give Saul another glare and whisper, "*Stop it.*"

He shrugs.

"I mean it, Saul."

He grins so big his eyes practically disappear. Instead of finding it charming and irresistible, I want to punch his slightly too big nose and make it a little more crooked than it already is.

I add another plate to the table and get three wine glasses. Coen sets the food on the table.

"Thanks, Coen," I tell him gratefully. "I mean it, thank you," I whisper.

"I'm happy to meet some of your friends. You've seen part of my clan," he says. "In fact, my sister and Melissa are wanting to know when they can see you again.

I think they're trying to sabotage me." He laughs.

"I'd love to see them … and how could they possibly sabotage you? You're perfect."

I hear Saul snort at my comment right before we sit down.

"Oh, the sooner we get you together, the better … they may as well be the ones to break it to you," Coen says.

"What—your dirty secrets?" I tease. "Definitely. Should we call them right now?"

"No! Give me one more night of perfection," he says.

His eyes twinkle as he looks at me. Saul clears his throat.

"So what is it you're hiding?" Saul asks, looking directly at Coen.

Coen laughs until he realizes Saul is serious.

"Saul…" I start.

"What? What's wrong with asking that?" Saul practically growls.

"I'm not hiding anything," Coen responds. "No need to."

"Seems like if you have nothing to hide then maybe you haven't lived much," Saul says.

"I've lived plenty," Coen says. "So wait, which is it—bad if I'm hiding something or bad if I'm not?" He smiles at Saul and leans back in his chair.

"What are you—21?"

"Saul, enough with the interrogation!" I interrupt.

"I'm 25. How about you?"

Saul nods with a *yeah, that figures* expression on his face.

"Who wants some of this?" I interrupt again, putting

shrimp parmigiana on my plate. "This looks so good."

Coen seems fully aware of the tension now. I feel bad that I ever let Saul in the door. Saul doesn't bother telling Coen his age. He scoops food into his mouth and downs his wine. I take a couple of bites and try to think of anything to make this less uncomfortable.

Saul stands up from the table. "I'll get going. Thanks for sharing the pasta."

Coen stands up and holds out his hand. "It's all good, man. Hope to see you around again."

"Yeah," Saul mutters and grabs his coat.

I walk behind him to the door. "Thanks for the pizza," I say quietly. I hate to see him leaving upset, but I'm relieved that he's going.

"I shouldn't have stayed." He opens the door and turns to face me. "I wish you wouldn't do this, Maby," he says, barely above a whisper. "Why can't you see what's right in front of you? What's been right in front of you all along?"

My eyes fill with tears. "I don't know what to think anymore, Saul. Right now, though, it seems like too little, too late."

"Don't give up on me, Maby. Please. Not yet." And with that, he walks away.

I stand for a minute in the doorway and then walk back to the table. Coen looks up at me.

"I'm sorry about all that," I say quietly.

"I think I blew his plan for the night," Coen says and then cringes. "I-uh, are you seeing him?"

"No."

"Do you want to?"

"I used to," I admit.

112

I sit down at the table and push the food around on my plate.

"And then what happened?" He leans forward.

"I went out with you."

His eyes light up and he exhales. "God, so … I'm still in the running?" He quirks his head to the side and stares at me.

"Oh, you're right up there," I tell him.

He picks up my hand and kisses it. "That would explain his general disgust where I'm concerned," Coen says, gritting his teeth through his smile. "I can't say that I really blame him. I mean … you're lovely, Maby."

"Here's the thing. I'm not. I've got a lot of … weirdness. I'm pretty sure you'll run when you see that side of me." I try to sound lighthearted even though I'm speaking the cold, honest truth. "I have *not* had good luck with relationships. I haven't even gone on a date in a year. I'm not complaining. I'm just not exactly sane, Coen."

His eyes are so kind. I know that I can't keep it from him any longer. He deserves to know that he's trying to walk straight into the eye of a hurricane.

I take a deep breath and let the words rush out: "I count things." I watch his reaction and when there is none, I wait for what I said to register. "I count, like … *obsessively*. It takes over my life sometimes. Well, pretty much every day, it takes over in some way. And that's not all. I struggle with depression, especially this past year with my mom and all. But even before that … I'm a mess…" I trail off.

His thumb rubs circles on my hand while he waits for me to say more.

"It all sounds so trivial for me to say it outright, but

trust me, it isn't. I'm actually a huge risk that I'm not sure anyone should take." I bite my lip when it starts to feel the slightest bit wobbly. I'm determined not to wreck this confession fest by crying. That would just further solidify everything I'm telling him, and I'd prefer for him to have time to think about it, rather than driving the point home. Also, I know once I start, I won't be able to stop.

He's quiet for a minute or two, stroking the inside of my wrist until it makes me shiver.

"How about this?" he asks. "How about you let me decide the risk I'm willing to take? No one is perfect. I'm certainly not. I *have* had pretty good luck with my intuition though, and I've always had a *really* good feeling about you."

He stands up and gives my hand a tug, so I stand up with him. He leans his forehead on mine.

"Thank you for telling me, Maby." He leans back so he can look in my eyes. "And remember how we were talking about my balls earlier?" he whispers with a grin.

I nod, turning a deep red.

"I'm not afraid."

We kiss then and it's so good, my legs threaten to buckle. The guy makes me go weak all over. His full lips tease mine and I lose my mind in his tongue. But a tiny, nagging thought whispers away at me as we kiss.

I have enough fear for the both of us.

19

Ecstasy And The Abyss

WE MOVE OVER to the couch, never breaking the kiss. He leans me back and kisses my neck.

"I've been dying to do this since you cut your hair off," he whispers. "Your skin feels like satin."

He unbuttons a couple of buttons to my shirt and slowly works his way lower. I hold onto his curly hair and when he presses the full length of his body on mine, I think I'm going to come unglued.

I can't help it, I moan. "Mmm, you feel *so good*."

I feel his body respond to that and he looks at me, dazed, before crushing me with his mouth. The lower half of my body is drawn to his and we both strain to feel as much as possible through our clothes. It would all be very high school except I didn't feel anything close to this in high school, college, or in a single make out session with Dalton. He was never as leisurely as Coen is being. Coen

115

is unbuttoning more buttons and his tongue is gliding down with each new opening of my shirt.

I pull off his shirt as he unbuttons my last button. His skin is smooth and muscled. He pulls back to open my shirt all the way and I stare at him in awe.

"You're gorgeous," I whisper.

He's staring at me the same way. What the hell is happening here?

He runs his fingers down my skin ... over the swell of my breasts, down my stomach. His eyes wander back up to my breasts and he fingers my nipples through my bra. My eyes close of their own will and I arch my back to give him more. Before I know it my bra is on the floor and his mouth is taking me in.

"I want my mouth on every inch of your skin." His voice is a low, seductive rasp. "I can't believe I'm here with you right now. You're perfection." He kisses down my stomach and then looks at me. "I didn't come prepared tonight, Maby. I didn't expect—" His dimple deepens. "This is so much *better* than I imagined."

He runs his hands over my breasts and kisses the spot just below my belly button. "I *need* to make you feel good."

I'm feeling beyond good. I'm not sure if I say it or just think it.

"Please let me taste you..." he whispers against my stomach.

Something like a squeak escapes my mouth. I nod, biting my lip and staring at him wide-eyed.

He pulls my leggings down and admires my cute black underwear with tiny blue skulls before pulling them off.

Here we go, I think, prepared to go into my trancelike state of trying to relax and be okay that a man is going down on me. I start to do my routine count. One time with Dalton I counted to 537 and still never 'got there'. But the moment Coen's tongue makes contact, every nerve ending comes alive. He explores me with a primal hunger, on a mission to learn my body. He quickly knows it better than any man ever has before.

I bliss out on wave after wave. When he finally comes up for air, I'm limp and completely sated.

He laughs at the expression on my face. "You look … drunk."

"I am." I giggle.

"I'm the one drunk on you," he says, licking his lips and giving me a huge grin. "God, Maby, will you think I'm weird if I tell you this is the best night of my life?"

"Ha. No." I shake my head. "I've never … well … pretty much best night of mine too."

He kisses his way back up my stomach and breasts and stops at my neck. "Where I started," he says, planting soft kisses just below my ears. "I meant to be a gentleman tonight, Maby, I really did."

"I'm *so* glad you weren't."

Much later, upon reflection, I'm really grateful for all the pineapple I've consumed recently. It was not planned. I didn't expect this miraculous event to occur. Mark it down to something finally going very, very right.

❧ ❧ ❧

I WAKE UP in a dreamy state thinking about Coen. Last night ended so blissfully. He had to get up really early this morning, but still stayed late. It seemed like it was torturing him to go. I stretch out in my bed, still getting warm when I think about how he made me feel. It was truly mind-blowing...

I glance at the clock. Shit. I overslept! Normally I would already be on my way to work. I can count on one hand the times I've been a couple of minutes late to work. This is bad. I'm at least 30 minutes behind and Anna will kill me if she finds out I opened this late. I press down every urge that is bucking up inside for me to go back and count steps. I need a do over. I fight it and my hands start shaking.

Beads of perspiration take over my forehead. I run to the front door of the shop and try to unlock it, but it's already open. I put my hands on my knees and take a deep breath.

Anna is standing in the middle of all the beautiful things I've been filling the store up with. She looks *angry*. Peggy is standing beside her. I'm fairly certain it's not Peggy's scheduled time to be in the shop.

"You're late," she says and flings a folder on the counter. "And you left this hanging last night, Mabel. And do you know what else? You missed a huge shipment this morning. It was a COD, so I got the call when they couldn't stick around waiting."

My eyes get huge as I pick up the file. Oh no. It's a difficult vendor that I've been trying to woo for months. They only deliver to a small handful of shops in the city, none that are close to each other. It took a long time to get them to agree to add our store to the list.

"What happened?"

"They decided to go with Allen Price's shop."

"You've gotta be kidding. Allen is a prick!"

"Well, I know that and you know that, but … looks like *they* don't mind." She points wildly at the file. "I don't know what's going on with you, Mabel, but I can't handle the risk any longer. You've never been stable and now you're not reliable with your job either. I can't risk losing business." She glances at Peggy and then back at me. "You're fired."

"What? *Fired?* Anna, no! I can talk to them, try to change their minds. And we don't need them anyway! We can find something else that will sell just as well," I say in a panic. "Allen must have done something slimy to sway this one. I *had* them. You *know* I'm good at my job."

She shakes her head. "I need you to leave your keys, the laptop … your cell phone."

"What the fuck, Anna?" Any professionalism I had went out the door when my former friend completely sabotaged me. "Cell phone? Seriously? No."

"I gave you that phone to do your job. Hopefully you have a backup."

"Unbelievable. Un-fucking-believable. I've *made* this store what it is. I was here from the beginning. You think you can keep it going on your own?" I wave my arms toward her. "I've been doing your job for the last three years." I nod at Peggy, bearing her no hard feelings. She's been given the unfortunate job of being a witness to this. "I give you six months before you go under."

I hold up my phone. "I'm not giving you my fucking phone. Do whatever you must. I'll be happy to have a little conversation with Peggy here about those trips to the B&B

you've been writing off every year. Or a little conversation with Joey about those." I point to the fake boobs Joey never realized he'd bought. She'd blamed her new curvaceousness on a rapid weight gain and Joey had been naive and lust-driven enough to believe her. Now she could blame it on a baby and he'd be none the wiser yet again.

Anna's face goes white. "Get out. You have 10 minutes for me to see the back of you headed out that door."

I flip her off. Both hands.

I never said I was mature.

She is physically shaking when she abruptly turns and stalks off.

I get to work on my desk. I don't have many personal items lying around, but I gather the little there is in a pile. I take the tiny hard drive that I keep in my purse and quickly move some of my pictures and documents off of the laptop. While I'm at it, I make sure the new vendors I've been working with are also transferred to the hard drive. I'm not doing anything to make Anna's job easy when she's just fired me.

I don't bother saying goodbye. I've invested all my time in something that has never given anything back. When I step outside, the tears fall. As I shuffle down the street with my purse and a meager three years stuffed in a box, I realize I've felt every possible emotion in a single day.

Alone, again.

20

It's Not You, It's Me

I'M NOT EVEN out the door when I feel my arm being yanked out of its socket. At first I think I'm being mugged and drop everything. My box falls on a foot and a girly scream comes out. I'm so surprised it isn't a man, I turn around to look at my attacker.

"Courtney!" I take in her tiny baby bump and bleached blond hair all in one glance. "What's going on?"

I rub my arm and glare at her. She kicks my box and gives me a scathing look.

"I want you to tell me," she spits out.

"Tell you what?" I shake my head.

She holds up her phone and shows me a picture of my boobs. I immediately feel feverish.

"You just couldn't let us be happy, could you?" She starts to cry.

"Believe me, I can let you be happy. The two of you

121

deserve one another."

She grabs my arm again and gets an inch away from my face—close enough that when she talks, she spits in my eye.

"Listen to me, you bitch, stay away from Dalton. You have never been good enough for him and you never will be. I don't know what possessed you to think you could start something back up with him, but let me tell you, he's over you."

"I didn't start anything." I feel like the wind is knocked out of me. "I thought you were my friend," I whisper.

Tears roll down my face. The last hour has caught up with me. My body is shutting down from the stress.

"What did I ever do to you, to make you hate me so much?" I ask her.

She lets go of my arm and backs up a little. "You made him miserable. All he ever did was complain about how crazy you were. It's your fault you lost him. Your fault that you can't stop doing stupid shit. You need help, Mabel." She does the crazy finger motion around her brain.

I nod. "I do. Because God help me, I was a lunatic for ever trusting you or Dalton. I might be crazy, but at least I'm a decent person. I'd rather have no one than have snakes in my life."

She holds up her phone again with my picture. I cock my head to the side.

"They look pretty nice." I point to hers. "He must have been missing them to beg me for this picture."

Her face drops and she goes red. I instantly regret what I've said. I've just stooped to her level.

"I'm sorry, Courtney. I've felt horrible for doi—" I step toward her.

She grabs my shoulders and slams me against the brick building. She's at least 5 inches taller and could easily take me in a fight.

"Stay. Away. From. Him," she says between clenched teeth.

"I promise you: I. Don't. Want. Him," I say, teeth equally clenched.

"You pull this shit again and I'll come after you," she promises me. She backs away, holding both hands in the air.

"Isn't that what you just did?" I mock her. "Feel better?"

She looks like she's going to hit me and I stand tall, staring her down.

"I'm gonna say one thing to you, Courtney, and then you need to get the hell out of my sight. I'm not the one you need to be having this conversation with. Got it?" I pick up my box and my purse. "Your boyfriend has a problem, and it's beyond either one of us. Good luck with that."

And with that, I walk away. I hope my shakes aren't showing, but I think they probably are.

It feels good for all of 6 seconds. I've told Anna off, and finally Courtney, too. All in less than a half hour. It's been a long time coming. But the further I get, the more devastated I am. I've lost my job. What am I going to do? No one is going to hire me. They're right—I'm crazy. And what *ever* made me pick them as friends? What's wrong with me that I would be drawn to people like them? What does that say about me? Just further proof that I'm unstable.

Every friend I've ever had has let me down. I see Coen's smile and think that he doesn't count. I'm pretty sure he really is as wonderful as he seems, which is exactly why I can't see him anymore. There's too much wrong with me—even someone as grounded as Coen is would lose his way with someone like me.

I damage people.

I stop walking as the truth hits me. It's *me*. I'm the one that turns people. They must have all started out good to begin with … *I'm* the weak link here. I'm the bad seed. *I'm* the true snake.

In a fog, I get on the subway and fall into a seat. The trembling gets worse. I put my head between my knees and will the nausea away. *I can't throw up here. I can't throw up here. I can't...*

"You okay, miss?" A voice asks, with a hand on my shoulder.

I nod, but feel the sweat pouring out of my body. *I'm not okay. I'm not okay. I'm not okay. I'm not...*

"Can I help you?" he asks again.

"Sick," I mumble. "I'll be okay." *Just please don't ask me anything else. I will throw up all over you.*

I stand up at a stop that isn't mine and stumble off the train. I throw up under a tree and don't look at anyone around me. They probably think I'm a junkie. In a way I am. I've just thought it didn't really hurt anyone else for me to be consumed by OCD, but turns out, it hurts everything and everyone I touch. My stupid compulsions make people run from me. They make boyfriends turn to other lovers. They make girlfriends who have stolen said boyfriends shove you into brick buildings while they tell you how worthless you are. They make the steady and rock solid friends avoid you for a year even after you've lost everyone.

It's me.

Shout Whispers

THE SIDEWALK APPEARS larger than it really is. The cracks scream at me, until I have to go back and walk the last 7 tiles again. I walk it 7 times—left foot, right foot in each tile—until it feels right and I can move on. I walk past my corner deli and end up dropping my box from work in the trash. There's nothing in there that I want to bring in to sully my apartment.

My grandma would kill me for throwing that box away. For her sake, I contemplate going back and trying to retrieve it, but the thought of all those germs … there's no way I could touch that box now.

For a fleeting moment, I nearly stop by Dr. Still's office to see if she might have an opening. I already know what she would say though. She'd say there is hope and that I don't have to fall into this downward spiral. She'd try to convince me again to give Cognitive Behavior Therapy a try. She'd ask why I haven't been in to see her in a while and why I stopped taking the medicine. Again. I don't have Dalton to blame this time.

I can't think about that right now. Nothing is ever going to help. I don't know why I ever think it can be any different. Medicine doesn't solve it. I can't prevent stress from happening. Some people are just disasters from the start. A continuous cloud hovers overhead with a steady downpour. The precipitation lets up a little once in a while, and then the deluge hits. Every now and then a sprinkle fools me into thinking I can manage it, but it's a trick. My cloud will never go away.

When I look up and realize where I am, my shoulders drop. My feet ache and a new blister is yelling at me. I sit down on the front step in front of Saul's apartment building. I put my head in my hands and force myself to breathe through the panic that's taken over my body. I'm not sure how long I sit there, but I heard once that panic attacks really only last 15 seconds. I don't know if I can believe that because every second feels like an eternity. My skin wants to crawl off of my body. The moment the air finally reaches my lungs, I realize I *cannot* let Saul see me like this. It would basically *confirm* my crazy. Force of habit brought me here, but that doesn't mean I can stay. I get up and run like an army is chasing me down. I know I'm looking even more manic than Tom Cruise—if I were him I'd fire whoever keeps making him run in every single movie—but I can't stop.

I don't know how I make it to my apartment without collapsing. My chest burns. Everything hurts. But somewhere along the way, adrenaline kicks in. I manage to keep running all the way up my stairs. I close the door behind me and lock it. Unlock. Lock. Unlock. Lock. Unlock. Lock. Pause. Check one more time to make sure it really is locked. And then once more, for good measure.

I pull my clothes off as I walk to the shower. Turning the water as hot as I can stand it, I scrub and scrub and scrub until my skin feels like it's going to explode into fiery embers, sparking red and gold and black. Charred.

When I get out, the clock beside the bed says 12:30 PM. It seems impossible—I've already lived a lifetime today. I crawl into bed in my underwear and pile the covers up to my chin.

Staring at the ceiling, the tears roll back into my hair and ears.

"I can't do this," I whisper to my mom. I'm not sure if she's up there or in the ground or all around me, but it just feels natural to look up. "I don't want to live without you anymore. I can't do it. You know I can't."

The whole bed shakes as I cry a hard, ugly cry.

MY CELL PHONE wakes me up a couple of hours later. I let it go to voicemail, seeing Coen's name scrolling across the screen. My temples pound like they have a mind of their own. I'm so stopped up I can't breathe. I know without looking that my eyes will be puffy slits. My eyelids burn. The tears start right back up and feel warm as they roll down my face.

Coen needs someone far better than me. Younger, innocent. He deserves a tall, perky model type. Someone not too smart, but smart enough … who hasn't lived a thousand gross lives, but radiates sunshine, and weaves daisies in her pretty brown hair. In other words, the antithesis of me. I can just imagine them making terrariums together and my gut squeezes with a pathetic ache.

The phone dings with a voicemail and even though I know I have to end it with him, I can't resist hearing his voice.

Hi, Maby. You have driven me to a whole new level of distraction today. I just wanted to thank you for the smile that hasn't left my face since I left your place last night. The only thing that would make this day better is for you to call me back. I mean, not to invite myself over or anything, but ... yeah, I'm totally inviting myself over. Oh, hey, this is Coen, by the way.

I can hear the laugh in his voice. It's one of the cutest things about him.

I cover my head with the blankets and will this day to be over.

Another dream—the awful kind where I keep thinking I'm going to see my mom, but I never quite do. She's just always dancing on the peripheral outskirts of my dreams. I can *nearly* imagine that I hear her, and if I could stand on a stool or see around such and such, I would be able to see her ... but it's like my eyes are in slow motion or quicksand. The circuits never connect. Eventually my cries reach her and she crawls into bed with me and holds me. It's so real I can feel her breath on my neck as she spoons me.

I know that if she'll just stay with me like this, I'll

never have to wake up.

❖ ❖ ❖

DAYS PASS AND I'm still under the covers. I know I should get up. I'm *ashamed* I haven't gotten up. I just *can't* get up. I can't even eat. The vain/morbid part of me hopes that I'll die here and when they find me I'll at least be skinny.

Coen's voicemail messages have become increasingly shorter, with the 4th simply saying, "I'll just wait for you to call me. Hope you're okay, Maby."

I'm impressed and guilt-ridden that he's still trying.

Saul has also left messages and texts. Anna apparently told him the same day I was fired. He's been by several times, banging on the door like the brute he is.

I've also heard from Paschal and think fleetingly that although I've needed girlfriends, Paschal is like 3 of the best girlfriends put together. I hope he meets some other girl who gets a short hair makeover and that they can become instant kindred spirits like we were.

On the 3rd morning, I know I'm losing it.

If I were brave enough, I'd end this. I don't want to live and I'm too afraid to die.

My stomach is gnawing on itself and my throat feels like I've gone too long without water … because I have. I don't know if my mind is playing tricks on me or if I'm dreaming again. I can't make myself care.

I can't do it anymore.

My mom sits on my bed, making the mattress sink a little with the motion.

"Mabel," she whispers.

Her hand caresses my face and I close my eyes, leaning into her hand. It smells like lemons. She drinks water with half of a lemon every morning and her hand always smells faintly of that lemon.

"Mabel," she says louder, giving my shoulder a shake.

I jump and open my eyes, looking for her. She's gone. I look around the room and swear I can smell lemons. I drift back into a deep sleep and it happens again.

"Mabel, get up," she says. *"Mabel!"*

I feel her shaking me, but I know she's not really there. I don't want to ruin everything by opening my eyes and seeing the truth.

"You have to live, Mabel."

It's a whisper, but it echoes through the room as loud as a shout. I shiver and slowly open my eyes, sitting up.

The curtains flutter like a breeze has just gone through the room and I blink.

Signature Statement

ON SHAKY LEGS, I make my way to the kitchen and open a can of chicken broth. I don't even heat it, I just take a few sips and let that settle in my stomach before I eat or drink anything else. I nibble on a saltine cracker then and take a water bottle into the bathroom with me.

Feeling too tired to stand in a shower, I run a bath and sink into the hot water. It feels good. The broth hits my stomach and I get on my knees in the tub and throw it up in the toilet just in time.

Thinking back over the last few days, I don't know what is real and what is imagined. I do know that I can't let a stupid job do me in. The tears start again and plop into the bath water.

It was never that simple. I have to make a decision. Today.

I pick up my razor and my hands shake as I hold it

over my skin. *Coward*. I drop it in the water.

Either I kill myself and end the madness. Or I decide today to let my madness work for me.

I repeat those words to myself 6 times.

Let my madness work for me. Let my madness work for me. Let my madness work for me. Let my madness work for me. Let my madness work for me. Let my madness work for me.

After I've washed my hair, I dip my head under the water again and stay submerged, reveling in how my entire body finally feels warm. I'm about to lose my breath when I feel hands on my arms, yanking me out of the water. Completely out of the water.

I sputter and open my eyes.

"Saul! What the fuck?"

He's in the process of laying me out on the floor, while I'm fighting to cover my naked body.

"I'm not gonna let you kill yourself!"

"I was washing my hair! *Geez!*"

"Didn't look like that. You weren't coming up."

"You were staring at me while I *took a bath*?" I shove him and in removing my hand from my body, reveal a breast. My eyes narrow when his gaze flits down for a millisecond. "How did you get in, anyway?"

"I kicked the door in," he says like it's nothing.

"You've gotta be kidding me," I groan.

"I was worried, Maby. When Anna told me you were fired and then I couldn't reach you, I thought…" he trails off.

"Maybe earlier, but not just then," I admit sheepishly.

He averts his eyes and hands me a towel. "Well, I can't say I'm sorry then. I've been over three times. I knew you were in here."

"Sorry I've been avoiding you. I've … been a mess." My voice comes out in a croak. I can't look at him. I'm ashamed of where my mind has been and what I know I'm capable of doing to myself.

"This with your job—look at it as a blessing. You hated working for her anyway. You did everything and she got all the money. It's only gonna get worse with the new shop. She would have driven you into the ground."

"Can we talk about this when I get some clothes on?" I snap, shivering under the towel.

"I'm fine like this." He shrugs and I see him grin out of the corner of my eye.

I roll my eyes and even that takes a huge effort. So weak. "Well, I'm freezing. And I had just finally gotten warmed up before you burst in here going all Incredible Hulk on me."

Before I know it, he's hoisted me over his shoulder and is carrying me to my room. He flops me on the bed like a rag doll and walks to my dresser. He quickly takes out T-shirts and jeans.

"What are you doing?"

He's in my underwear drawer now and grinning at my colorful skull and dagger-themed panties.

"Saul! Get out of my underwear."

He moves on to my pajamas and socks, putting it all in the growing pile in his arms.

"What—?"

"You're coming to my place for a few days."

"Like *hell* I am."

"I don't trust you right now." He points at me, punctuating each word. "I need to keep an eye on you."

134

I get off the bed, slowly, feeling lightheaded. My hands have a tight grip on my towel, making sure it doesn't flap open. I stand a foot from him and up on my tiptoes, so the distance isn't so great and he'll know I mean business.

"I'm not going anywhere with you. I decided to not kill myself today and I'm going to be fine now." I dig into his chest with my finger at that last word.

"Well, excuse me for that not making me feel any better," he yells. He drops the pile of clothes at my feet and puts his hands on the top of his head as he stares me down. "Either you get some clothes on and come with me, or I will get you dressed myself and carry you out of here."

We stare at each other, chests heaving with angry breath. I want to squeeze his massive neck, but my hands aren't big enough. I'd probably need to eat something first too...

Finally he blinks and says, "So what's it gonna be? I've got your clothes right here." He holds up the hot pink underwear with the teal daggers.

I snatch them out of his hand. "Give me those."

I go to my closet and pull out a sweater dress instead of the jeans he's holding and raise my eyebrows, daring him to try to tell me what to wear. I walk to the bathroom with as much dignity as I can muster with a bath towel barely wrapped around me.

Before I close the door behind me, I give him the finger. It seems to be my thing.

❦ ❦ ❦

NEITHER OF US says a word on the short cab ride to his apartment. Once I've dragged myself up the stairs, I can feel his anger settling into something a little closer to bristling uneasiness. He unlocks his door and sneaks a look over his shoulder at me. I shoot another handful of scowls at him and he gulps.

"I don't like it when you're mad at me," he says, sighing. "Come on. It'll be like old times. We can watch movies tonight. I'll order pizza…"

"We can't just magically have it be like old times, Saul. Too much has happened. Too much *time* has passed," I tell him with a clipped voice. I look around the room. "Dammit, I left my laptop."

"I've missed having you here," he says softly.

"Yeah, well, I never went anywhere, buddy. *You* did."

"I'm not going anywhere now, I promise you that."

I look up at him and suddenly feel blood rush to my face. His eyes are so full of emotion, I'm the one gulping now. Whatever used to be holding him back is not there any longer. I seem to be the only one holding up the enormous barrier between us.

23

I Think I Can't

I EAT A slice of pizza and then pick at another.

"Not feeling well?" Saul asks.

"Not very hungry," I tell him.

I fail to mention that after just breaking a 'fast' with a few sips of chicken broth, pizza might not have been the best choice for me.

He frowns. "That doesn't usually stop you."

I bop him on the head with one of his couch pillows. "Shut it."

It's the first laugh I've heard from Saul in a while. His eyes disappear with his laugh.

"You know it's true," he says.

"I'll eat when I'm hungry." I stalk to his garbage can and toss the crust and olives in the trash.

"You're so *volatile*." He sees my empty plate when I walk back to the couch. "Did you just throw that away?"

he asks in shock.

I nod. "What?"

"Why'd you do that?" He demands, looking wounded.

My eyes widen. "*Oh*—I wasn't thinking. Sorry…"

He shrugs, but I can tell he doesn't really believe that I didn't do it on purpose. He used to give me all the mushrooms and I'd give him all the olives. I look at his plate and there's a small pile of mushrooms on the side of his plate.

"I was just making sure I got them all before I gave them to you," he mutters.

An unpleasant silence hangs in the room. I lean back on the couch and mentally groan. I don't like being angry with Saul. And I don't like being mean to him either. I'm not used to feeling this way. He's always been able to snap me out of any bad mood and make me laugh. No matter what. Even the times when I should have … I just can't seem to stay mad at him.

He's staring at me.

"What are you thinking?" I ask.

He hands me a glass of wine and holds up his beer bottle. "To new beginnings."

I sigh. We clink and take a drink.

An hour later Saul is laughing at everything I say. I'm even finding some things humorous. I'm trying really hard to shelve the dark that's taken up residence in my brain the last few days and just enjoy a night. I'm still hurt, still bitter, still broken, but … there's a good looking man who is trying to do everything possible to make me feel better. I have to at least fake it so he'll let me go home soon.

138

He's been steadily filling my glass and drinking right along with me. I've gone on a few Anna rants, impersonating her to the point of perfection. That's what Saul says anyway. He has me do it over and over, laughing until he's wiping his eyes.

"I think she's always been jealous of you," he says when we're taking a breather.

"No, she's not—I have nothing for her to be jealous of!" I shake my head.

"You're everything she's not—of course she has something to be jealous of with you!"

I scoff at him. "Don't be ridiculous."

"You're beautiful, Maby."

"No, I'm not. She's the beautiful one!"

He raises an eyebrow and gives me a look. "I saw her once without her makeup. It's *ter-ri-fy-ing*. You look amazing just rolling out of bed…" He gets a far off look in his eyes and my heart pounds a little faster. He has a heated expression when he looks at me again. "You're smart, kind … you have the best a— … you're kind," he repeats, flustered. "She's … well, she's a viper."

"Guys tend to not mind the viper qualities. I mean, look at Courtney. Back when I first started bleaching my hair, she made so much fun of me. And then after she stole Dalton, she bleached her brown hair to match mine…"

"Because Dalton loved when you did that. He thought it was so bold."

"He's such an idiot," I groan.

"Wuss."

"Pussy."

"Wanker."

I lose it then and laugh until I'm wheezing. Saul

pounds my back. Once I catch my breath, he pours the last of the wine and gives my glass another clink.

"To finding our way back," he says.

We sip and both set down our drinks at the same time. The current shifts between us, but I'm still a little late in realizing that Saul is coming in for a kiss. His mouth claims mine and he kisses me like he wants to prove a point. I think fleetingly how different this kiss is from Coen's. That kiss was straightforward. Pure and meaningful. This one is loaded with intent. It's a little jarring. I'm not sure I want to go backwards to complicated.

But it's Saul and he's the one I've pined over for so long. He's familiar and comfortable. I second-guess my thoughts as rapidly as they're happening. This is what I've wanted all along. Right? To have Saul's heart?

Everyone makes mistakes, I reason with myself. He's trying to prove himself. God knows I fail miserably every day. I should be willing to give someone another chance.

Any other thoughts that sneak in about where he's been all this time, I push away. I'm too weak. It feels too good to be touched.

I match his fervor with my kiss. He groans and pulls me tight against his chest. He tugs on my sweater dress.

"Can I please take this off?" he asks.

"We're drunk, maybe this isn't the best time, Saul..." I start, but his lips take the words and then he wipes them out with his tongue.

It does feel intoxicating to have Saul so boldly taking what he wants. I let myself be caught up in the moment. I think we'll never really know what we can be with each other if we don't see where this goes.

He picks me up and carries me to his bedroom. I sober up quickly when I see his bed. He lays me on the bed and pulls my dress over my head. My hair gets static cling and he chuckles when he sees it going every which way. He gives it a tug.

"You're so sexy, Maby."

He makes quick work of my bra, unclasping it and throwing it across the room. He buries his head in my breasts and then takes his shirt off. With one hand, he rubs one breast, and with the other, he unbuttons his fly.

"Saul," I whisper. "Slow down."

He pauses, stretching the waist of his boxers out. "Do you not want this?"

"Do you?" I ask.

Part of me will never get over him turning me away before.

"Of course I do. Can't you tell?" he jokes.

His penis looks big and a little angry. It intrigues me, I'm not gonna lie.

I feel the need to count something, anything, stronger than I've ever felt it before. I squash it down.

I will not do it. I will not do it. I will not do it. I will not do it. I will not do it. I will not do it. I will not do it. I will not do it. I will not do it. I will not do it. I will not do it. I will not do it. I will not do it.

There.

I will not do it.

"What?" Saul asks, his eyebrows meeting in the middle.

"I'm not going to count. I will not do it."

"Okay, Maby," he says as he comes in for another kiss.

This kiss is the best one so far. It almost makes me

forget everyone and everything. Almost.

It isn't until a little later, when we're both coming and I'm moaning, "Harder!" that I truly do get lost in Saul's arms.

Resembling The Twigs

AND THEN I wake up. My shoulder is prickling; the pain is like a thousand tiny knives digging into my skin. What the hell?

I turn and see Saul's chin resting on my shoulder. His stubble is rubbing my skin raw. I try to shift underneath him, but he's so heavy. Whenever he moves, it feels like he's taking off another layer of my skin.

My face feels the same way. I have sensitive skin, though, so it's not like he was doing anything wrong. It's just that I'll have the marks proving what we did. I bite my lip. I can't believe I just had sex with Saul.

Coen! Oh God. Coen. My lips tremble and I bite down harder. It's not like Coen and I were exclusive or anything, but...

I can't believe I had sex with Saul!

My stomach drops and I try to remember if we used a

condom. We were going too fast and then it got better. Really nice. I look over at the side table and see the wrapper there. We did. Thank God. That's all I need—a little psychotic baby with my genes.

I lift Saul's arm and he lets out a little snore. He is *out*. I slide lower and lower until I'm completely under his arm and can get out. I sit up and try to lift his leg off of mine too.

I throw on one of his nicely pressed dress shirts and walk to the bathroom. After I've brushed my teeth, I sneak to the kitchen and start the coffee. I'm buttering toast when he stumbles in, rubbing his bare chest. He looks like a little boy giant with his messy hair and sleepy eyes. He grins when he sees me in his shirt.

I smile and get back to the toast. "Got any peanut butter?"

"Of course." He reaches into the cabinet and pulls it out.

When he gets to me, he sets the peanut butter down in front of me and pulls my back into his chest. He hugs me tight and I close my eyes, trying to fully enjoy how sturdy and safe he feels.

He turns me around and leans down to kiss me. I kiss him back, but when he lifts me up and wraps my legs around his, I stop.

He leans his head back and looks into my eyes. His eyes crinkle as he smiles at me and that has always been my biggest weakness with him. My heart never fails to squeeze just a little bit when he looks at me this way.

"You okay, Maby?" he asks softly.

I stare at him and give a tiny nod. It's hard to think about anything when he's squeezing my ass that way.

144

"You sure?" he asks again.

I look at him gravely and a million thoughts rush through my head at once.

Do I feel the way I used to about him? What does he really feel for me? Should this be feeling different/better/easier/harder/mushier than it does? Is being wrapped up in his arms like I'm hugging a teddy bear really the best thing I've ever felt?

Coen.

I shake my head and try to stop the jumbled heap of questions.

And still Coen. Sweet, beautiful, kind Coen.

I might not know much of anything, but I do know that I cannot ruin Coen. He's too good. I can't be the one to mess him up. I don't want to ruin Saul either, but he's 30 and he knows all my mess. If he can't step up and handle it by now, no one ever will.

I put my forehead to Saul's and kiss him back hard.

THIS TIME WHEN we have sex, I'm fully aware of *everything*. He knows what he's doing. When we're done this time, I can't believe we *haven't* had sex before now.

He kisses my hair as I lay on his chest.

"You've been holding out on me, Mr. Saul."

"I could say the same about you, Miss Maby."

"Ew, I just realized we'll never be able to marry each other." I turn to him with my nose scrunched.

He laughs. "Uh, why not?"

"Maby Mayes—that's the worst name ever!" I rub my

145

face where his stubble has been.

He cringes. "Ow, you're all red. Sorry about my scruff." He runs his fingers softly along my chin. "And I think Maby Mayes is pretty sweet, actually." He tries to kiss my lips without any of his beard touching my skin. "Maby Mayes, Maby Mayes," he whispers. "Or maybe I could go by Saul Armstrong. That's much better!"

"It was a joke! Don't be getting any ideas!" I yell as he goes under the covers and nuzzles my chest, tickling my sides.

❧ ❧ ❧

AFTER MY SHOWER, I tell Saul I'm going home.

"No—stay here. We're having fun, right?"

"Yes, it's been fun, but I have to start figuring out what I'm going to do about a job. I have calls to make … all that."

He looks wounded. "I hoped we could just stay here. I took today off. Weekend is coming up. I thought maybe we could … not leave the bed…" He smiles, but it falters when he sees my expression.

I look away to avoid his eyes. Just a few days ago, I couldn't see past that very second, and now I … well, I'm finding life more bearable, that's for sure. But I feel antsy too, and I'm not sure what to make of that. Maybe I just need time to process this whole change of events.

"Are you regretting being with me?" he asks quietly.

"No!" I respond quickly. "No, I'm not … I just … I don't really know what to think about it yet."

He nods. "I've wanted to be with you for a long time,

146

Maby. I wish I hadn't wasted so much time."

"That's just it. Maybe it wasn't a waste. Maybe it had to go like this. I'm still not sure why you want to be with me now … or even that you really do." I look at him before zipping my bag.

His jaw ticks as he watches my hands. He doesn't say anything, just stares into nothing. There's the non-committal Saul I know and love. I slip on my shoes.

"Thanks for the overnight," I say nonchalantly, giving a little wave.

"Wait, you're going right now?"

"Yep."

"Let me walk you home."

"No, it's okay. Thanks, though. I'm good. Bye, Saul." I stand on my tiptoes and kiss his cheek.

"Why do I feel like you're never coming back?" he asks.

"You know I can't quit you, Saul." I give him a wobbly smile.

He smiles back and gives me another hug. "You better not. I have lots more I need to do to this hot little body you've got going." He gives my butt a slap and I jump.

"You're such a child," I grumble, rolling my eyes.

"That's not what you thought this morning," he whispers, grinning.

He pulls me in for another kiss and makes it count before I walk out the door.

Zero, Zip, Zot. Bottom.

WALKING HOME I scroll through my missed texts and voicemails to avoid … myself. I'm feeling a really weird urge to yank on my hair that I'm trying to avoid. Not just a tug, but a full-on, pull-it-out-to-the-roots kind of yank. Nervous energy is pumping through my blood and it seems like it would ease it a little if I pulled out some of my hair. As I think it and want it, I simultaneously realize that the thought is not something I should entertain. I just can't stop imagining the relief. Even though my bag and purse are flapping on my arm, I start jogging. It's uncoordinated and probably completely unsightly, but it helps. I count my steps while I jog, but suddenly that seems like nothing. It certainly seems a lot better than pulling out my hair.

I want to roll my eyes at my own logic.

I decide right then to go see Paschal after I've dropped off my bag. Maybe I'll have him add some pink when he touches up the blue. Besides missing him, I know that I need to keep doing things that help. I don't want to get all vain, but something little like making my hair fun so I don't pull it out might help. I can't afford to let my compulsions start affecting me on the outside as well as the inside.

There are a few texts from Dalton, growing increasingly hostile with each text.

Dalton: I can't believe Courtney knows. Sorry I didn't give you any warning. She took off before I could think straight.

Later...

Dalton: What the hell did you tell her?

Later...

Dalton: Answer me, dammit! Why would you do that? Son of a bitch! I knew you were a vindictive bitch, but this is too much.

That does it. I answer him back.

You've gotta be kidding me. Take a long look in the mirror, you flaming wuss. You're the one who caused this mess. I didn't tell her you texted me incessantly for weeks! I didn't tell her you whacked off on video! I told her you asked to see me. That's it. You got off easy, jerk off. Now leave me the hell alone.

He starts calling then and I decline his call. I'm not giving him a single second longer of my time. Of all the arrogant bastards. I can't even believe I *ever* thought I loved him. I have a full body shiver at the thought ... and *not* the good kind.

He calls again. And again.

Okay, I'll give him one more second after all. I text him one last time.

When I say leave me the hell alone, I mean, DO NOT CONTACT ME EVER AGAIN. Got it? I HOPE I NEVER SEE YOUR TINY HEAD ON YOUR TOO SHORT OF A BODY AGAIN. Your mini legs can walk themselves out of my life FOREVER. Get LOST.

I start laughing then and can't stop. I can't believe I just said that, but fuck it all, it feels damn good. The lady I pass on the street watches me carefully out of the corner of her eye, but I don't care. I know that I'm losing my mind, but at this moment, it's not all bad. It feels like spring ... like I've shed my scales and am going to get new skin. My apartment is just ahead and I lean against a nearby tree, tilting my face to the sun. I giggle again over the short comment and walk toward my building.

Before I go inside, I call Dr. Still's office. "Does she have an opening soon, by any chance?"

"She had a 2:30 cancellation. Are you able to make that?"

I look at my watch and have just enough time to eat lunch and go. "I'll be there," I promise.

❧ ❧ ❧

DR. STILL SMILES, BUT it doesn't quite reach her eyes. I feel like a little girl getting scolded when I sit down across from her.

"So, you've missed your last handful of appointments. You lucked out getting in today on a cancellation," she says.

"I know. Thank you so much for seeing me. I'm sorry for missing—I'm going to do better." As I say it, I surprise myself by meaning it. "I'm going to make every effort to come regularly. And to stay on my medication. I had a good stretch and it made me think I could handle not taking it."

I look at her sheepishly and fold my hands in my lap. She nods and waits to see if I'll say more.

"I then hit bottom, I guess you could say … and I know I'm probably never going to be normal. I mean, who is normal, anyway?" I laugh awkwardly. "But I don't want to sabotage all my relationships anymore. I don't want new compulsions to start. Today I wanted to yank my hair out just to get rid of anxiety. It's part of why I called to see if I could come in. I know once I start something like that, I'll just have a new issue to try to get rid of…"

"Obsessively pulling out hair is known as trichotillomania. It can be fairly common for people with OCD, but you've never mentioned feeling this compulsion. Is this new for you? Did the feeling go away or did you give in to it?"

"I started running instead and it helped get my mind off of it."

Dr. Still leans up in her seat. "Good. You're still not fully answering me, though—have you ever wanted to pull your hair out before?"

I shake my head no.

"Okay. I'm glad you distracted yourself. Exercise is actually a powerful tool that works. I know it sounds trivial to simply start running, but you did the right thing. I've mentioned you trying yoga before, but if you prefer to run, I'm good with that. A dance class would be great too. Do you like to dance?"

"I like it, I'm just not any good at it," I admit.

"All the more reason for you to take a class," she says with a smirk. "I'd like to talk to you about some relaxation techniques I think will help you. I'll refill your medication today and I hope you will take it. If you take the medicine, it will help you carry out the other tools I'm trying to give you. Okay?"

I nod.

"It would also be good for you to start journaling. Some find that it helps to write out their anxieties and compulsions as they come. If writing about it just makes you want to live out what you're writing, start writing a story, a poem, anything else that might get your mind off of it. Do you think you can do that?"

"Yes."

"Okay. I hope you really mean it this time, Mabel, because I have hope that you can get better—IF you take action." She looks at me sternly.

I nod my head again.

"*Now* ... what got you to rock bottom?"

26

Mental Marathon

I REFILL MY prescription and go see Paschal. He yells when he sees me.

"You disappeared on me," he moans as he gives me a hug.

"I'm sorry. I've been going through a bad stretch. I'm here now though, and you're not getting rid of me." I grin.

"I have a client coming in soon, but I want to see you—come back and I'll touch up your color." He fingers the fading blue.

"Okay, I will. Would tomorrow work?" I ask.

"Yeah, come in around 11:30—maybe we can go get lunch too?"

"I'd love it!" I give him another hug goodbye as his client walks in the door.

I step outside and start walking toward the coffee shop. I don't know if Coen would even be working right now, but I've avoided him long enough.

It's late Friday afternoon, and so nice outside. Spring has finally decided to show up. I pull off my sweatshirt as I stand outside the shop and try to casually look in the window. My heart drops. He's in there. I watch him for a while, until he notices me. *Shit.*

I turn around and count to 14.

"Maby?" he says quietly. He's holding the door open.

"Hey, Coen." I turn to face him and lift my hand in a small wave.

"I thought that was you." He smiles tentatively and opens the door wider. "You coming in?"

"Sure. I may as well." I tilt my head up to the sky and hope that my stupidity will be carried off with the angels.

He lets me in and heads toward the back of the shop, looking back to see if I'm following. All of a sudden, he stops walking and I bump into him. Again they fail me— why do I still hope in the supernatural?

Coen puts his hand on my arm. "Did I mess everything up, Maby? I went too fast, didn't I?"

His eyes look so sad and so earnest, I want to take up that running regimen and run miles and miles away from here.

"You were perfect, Coen," I whisper.

His hand finds mine then and he pulls me to a table in the back.

"Then why do I feel like you're done with me?"

I put my head in my hands. "You're way too good for me," I make my voice sound like the cold bitch that I am.

"You're deciding for me again. I get a say in this, you know."

"I know." I discreetly wipe my eyes before I lift my

head. "Just trust me. It's good if you get out of this," I wave my hand between the two of us, "before it ever even gets started. It's for the best."

His long, curly eyelashes sweep up and down as he blinks, trying to comprehend all I'm *not* saying.

"Let me get this straight." He scoots his chair closer to mine and gets in my face. "So ... I like you. I *think* you like me. We have this," he waves his hand between the two of us, mimicking me, "crazy spark when we're together ... but, what? You're scared? Is that it? Did something happen to change your mind about me?"

"It's not you. It's me."

He rolls his head up to the ceiling. "Oh, Maby. Do you know how overused that line is?"

"But it's true," I sputter. "There is absolutely nothing wrong with you. You're ... wonderful. Any girl would be so lucky..." I stop when he holds up his hand.

"Stop! If you don't want to be with me, just say it ... you don't need to sugarcoat it with all this crap."

"I'm not trying to sugarcoat it!"

"Is it because I'm too nice?"

"I love how nice you are!"

He leans back in his chair and studies my face.

I clear my throat. "I like you. A lot. I just—I lost my job, everything feels so unpredictable with me right now, and I can't stand the thought of taking you down with me." I shake my head. "I won't do it."

I don't say anything about Saul because I'd decided to end things with Coen before that even happened with Saul. I still don't *really* know what is happening with Saul.

We stare at each other and Coen takes my hand. He laces his fingers through mine without breaking eye contact.

"Do you have plans this weekend?" he asks.

"Uh, not really."

"Come with me tonight. I have to go to my parents' house. We can come back tomorrow night or Sunday, if you'd like."

"Have you heard a word I've said?" I ask him, taking my hand back.

"I have. I've heard every single word." He gives me the grin that makes my insides drool and picks up my hand again.

His wavy hair is so perfectly messy, I have a hard time looking away. But I do. He gently nudges my chin until I'm looking at him again.

"Now, would you listen to me?" he asks.

I blink in agreement.

"I'm not trying to marry you or anything—not that the idea is *grotesque*—but I would like to … hang out?" He lifts his eyebrows, trying to gauge my reaction. "I'd like to be with you … whenever, however, whatever you might be okay with. *If*," he holds up his index finger, "you like me at all. If you *don't* really, we can go on and I can let the baristas do their job so they make your coffee from here on out. I can give you a friendly hello and that will be that. We'll have a nice little memory of a couple fun times. I, in particular, will always have one *very* fond memory with you." He slowly gives my body a once over and I blush. "But if you *do* like me at all," his smile fills up his whole face and I nearly squint from the light, "give me a fucking chance."

My eyes get wide. He does like to throw in a surprise here and there, what with the whole balls conversation and now this. I like it. I like it a *lot*. I like him a lot. Even if I don't want to. I just do.

It's like he hears every thought I'm thinking because his smile gets bigger and bigger. My heart is about to palpitate out of my chest and I don't think I can breathe until I—

"Okay!" I yell.

"Okay, what?" He bites his bottom lip, and his dimple gets so deep I want to lick it.

"I'm not promising anything," I tilt my head to the side and try to hold back the smile that's fighting its way out, "but I'll give you a fucking chance."

He squeezes his eyes shut and starts nodding his head. "Yes. That's -"

I cut him off. "But I can't go with you this weekend."

His forehead creases with his frown. "Why not? You said you don't have plans."

"I'll give you a chance, but I can't rush into anything, Coen. I'm not kidding about being a mess. I've been so up and down, and..." I look away, embarrassed but also determined to tell him the truth. "I'm just not ready to make any decisions right now. If you're not okay with *that*, then we can just have a nice little memory of a couple fun times," I repeat his words back to him.

"Fair enough," he says. "Would it change anything if I said I'd keep my hands to myself this weekend?"

I laugh. "I'm not sure we're capable of being around each other and keeping our hands to ourselves."

"Come on." He gives me a lopsided grin that makes my gut twist. "It'll be fun to try."

"Maybe another time," I promise. "I have to go see Paschal tomorrow anyway … forgot about that."

He sighs. "Okay."

I take a deep breath and know that I have to come out with the rest. "And some things happened with Saul the last couple of days that I still need to process."

The fun is instantly zapped right out of the room. He flinches, as though I've hit him.

"Oh, so that's what this is about." He stands up and pushes his chair back.

I stand up and resist touching him. "No, I told you the truth. You're too good for me. It's only a matter of time before you realize it."

"What, and he's not?" He looks away and rubs his chin.

"Saul knows what he's getting into. You don't."

"So, he's safe," he says flatly.

"Maybe."

He shakes his head and then catches me off guard by leaning down and kissing me. Not a sweet kiss. A scorching, send my heart soaring kiss that makes me lose my air and all reasoning. My hands are wrapped in his hair where they've been dying to be, when he stops abruptly.

"Does he make you feel like *that*?" he asks before he walks away.

He turns around as he gets to the door of the kitchen. "I'll call you later. No more running, okay?" He smiles, kisses his fingers, and holds them out to me.

I've never seen anything any sexier.

Get A Handle On All That Love
Or
Love Handles

WELL, I THOUGHT my life was confusing before. I shuffle home and walk slowly up my 36 stairs and softly close and lock the door behind me. I look around at my apartment and decide I'll find a yoga video to do online. I need something to occupy my mind.

I find a short video and get after it. As I'm twisted over in one move, I see my belly bulging over my waistband and speak to it.

"You're not gonna be around much longer."

My flab is actually significantly smaller than it was a few weeks ago, but I can hardly take credit. I've gone about it all the wrong way. I stretch and think that it feels so nice to finally do something right for my body, I'd love to lose the chub in a healthy way. I see the tips of my fingers in the mirror as I raise my arms high over my head in another stretch. I vow to myself to make it a priority every day to treat myself well. No more junk, no skipping meals, no more binge eating, no more negative thinking, no more hate.

I stand up and press my hands together, breathing in good thoughts and blowing them out into the room. I feel so silly, I giggle, but my eyes burn with moisture too. This has been one of the most topsy-turvy weeks of my life.

"It's time to get your shit together, Maby. And you can quit talking to yourself starting now."

I take another shower and collapse into bed.

THE PHONE WAKES me up the next morning. I answer groggily and peer at the clock through squinted eyes. 9:47. Wow. I slept hard.

"I hope I didn't wake you," a girl's voice says. "It's Melissa."

"Uh, it's okay. Hi…" I rub my forehead and try to remember who Melissa is. "Oh! Coen's cousin, Melissa?"

"Yeah. Sorry. I can call you back later if you're not awake yet."

"Oh no, I'm awake now. How are you?"

"I'm really good. I'd hoped we'd all do something to-gether by now, but Coen's taking too long to set it up. Jade and I are getting impatient, so we thought we'd see if you want to go get drinks with us tonight."

"Did Coen put you up to this?" I ask, frowning.

"No! To be honest, I didn't even tell him I was calling

you. I went to get coffee and he wasn't there this morning, so…" She sounds unsure of herself.

"I'd love to get drinks with you and Jade," I jump in. "Sounds … really great!" Good lord, I sound perky. Gotta nip that so she doesn't expect Little Miss Sunshine. "What time?"

"Are you opposed to The Village Idiot around 5?" she asks.

"Not at all." I laugh, knowing I can at least afford that place.

"Awesome. See you there!"

I'm pretty sure she *is* Little Miss Sunshine, so this should be interesting.

❧ ❧ ❧

SAUL CALLS AS I'm walking to the salon. I almost let it ring, but know part of becoming stronger involves me facing things head on. I think back to Coen saying, 'No more running' and how ironic it was that Dr. Still encouraged me to run on the same day. Two very different messages, but I heard them both clearly.

"Hi," I answer.

"Hi. What are you doing?"

"Gonna get my hair done…"

"Ah. Well, I just wanted to … see if you were okay. I didn't know whether to call you last night or give you space."

There are a few tick-tocks of awkward.

"I went to bed pretty early."

"I wish you'd stayed, Maby," he says.

"I need to work some things out on my own, Saul. It's time." I clear my throat, not knowing what else to say.

"We can work it out together," he says it almost as a question.

"I never quite know what you really want, Saul. I said it yesterday and you never set me straight."

He's quiet.

I feel the frustration build when I think of all the second guessing I do with Saul. It's always been that way. For someone so honest, it would seem like he's an open book, but he's far from it.

"Either way, I have to figure out what *I* really want."

"Sometimes I'm not sure what you really want to hear," he admits.

"The truth, for starters." I round the corner and stand outside the salon. "I'm gonna keep seeing Coen, Saul."

I hear his intake of breath.

"*What?*"

"I told him I had some things to process about you, but that I want to give him a chance too."

"Too? Like, you want to date *both* of us?"

"I don't know. More like, I need to figure out if I want to date either one of you."

"Shit, Maby. What's it gonna take for you to figure it out?"

"I don't know, Saul. When I figure that out, I'll let you know." I hang up before he can make me any angrier.

❦ ❦ ❦

I SQUEEZE INTO some jeans that haven't fit for a while. I know I should just be excited that they're fitting at all, but the muffin top keeps it real. I wear a loose shirt to help cover up the flab and extra makeup to bring the self-confidence up just a few notches.

Melissa and Jade are both gorgeous. Tall and willowy like models—Jade with her long red hair and Melissa with her dark brown curls—I'm going to feel like a hobbit next to them.

I'm more nervous than excited. I'm not sure why they want to get to know me. And, if I'm being honest with myself, I'm a little gun-shy. I haven't had the best luck with girlfriends.

They're waiting for me when I get to The Village Idiot. Both of them stand up to give me a hug, and I blush like a schoolgirl. They have lemon drop martinis and I order a gin & tonic just to be different. The martini looks better.

"So glad you agreed to meet up with us," Jade says with a grin. "Has my brother scared you off yet?"

"Ha! No—I'll probably be the one to do the scaring off," I admit.

They laugh like I've made a joke, but I know I'm telling the truth.

Jade shakes her head. "He has it *bad* for you. I told him I was seeing you tonight and he gave me a list of things we couldn't talk about."

"Well, of course, that's what we need to start with," I say and clink their glasses with mine.

They laugh again, but again I was serious. It seems no one is used to straight up honesty anymore.

"I just love your hair," Melissa says. "And the pink is

so great. Did you just add that?"

I nod.

"I could never get away with it."

"Are you kidding? Your hair is perfect." I tell her.

"So what do you do for fun?" Jade asks.

"Uh, well … I'm not very exciting. I'm trying to get back … out … there," I mumble.

God, I'm such a dud. They're going to regret ever inviting me.

"Did you have a bad breakup or something?" Melissa asks.

"Yeah, you could say that." I smile. That's it. Among other things.

"Coen mentioned your mom passed away, too. Maby, I'm so sorry," Jade says it softly, but puts her hand on my arm, solidifying her words. "I can't imagine."

I look at them both and am moved that they seem to care. "Thank you. It's been over a year, but I still can't seem to get past it. I'm trying." I give them a wobbly smile.

"I don't think that's something you ever get over," Jade says.

We're all quiet for a moment.

"If you ever want to talk about it or to just get out and try to clear your head for a while, call us!" Melissa puts her hand where Jade's was.

"Thanks, I will. So, what do *you* do for fun?"

They launch into a couple of hilarious stories about the dives Jade sings in. We quickly lose track of time. They're kind, funny, beautiful, smart women. I sort of want to be their best friend forever.

My mom must be working some kind of deal with the

big guy up there. Men, and possibly friends. Now, if she could just work out a job for me, that would be too good to be true.

The Bird and Peacocks

SOMETIMES THERE'S AN in-between place between being asleep and awake where I forget. I feel at peace. There is nothing clouding my mind. No numbers, no crazed need to clean or organize or declutter. My mind is an open field of possibilities. And then suddenly, it hits me like a bomb detonating deep inside my chest.

She's dead. My mother is dead. I can't breathe. It hurts too much.

I do this over and over and over. You'd think I would realize by now that she's gone, but it's like it's a new revelation every day. I wonder if that will ever go away. It's like even my grief has OCD.

❦ ❦ ❦

ON SUNDAY, I jog to the corner and pick up a paper. When I get back, I settle into my comfy chair and study the options. I decide to go old school with it, circling jobs that sound even halfway interesting with my pink highlighter. Most of them still sound like duds. I enjoyed my job. Minus Anna, it was a great job. I loved finding merchandise that was unique, especially from local vendors. Anna left all of that up to me. I'm not even sure what she would pick out at this point.

I mull over the ads for an hour, sipping coffee and picking at a bagel. After a while, my skin is twitching. I'm anxious and feel that oh-so-familiar tug. I put on my tennis shoes and run out the door before I can give in to my urges.

Four miles or so later, I get back to my apartment, dripping with sweat and sore from being out of shape. I shower and look around my apartment like a lost dog. Sometimes the loneliness is so thick, it threatens to choke me. It seems like I should be set for a while after my fun night out, but it's almost worse. Now I know there's life out there being had without me.

On a whim, I text Coen.

Did you have a nice weekend at home?

His reply is quick.

Coen: I did. Would have been better if you'd come with me, though.

I type a smiley face back and stare at my walls. They're closing in on me. I look at my bed longingly and

167

shake myself. I can cave and get in bed and cover my head, or I can fight this depression that's threatening to eat me up alive.

Coen: Any plans today? I'd love to see you.

I pause for a minute, simply so I won't seem too eager and type: **Let's do something.**

Coen: OK. :) What did you have in mind?

I have nothing in mind and am too sore to do much more than sit around, but I don't tell him that.

Uh … anything?

Coen: Well, that leaves our options open. I like it. Anything.

I giggle and it bounces around the room.

I know! Let's go to one of those wine & paint places. I've always wanted to try that.

Coen: Do guys really do that? I mean … okay. I did agree to anything, after all.

I'm already looking online to see if we can even get in somewhere still today.

Oh! Perfect! Party Paint is painting a "Pretty Peacock" today. See? Meant to be.

Coen: Pretty Peacock. Have you been drinking?

I giggle again and look around, embarrassed, like my walls are going to rat me out.

Noooo. But I will at Party Paint! It starts at 3. Can you make that?

Coen: Oh—that's soon! I'll pick you up in 30?

Perfect.

I scramble to the closet and throw on a short black skirt and black t-shirt. I try to find colorful jewelry, but my jewelry is seriously lacking, so I loop a thin pink scarf around my neck instead. Paschal gave me some new hair product to try and I like how it spikes my hair and makes it piece-y … something I never knew was possible when my hair was long and fuzzy.

Coen buzzes exactly 30 minutes later, and I run down the stairs instead of inviting him up. I suck in my jiggle as I run, hoping it can substitute as sit-ups. My new fitness phase is already annoying me, but I'm determined to get back in shape. Besides, I don't want to scare Coen if my belly runs ahead of me. So far, he hasn't seemed to mind that I'm not a size 6. Maybe he'll appreciate it when I am, though. If he's telling the truth about liking me all this time, he's seen me tiny.

I wonder again what in the world it is that he sees in me.

I have to stop this train of thought or I'll have to turn around and go to bed.

Coen looks edible with his jeans and wet hair. He kisses my cheek and we grab a cab.

We're nearly to the place when my phone starts going off like crazy.

"Geez. Sorry. I need to turn it off." I look down and see Dalton, Dalton, Dalton. Five missed messages from Dalton.

"Must be important. Check it. We're not there yet."

Dalton: You really hurt me with all those insensitive remarks the other day. We had a history together. I thought that counted for something. You didn't seem to mind how short I was when you lived with me for TWO FUCKING YEARS.

Dalton: Courtney has kicked me out, thanks to you. I hope you're happy.

Dalton: You deserve to be alone. It's not like you're even all that special. Acting like you're better than me while you're counting all the days you're alone...

Dalton: And as you're going to sleep alone, AGAIN, I hope you remember that you've fucked up everything you've ever done. You can't keep a job, can't keep a man, can't keep your sanity...

Dalton: I was a fool to get caught in your web again. I'm going to enjoy my time as a free agent and when the baby is born, I'll be there for Courtney. She'll take me back. You haven't cost me anything.

My hands shake as I read through the texts, but I feel a wave of hysterical laughter building in my gut.

"Everything okay?" Coen asks.

"Oh yeah. Fine."

We pull up to Party Paint and when we get out, I grab Coen's arm.

"Take a picture with me?" I ask him.

He smiles down at me. "Of course, gorgeous."

I pffft his comment and he holds the camera out and clicks. We look at the camera. Click. And then at each other. Click. Coen leans down and kisses me. Click. His tongue reaches out for mine. Click. I giggle. Click.

"Okay, okay, give me that." I laugh and take the camera.

We scroll through and our smiles get bigger and bigger with each picture.

"There you have it," he says and taps on the kissing picture. "You can't deny that magic, Maby."

I look at it intently. No, I cannot. I give him another quick kiss and wish I could just take him home with me and keep him there. There's just something about him that makes me feel … free.

I subtly forward the kissing picture to Dalton and say: **Not suffering at all over here, believe me. And FYI: I always minded how short you were.**

I wish there was an emoticon with the middle finger up… maybe that could be something I look into next: creating foul emoticons.

29

Almost

"YOURS TURNED OUT way better than mine." I hold my painting up to Coen's. "My peacock looks angry."

Coen tries to shake his head, but he takes another look at mine and bites his bottom lip. "Yours *is* very … expressive."

I snort. "That's one way to put it. Mine looks more like a raptor."

Coen's dimple curves in as he gives up. "I guess it's true what they say about interpreting art differently."

"You're so nice. Are you ever, *ever* mean?"

We're holding our paintings carefully and step outside the store. He looks down at me and shrugs.

"That whole 'nice guys finish last' thing just always seemed like a crock to me. I personally think it's a waste of time to be anything else. Nice isn't always boring—I like to have fun. It takes up too much bad energy to be mean."

I nod. "I agree, but I think it can be really hard to be nice. I don't like people as much as you seem to."

"You're nicer than you think," he says, leaning down to nibble my lip.

It makes my stomach drop.

"There is nothing boring about you," I tell him.

We stop walking and hold our paintings out as we kiss each other's face off.

"Get a room!" someone shouts.

"Why would I when I can do this?" Coen yells back.

I laugh and cover my mouth with my hand.

"Being with you makes me forget who I really am." I say it with a smile, but then get serious when I realize the gravity of my statement.

He crinkles his face, a little frown forming between his brows. "Maybe I just remind you of who you want to be ... who you are when you're not trying to be something else." His hand sweeps across my cheek and I lean into it, closing my eyes.

I wish he was right. When he looks at me the way he is right now, I can almost believe him.

THERE'S AN AWKWARD pause when we get back to my building. I clear my throat, wishing he'd come up and stay a while, but not wanting to be the one to say it.

He chuckles again as he looks at my painting. "Are you going to hang that in your apartment?"

I look at him like he's crazy. "No way. I'll be dumping it before it ever goes inside."

He scowls at me. "You can't! It's a memento of our night!"

"Oh, would you like to keep it then?" I poke his side and he jerks away, laughing.

"Thank you, but I have my own memento." He holds up his flawless painting.

"Nice work, Mr. Brady."

He gives a slight bow. "Thank you, Ms. Armstrong."

I look at mine again and can't stop smiling. "Maybe I will keep this guy. He is pretty amusing."

He opens the door and walks up the stairs with me. When we reach my apartment, he clears his throat and gives me a kiss on the cheek. "I had a great time, Maby. I'll see you this week?"

"Uh, sure."

I unlock my door and step inside. When I turn to look at him, he gives me a little wave.

"Night, Maby."

"Night."

❤ ❤ ❤

I TOSS AND turn, disconcerted by the way the night ended with Coen. The next morning, I wake up and feel so strange taking my time on a Monday. I consider getting coffee at La Colombe, but am not sure if I should go see Coen so soon, after we ended on such a weird note.

The sun is blinding and it's finally warm outside. I put on my camo shorts and start walking toward the coffee shop. I'm nearly there when my phone starts ringing.

"Hey, Saul. Whatcha doin?"

"I'm at Whatnot Alley and Anna is flipping out," he says. His voice is muffled.

"Are you *hiding*?"

"No! I'm just ... look, she's had a rough week trying to handle all the vendors without you. Some have pulled out of the new shop because they're worried about the risk. They don't like the way she runs things. Do you think you could ... smooth things over with Retro Mod?"

I close my eyes and breathe to 20.

"Maby?" he whispers.

"Are you serious right now? *She's* had a rough week? Saul!" My voice bites into the air and passersby turn around to see who's yelling.

"I know. I'm sorry, Maby. It just ... it affects my job too. If the big vendors keep pulling out, I'm afraid she'll lose the new building—I'm not sure she'll pay me if that happens."

"You can sue her if that happens!" I snap.

A door shuts and his voice gets louder. "You know I wouldn't ask if it wasn't important," he finishes.

"This is a shitty thing you're asking, Saul, just so we're clear."

"I know, Maby. It is. And I'll make it up to you, I swear."

"Retro Mod is wanting out? Vintage Textiles will want out too then."

"I'm pretty sure she's talking to them right now. Wasn't sounding good when I stepped out."

I roll my eyes and tug the top of my hair. "Ugh, Saul. I'll think about it."

"Please don't think about it too long, okay?"

I hang up on him and shake the phone in the air. Then I dial Cheri from Retro Mod. She picks up on the second ring.

"Hi Cheri. It's Mabel."

"Mabel, hi! I was gonna call you today. What's going on with Whatnot Alley?"

"Well, I'm taking some time off, but the plan is still to expand the mother store and the new shop will be ready soon. We're really counting on your merchandise in both stores! What's this I hear about you pulling out?"

"I heard you weren't there anymore. Mabel, you know I can't work with Anna! And when I've called this week, it's been one disaster after another. When are you going back? Because I don't feel confident moving forward with the way things are now."

"I understand. Anna has had a rough week, I hear." I fist the hem of my shorts in one hand and take another breath. "She's pregnant—did you hear that?" I say it conspiratorially, like Anna might hear me if I say it any louder.

"No, I hadn't heard. Well, that makes some sense. But still, I'd rather not deal with her."

"The new shop is going to be spectacular. I really hope you'll reconsider."

"As long as we can work with you, we'll reconsider. Elaine agrees with me on this. We've always worked with you, and it needs to stay that way."

I bite my lip, not sure what to say. "I'll talk to Anna and give you a call sometime next week."

"Thanks, Mabel."

I hang up and exhale. I could have told her I'd call back sooner, but Anna and Saul can both squirm for just a

176

little longer. The more I think about it, the madder I get. Anna would flip if she knew Saul called me, and that does a little something evil to my insides, but the fact that he would even ask me to help her—I want to shake him until his teeth rattle.

30

Oh Snap

ON A WHIM, I grab a taxi for the few blocks to Anna's Soho location. It's a prime spot. If I could pick anywhere to have a shop, it would be this place. In fact, I *had* been the one to suggest this location. I saw it in the paper, went to check it out, and called Anna that night to tell her she needed to open another shop here. That was what stung the most about getting fired—I did all the grueling work and she continuously reaped the benefits. And for what? So she could fire me over one mistake? A mistake that I could have fixed in one conversation? It just wasn't right.

The windows are mostly covered, but I can see in through a tiny flap that was left open. It's nearly done and is already beautiful. It seems like it could be open within a couple of months, at most. I wish I'd asked Saul how much is really left to do.

I pace the sidewalk and chew my lips, trying to decide what to do. After much thought, even though she's been cruel to me, I decide to give her a chance. I call her cell before I can talk myself out of it.

"Hello?" Even her hello is snappy.

"Hi, Anna, it's Mabel. Got a minute?"

"What do you want, Mabel?" She sounds frustrated before I've even said a word.

"I'd like to take over the Soho location," I say, more confident than I really feel.

"Have you forgotten that I just fired you?" She laughs. "*No*, you're not *taking over* the new Soho location."

I grind my palm into the brick wall and breathe. "Okay, I thought you might say that. I just hoped you would say something different."

"What do you *want* me to say, Mabel? I can't lie to you—getting rid of you was the best thing I ever did."

"Really? Then why are vendors calling me? Why do they say they'll go with me wherever I decide to go? Why do they say they'll never work with you, no matter how hard I try to convince them to?"

It's quiet for a moment. "Who said that?" she snaps. "You're lying."

"No, Anna. I can't lie to *you* either. Since I'm the one who made their business what it is, I have some really loyal partners. I'd think about it, if I were you, Anna. Otherwise, *both* of your shops just might go under. Don't say I didn't warn you. *Or*, you could let me take over the Soho store and we'll call it a day."

"Who, Mabel? Who said that? What do you—"

I hang up on her before I'm tempted to say anything else. Let her wallow in that a while.

I head back to my apartment and spend the rest of the afternoon on the phone. I don't beat around the bush, I say exactly what I'm planning and the help I need. It really isn't that hard to convince them.

That night I take a long look at my money situation. I haven't made much, but I don't spend much either, and I do have a small savings that I've left alone. I've made a couple investments that I also never pay any attention to, but I open an online account and look at all the numbers. I have more than I thought I did; not enough, but I'm not as poor as I thought. Still, it will take people who trust me to make this work—and a business loan.

I'M SHUTTING MY laptop when the door buzzes. I push the intercom.

"You up for company?" Coen asks.

"Come on!" I buzz him up.

He seems shy when I open the door. His smile isn't as bright as usual.

"You okay?" I ask him.

"Sorry to drop in." He holds out a takeout box. "Thought we could share this."

I open the box and inside is enough carrot cake for a giant. I squeal and then grab his arm and pull him into my apartment.

"You are always welcome with carrot cake. I will eat anything with cream cheese frosting … always." I hurriedly get two forks out of the drawer and practically skip to the couch.

He laughs and the nerves seem to fade with it. He sits next to me on the couch and we take bites from opposite ends of the cake. My eyes roll back. The frosting is perfect and the cake is delicious.

"Where did you get this?" I ask with my mouth full.

"My mom sent some back with me. So ... how did it go with Jade and M—"

"Your *mom* made this? Why didn't you tell me she baked like this? I totally would have gone this weekend."

Coen chokes on his bite, laughing, and I venture to his side of the cake while he's distracted.

"Oh my God, this is the best cake I've ever tasted. Seriously. I can't believe you didn't tell me. This has to go in your coffee shop one day." I point wildly at the cake with my fork and sneak another bite from his side.

He grins and holds the container while I keep moaning.

"So ... Jade and Melissa?" He tries again. His Adam's apple goes up and down slowly as he waits for my answer.

"Why are you so nervous?"

"I'm not, I just—"

"You totally are. What are you hiding, Coen Brady?"

"I just didn't want them to wreck my chances with you," he spits out quickly.

"What? Why do you think that?"

"Because they know how ... crazy I am about you," he says. His lips move up in an embarrassed smile. "I mean—I know you know it, but I thought they might just *dig it into the ground*."

He hasn't taken any more bites and I'm not bothering to remind him. Until the guilt kicks in. I pick up his fork and offer him a bite. He shakes his head. He doesn't have to tell me twice—I finish the cake. Once I've settled back on the couch in a sugar-induced high, I study him out of the corner of my eye.

"You're crazy about me, huh?"

He props an elbow on the back of the couch and stares at me. "Don't act like this is news to you."

"What would I have to do to make you *not* crazy about me?"

"*What*?" His eyebrows crease in the middle.

"What am I gonna do that will send you running like everyone else?" I turn to fully look at him. "Because I know I'll do something…"

"The only thing I can think of is if you don't want me." He rests his hand on the side of my neck and rubs my cheek with his thumb.

"I'm getting ready to do something pretty evil," I tell him.

"I'll believe it when I see it," he whispers, leaning in to kiss me.

I forget everything I've plotted throughout the day, and only think about how I want to get lost in his sweetness. He makes me believe I can be good. Or at the very least, that my ugly is really not so ugly at all.

❦ ❦ ❦

COEN AND I kiss for a long time on the couch. He pulls me on his lap but he's still being less handsy than before and it's driving me mad. I want with every hormone in my body to ask him to stay the night when he whispers that he should go.

"Really? Now?" I whisper back.

His pupils look gigantic as he leans in to kiss me again, his tongue teasing my mouth back open. I shiver as his hands slide up my legs, grip my panties, and then he stands up, still holding me, and sets me back down on the couch.

"What … are you doing? Don't go."

"I … I have to."

"Why?" I cover all the skin that's showing and look up at him.

"I've … made a promise to myself," he says quietly.

"What is it?"

He puts a hand on his forehead and drags it back to the top of his head. "I'll tell you later." He leans down and then thinks better of it. "Your lips are like a drug. I've gotta get out of here."

He gives me a wild-eyed grin and is gone before I can blink.

You Are Not It

OVER THE NEXT few days I call everyone on my favorite vendors' list and get an unbelievable response. After a run of three days in a row of being so elated, I'm tempted to forgo my medication and just ride this high. I don't, but I'm tempted. As a backup plan, I've contacted a real estate agent and have an appointment with the bank this afternoon to see about a business loan.

I've taken over the back table at La Colombe and shoot Coen flirty eyes every time I see him looking my way, which is a lot.

"What are you up to?" he asks, turning a chair around and sitting in it backwards.

"What do you mean?"

"I've never seen you look so … *what* are you up to?" He leans across the table and kisses me.

I hold up my hand. "I can't think when you do that."

He kisses me again and sits back in his seat, grinning. "Talk to me."

"Well, I did warn you I was gonna do something evil," I say cockily.

"Okay, now you really have to tell me."

I shrug my shoulders. "This may be our make or break test."

He groans. "Would you quit with that? Half the time I can't even tell if you really like me, and yet, you're always finding a way to get out of *this*." He points between the two of us. "Is this really your way of saying you want me?" He licks his lips and I watch, transfixed.

Shaking my head, I crinkle my face up. "Shut it. That's not even … shush." I can't help smiling though. I lean in and whisper, "*Wanting* you has never been in question."

Coen laughs. "You are so confusing." He leans over and kisses my cheek.

"Thank you. Now wish me luck. Anna is going down in … oh, it's probably already started."

"Wait, start over."

I look at my watch. "Sorry!" I put everything in my bag and stand up. "I've gotta run."

"Where are you going? Hey, come home with me this weekend? Tomorrow night?"

I pause and look him over. "Uh. Maybe. Ask me tomorrow?"

His face falls a little, but he recovers quickly, holding his hand up in his customary wave. "Tomorrow. Bye, Maby. Good luck with your evil plan."

❤ ❤ ❤

185

Saul: Are you mad at me?

Yes.

The phone rings just as I'm getting ready to walk into the bank. I turn it off and go inside. I've done my homework and know what they want to see from me. I've made a thorough business plan and spreadsheets of my projected rate of growth for the next year. My folder is at least an inch thick with all of it—my tax returns and credit report included. Justin, the loan officer, looks over everything thoroughly and we talk for almost an hour going through the file.

As we're closing the meeting, Justin tells me he'll get back to me within ten business days to let me know if I've been approved. I think I'll die waiting that long, but I smile and thank him for his time. I'm still hoping I won't need a business loan, but it's best to have everything covered, just in case.

❦ ❦ ❦

THE CALLS START at exactly 9:05 AM the next morning, just as I thought they would. I let it go to voicemail. The next one is at 9:35, and approximately every half hour until the last one at 4:05 PM.

Fifteen Missed Calls: Anna

Between her irate voicemails that I ignore, I'm getting calls from the nine companies that have pulled out of

Whatnot Alley. In their own way, all nine companies informed Anna that upon hearing of my firing, they were free to pull out of any and all future agreements since I was the one who secured their business in the first place. Not just any nine, but the top nine that Anna has used to fill Whatnot Alley. Actually—scratch that—the nine that *I* found to fill Whatnot Alley. They all signed contracts with me at 8 AM this morning stating they will give me exclusivity of their new merchandise for the next year. Not only are they out of the Soho location, but six of the companies have said they'll pull out of the current location once their product has sold, citing the inability to work with Anna.

The only catch is I have promised I will open my new store in two months, so there's no lag time in their business. I hope I can pull this off.

I don't know why I didn't think of it before. I wasn't just spouting out nonsense to Anna, it's the truth: she can't run the shops without me. I've helped make these nine companies successful too—most were just starting out when I discovered them, and the others needed the boost that Whatnot Alley gave them. As long as I can continue selling their products without any lull for them, they'll be on board with whatever direction I take.

Any guilt I feel is squashed by the elation that I feel at finally giving Anna a dose of her own medicine.

❧ ❧ ❧

THE LAST MESSAGE from Anna is: "Mabel? Can we talk? I'm ready to have a conversation with you about the Soho location."

I don't return her call. I still need time to think about what to do.

There's one text that I finally answer…

Coen: How about it? Pick you up at 6?

Yes.

I throw a few sundresses, cardigans, and pajamas in an overnight bag and remember my makeup bag at the last minute. I don't really know what to take to a guy's parents' house. I've never done this. Dalton's parents rarely came through town and he never took me for a visit. That should have been a huge clue about our relationship. It does feel a bit early to be going to Coen's, though. Maybe this is just what friends do. I wouldn't know much about that either.

I have a few minutes to spare and call Paschal. He must be with a client; it goes to his voicemail.

"Hey, it's Maby. Wish me luck—I'm going to Coen's parents' for the weekend! EEK! I'll call you when I get back. Has it only been a week since I've seen you? Feels like forever."

My door buzzes at 5:55.

"You're *early*." I tease him.

"What? Hey, you're home."

"Saul? I'm on my way out."

"Come on, Maby, you can't avoid me forever. We had *sex*, it doesn't have to change everything."

"That's not what—"

I hear another voice and my stomach drops.

"Hey, man." I hear Saul say.

I buzz them up and put my head through my knees to prepare for whatever is coming.

COEN LOOKS WHITE, despite the fact that he's just walked three flights of stairs. Saul looks smug. I'm fairly certain I look ill.

"Come in." I hold the door wide. "This is just … too much. Twice?"

I point at Saul. "You … quit dropping by without calling first." I look at Coen. "I'm sorry this keeps happening."

Coen swallows and starts to say something when Saul interrupts.

"What happened, Maby? We know now that we're *great* together." He lifts his eyebrows when he says 'great' and puts his hand on mine. "Why are you getting second thoughts now? We can finally be together."

I sit down and look up at both of them. Saul, who has been my rock and my fun-loving partner in crime, and Coen, who makes me laugh and lights me up from the inside out. Saul, with his smiling eyes that melt me, and Coen, with his open heart that makes me hope in things I didn't believe I could. Saul, who doesn't seem to know he wants me until someone else does, and Coen, who has just wanted me, period.

My long exhale seems to echo in my apartment. I clear my throat. They both stare down at me, waiting.

"I'm sorry, Saul. If Coen will still have me this week-end, I'm gonna go meet his family. If you still want to talk, let's talk on Monday."

Saul's hands flex and his veins pop out. "This is stupid. I'm tired of waiting for you to see what's right in front of you." He steps closer to me and his face looks flush.

"I think that's just it, Saul. I think I finally am."

He looks like I've hit him and turns around, stalking out of the room. The door rattles as it slams.

Pin-Up

COEN STARES AT me for a long time without saying anything. I can't tell if he's mad or sad, conflicted or done. I'm distracted by those brown eyes that look at me like I'm *something*, even when I don't know what that something is.

"Is it a mistake to take you home with me, Maby?" His lower lip is slightly bigger than his top lip and I can't stop looking at it. "Is it?" he repeats.

"Uh-I can't answer that, Coen."

"What do you feel when you're with me?" he asks.

"Light," I answer without hesitation.

"Light," he echoes.

He runs his hands through his hair and stretches both arms to the ceiling. When he looks back at me, one fist is at his mouth and the other is still on his head. It's silent, except for the traffic outside. And the clock, tick-tick-

ticking.

Finally, he looks around, sees my bag and picks it up.

"If we go now, we'll still make it for a late dinner."

My stomach growls in response.

"Sounds like we better hurry," he says quietly.

I smile up at him and he gives me a small smile in return. It's then that I know I would do *anything* for Coen Brady. I only hope that I haven't ruined everything before we even truly start.

THE DRIVE IS very quiet. It's not that it's awkward or angry silence, but neither of us is able to fill the time with small talk. Coen seems to need to think some things through, and I don't blame him. He's in a SUV that I've never seen before, and it's filled with terrariums of every size and shape. For a good part of the trip, I study all the ones I can see, still stunned that he is so skilled at something this unusual.

An hour into our trip, he says, "We're almost there."

"It's beautiful out here."

He nods and points ahead. "My favorite view of the Hudson River."

Mountains stand like bookends on either side of the river. I didn't know such a pretty place existed so close to my little world. I gasp when we keep driving into a picturesque town.

"It's right out of a storybook!"

"Do you like it?" He looks at me.

"What isn't to love?" I stare at the cute little shops

we're driving past. I don't see anything of Whatnot Alley caliber, but there are many places I'd love to explore.

We drive just outside of the town and I see the sprawling nursery ahead. Flowers, of every color and variety. A beautiful yellow Victorian house with a wraparound porch sits far back on the property.

"Is that your house?"

He nods, pulling into the long driveway and going past the nursery, toward the house. When he stops, we both start to speak at the same time.

"You go ahead," he says.

"I just wanted to thank you for bringing me here. And to apologize for what happened earlier with Saul."

I twist the hem of my short dress and wish I'd worn one of those sweaters I packed. My bare arms are suddenly chilled. I shiver and Coen puts his hand on my arm.

"I probably shouldn't have brought you here yet. It's soon and … you're still not sure about me … but … I'm glad you're here, Maby. And I want to talk about Saul eventually, but can we please *not* this weekend?"

I let out a long breath. "Yes. That sounds good to me."

He holds out his hand and I take it. He squeezes and then is out of the car before I blink. My car door opens and Jade pulls me out.

"Hey, it's a party!" she yells, hugging me.

"I wasn't sure if you'd be here—yay!" I laugh. "Is Melissa here too?"

"Not tonight, she might come tomorrow though."

Coen puts his arm around Jade and they look at me. Coen's eyes gleam with mischief and I squeak out another nervous chuckle.

"What do you think? Should we subject her to the torture?" Coen asks Jade.

"Why do your eyes look so vicious right now?" I ask him.

He opens them wide. "What? These eyes? Muahahahaaa—" He gives an evil laugh and Jade bops him over the head.

The door swings open and two pretty people walk out. They come and stand on either side of Coen and Jade and I am faced with the perfect family.

Coen's mom reaches out for a hug first. "I'm Janie. So glad you could come," she says.

"Scott," his dad says, giving me a quick squeeze. "Welcome. You hungry?"

"Starving!" I nod.

"You are just as beautiful as they said," Janie says as she leads the way into the house.

"Oh … um, no, that's…" I stutter.

The four of them turn to look at me and then smile their sweet, beatific smiles. Good lord, what have I done? I am surrounded by four perfect people. At least to me they are, with their easy, happy … *confidence*. They're all attractive, but more than that, they exude *joy* and that is fucking intimidating. I count the steps up the front porch, into the gorgeous living room, and back to the kitchen. The table is already set. Scott holds up a bottle of wine and a pitcher.

"Maby? Wine or a margarita?" he asks.

"Oh yes, thank you."

He laughs and pours out of the pitcher.

I ask for the restroom and when I pull the door closed, I take a long look in the mirror. After washing my hands for a solid minute, I start talking to myself in the mirror.

"Do NOT mess this up. Mabel Armstrong, get a grip. You might have a real chance at something wonderful here—please don't screw it up!" I get tears in my eyes and look up at the ceiling, still scrubbing my hands.

I hear a peal of laughter from the kitchen and jump. The water is scalding and my hands are scarlet, so I turn off the water and pat them dry.

"Help me keep it together just this once, Mom," I whisper. "Pull in whatever favors you have to."

I open the door and Coen is standing outside the door.

"You okay?" he asks.

I nod. He holds out his hand and we walk into the kitchen together.

"Sorry, we didn't even give you a chance to freshen up," Janie says.

"It's okay. Can I do anything to help?"

"Oh no, it's all ready. I hope you like enchiladas."

"*Love* them." I grin at Coen.

"If all else is a bust, you'll at least get Mexican food out of the deal," he whispers in my ear as he holds out a chair for me.

"Mind reader," I whisper back.

He holds his chest like I've wounded him and takes his seat next to me.

Once the food has been passed around, conversation flies at a fast pace. I'm not sure if they've had a head start on the margaritas or if they're just always this loud and witty. They throw out the normal questions to get to know me in quick succession and then move into the more intimate category.

"So what did our boy do to catch your eye?" Scott

says, elbowing Coen.

"Here we go," Coen says. "Good question, though. I approve, Dad." He lifts his margarita glass to his dad's and they clink.

"Thanks, son."

"Well, besides being *very* cute, he also makes a mean Americano."

"I'm pretty sure she only noticed my cuteness after a thousand Americanos, but I'm not bitter or anything," Coen adds.

"And for our first kiss, he made sure we were somewhere romantic—under the arch at Washington Square Park." I smile and then my smile falters when no one smiles back or says a word.

Everything goes silent for the first time since we arrived, until Janie says, "Wait a minute, you guys have *kissed*?" She looks horrified.

I stare at her and then look around the table. They all stare back at me. Coen looks down at his plate.

Janie starts cracking up. "I'm *kidding*! Kidding." Her shoulders shake as she laughs. "Sorry. That's so sweet! Nice move, Coen!"

Everyone laughs and I take a deep breath. Scott shakes his head.

"Don't pay any attention to that one," he takes his wife's hand," she's got a twisted streak in her. Don't you, babe?" He kisses her hand. "It's just … we've been hearing about this bombshell that comes in to Coen's work for the last—what, a year and a half now, right? Two years, maybe? So you can imagine, we're all just a little *excited* that you're finally here."

"Thanks, guys, you're terrifying her," Coen says. He

squeezes my hand. "So you thought that was romantic, huh?"

I start laughing and can't stop. Finally, when I can speak up, I say, "You're crazy. All of you. And *bomb-shell*? What did you tell them?"

Coen takes my chin and holds my face up in the candlelight. "*Yes*," he says, like that answers my question.

"You do have a bombshell vibe going with the hair," Jade says, "and the pouty lips, and the huge eyes … and the curves." She does the whole outline of a shapely body with her hands and looks pointedly at my breasts.

Coen clears his throat. My mouth drops.

"Damn, I know where Coen gets his say-what's-on-your-mind … ness," I end awkwardly.

They all laugh at that and I get a warm feeling in my chest that I don't fully recognize right away. Later, when my nerves are completely gone, I realize it's the feeling of belonging.

Sheath Slogan

OUTSIDE ON THE porch, after we've enjoyed at least one too many margaritas and the best homemade Key lime pie I've ever tasted, Coen says he needs to take the terrariums to the shop.

"I can take those for you this time, Coen," his dad tells him.

"I'd kinda like Maby to see everything while it's closed, without all the customers. You up for that tonight, Maby?" He looks at me and I'm pretty sure I'd go anywhere he wanted to go, *ever*, if he'll just keep looking at me like that.

"Of course," I say softly. "I'd love to see it."

He grabs a bag and we ride the short distance to the nursery. Coen backs the SUV to the gift shop door. He gets a crate and I start to pick up one.

"You don't have to carry anything. I don't want you

to get your dress all dirty."

"I don't mind. I can help." *If my therapist could hear me now*. I grab a smaller crate and stand by him while he unlocks the door and turns on the lights.

The gift shop is lit with small, delicate chandeliers hanging at various levels. My heart starts pounding and I have to hold on tight to the crate because it is such perfection, I actually feel weak in the knees. The furniture, the lighting, the gifts—everything I see is something I would have picked out. I recognize some of the brands and some of them are new to me. The terrariums magnify the charm of the room, their whimsy giving even more character in every nook.

"It's beautiful, Coen. I love every single thing in here, which has never happened, not even in the store I ran. This is so much *better*. Does your mom pick everything out?"

"Yeah, it's mostly all my mom. Occasionally, she asks our opinion on something, but she typically just follows her fancy—her words, not mine."

He sets a simple terrarium under the most exquisite chandelier. The light dances on the glass and makes it come to life.

"And she does the staging too?"

"Pretty much. She wants me to put the terrariums wherever I 'feel they should go' and sometimes my dad has opinions about the lighting, but yeah, she does the rest."

"I need to pick her brain."

He smirks at me. "Oh, she would *love* that. Be prepared though—you won't be able to get her to stop once you start."

I grin and continue to stare at the space while he

199

brings in the rest of the terrariums. He finds the perfect spot for each one.

"You're really good at this," I tell him.

"Thank you. I love it." He shrugs.

"God, you're gorgeous."

He stops in mid-stride, turning to look at me.

"It's the crate, isn't it?" He flexes his arm while lifting the crate up and down. He raises an eyebrow and gives me a cheesy grin.

"Okay, I take it back. I was dazzled by the chandeliers and thought for a moment there that you were ... *gorgeous* ... but now I see that you are simply a cute boy with ample crate skills. Silly me."

He sets down the crate and comes to stand in front of me.

"You've called me 'cute' twice in one night. I think you might mean it." He picks me up and places me on the lower part of the counter.

"Cute sounds *safe* and you are so *not* safe. You are in a whole other dangerous category..."

He leans his head down and kisses me softly. "Is this your way of flattering me, Maby?"

"Just saying the truth," I tell him between kisses.

He wraps my legs around his waist and picks me up, nuzzling my ear. He walks into the nursery and it has the charm of the shop, only wilder with all the flowers. I look over his shoulder.

"This place is huge. I can't get over how beautiful it is, Coen."

"I want to show you my favorite spot."

"That's what she said," I say under my breath.

"*What?*" He starts laughing and winds my legs

around him tighter.

"Sorry. Too many margaritas."

"If this is what alcohol does to you I need to open the bottle of wine now." He pulls it out of nowhere and winks.

"What the hell? Where were you hiding that?" I get both hands in his hair and tug it just hard enough that he has to look at me. He lowers me until I feel what's going on in his pants. I lift an eyebrow. "See? *Dangerous*."

"You don't know the half of it," he whispers.

He turns a corner and it looks like we're outside, but we're still inside the nursery. There's a dark wood chaise lounge surrounded by hanging vines and a small fountain. He lays me back on the chaise and sets the bottle of wine on the floor next to it.

"Can I tell you something and not creep you out?" he asks.

"That's never a good way to start a conversation."

"Yeah, well, here's the thing. I saw you a few times at La C and kept watching for you to come back in. The first time you really looked back at me—I dreamed about you that night. And you were lying here, just like this. Well, less clothes, but … yeah…" He crinkles his nose. "It was a lot smoother when I said it in my head."

I laugh then and pull him down. "Come here."

He groans when his body makes contact with mine and he hops up in an instant. "Not a good idea."

I squint at him and decide now is probably not the time for me to laugh at his tent situation. He's muttering something and looks like he's about to start pacing when I grab his arm.

"What are you saying?"

"What? Nothing." He shakes his head.

I lean up on my elbows. "Okay, there's only room for one weirdo in a relationship and I'm it. *What* are you muttering?"

"I can't … tell you." He bends down and opens the bottle of wine. "I don't know what I did with the glasses. Want some?" He lifts the bottle and I shake my head while he takes a swig. "Wait—did you say 'in a relationship'?"

"All right, that settles it. Tell me." I sit up and take the bottle from him, taking a long pull.

"It's just I've made an agreement with myself about you." He looks at me, embarrassed.

I stare at him and wave my hand for him to come out with it.

"You're killing me. Okay. No penetration until dedication." He says it really quiet and fast.

"What? I didn't hear you."

"No penetration until dedication," he mumbles. "It's just…"

"I still haven't heard what you're saying. Slow down and speak up."

He takes a long drink from the bottle. "NO PENETRATION UNTIL DEDICATION," he shouts, clearly enunciating every word this time.

I laugh until tears are falling down my face. Coen's laughing right along with me. He finally leans back on the chaise, facing me and we laugh until we can't breathe.

When we both finally try to catch a breath, he says, "I know I'm laughing, but I mean it."

And I lose it all over again.

Coen stands up and holds out his hand. "Come on, I've thoroughly killed the mood. I'll never look at this chair the same now," he says, still laughing.

We walk around the nursery and I comment again on how pretty everything is. We end up back at the shop and he holds up the bottle to me. I shake my head no.

"You've gotten me drunk and you're not having your way with me," I giggle, "I've gotta have a little self-respect."

Coen wraps his arms around me and gives me a huge hug. I soak it in and then back away, looking up at him.

"You do have to explain yourself with that line. Don't leave me hanging. It was hilarious, but I want to know what it's about."

"It's my one last ditch effort to maintain my head around you." He snorts and shakes his head. "What the hell, I've lost all my moves. Let me try that again. I am gone where you're concerned, Maby. *Gone*. And you're not there yet. But once I'm *inside you*..." He looks in my eyes when he says that and I get so lightheaded, I have to close my eyes. His fingers lift my chin and his lips touch mine. His tongue softly traces my lips and I tremble. "Once I'm inside you," he whispers, "I'm not gonna be able to let you go."

I look up at him and my eyes blur with tears. Fortunately, I think it's too dark for him to see.

"You're so perfect." I lay my head on his chest and a tear falls down my cheek.

"That didn't sound ... terrifying or ... stalker-y?" he asks, kissing the top of my head.

"It did, but I'm completely mad about you, so it just all sounded really wonderful."

Coen pulls back and puts his hands on either side of my face. He frowns when he feels the tears.

"You're crying? I'm scaring you, aren't I? Sorry."

I stand on my tiptoes and kiss him. "No. I'm trying to tell you I love you."

34

Traditions

COEN CRUSHES ME with a kiss and then picks me up and runs to the SUV. I laugh when he shuts my door and he leans in for another kiss when he gets in on his side. He speeds up to the house and I put my hand on his before he gets out.

"I didn't say that just so you'd take me to bed."

"Oh, I wasn't even thinking that, but thank you for clarifying," he says with a grin. "I just ... want ... hang on."

He gets out and runs around the other side to open my door and picks me up again. This time I don't even ask, I just hang on for dear life. We get to the porch and he goes around to the side and sets me gently on the porch swing.

"I just wanted us to be here when I tell you I love you back." He kisses each cheek and leans back so he can see me clearly. "I do, you know."

I smile so hard it hurts. "And you needed to be on this swing to say it?"

"Yes, my dad told my mom here first and my grandma told my granddad here first too."

I clutch his face and then crumble. I hold my head in my hands and bawl. At first, he gives my back a few rubs and then he holds me tight while I let it all out.

When I'm quiet, he whispers, "*This* has been the best night of my life. I know I said that before with you, but … this night just won."

"For me too," I whisper. I bury my head further into his neck.

"Come on, let's get you inside. Your arms are cold. But uh, first … my mom wasn't sure where to put you." He scrunches his face up. "I told her we aren't quite *there* yet, but … she laughed at me. Now that you've met her, I know you believe me." He rubs my arms. "There's a fancy room upstairs all ready for you. But she also put some things for you in my room, which is actually in the barn." He points at the barn behind the house that looks more like another little yellow house. "*Barn* sounds scarier than what it is, trust me." He looks at me for a moment. "I know where I want you, but if you're more comfortable in your own room, I completely understand…"

"If you're sure they won't get upset with me, I'd rather stay with you."

"They won't—and Maby? There's still no pressure for … you know, anything…"

"I know, I know." I give him another squeeze and sit up.

He kisses my nose and inhales. "I still can't believe you're here." He stands up and points at the door. "I'm just gonna grab our suitcases. I think they're still in the living room."

I stand up when he goes inside and look at all the stars. Heaven. I could get used to this.

❦ ❦ ❦

THE *BARN* IS really a 2-story extension of the shop, only with a masculine flair and definitely more lived in. Again, I'm speechless and inspired by the beauty of the place.

"Why would you ever want to leave all this?"

"Well, it's my intention to come back, remember? My dad and I remodeled the barn a couple of years ago and I love it out here. I've had to learn what I was doing at La Colombe before trying it out on my parents' dime. Now that I've saved and have some experience, when I open a shop here *I* can pay for it and hopefully make it *work*."

"How close are you to making that happen?"

"I could do it pretty much any time," he says with a smirk. "I've had a little something holding me back in the City for … a while now."

I grin. "I'm glad, but if you're wanting to be here, you should! Does the town stay busy? It seemed like it yesterday and we aren't even quite to the summer crowd yet, right?"

"Next weekend will be crazy with Memorial Day. Even in the winter, the nursery and shop stay busy with Christmas. It's busy year round."

"And a coffee shop would be perfect. Where would you put it?"

"There's space between the nursery and the shop that

207

I would enclose that can also be accessible to people who just wanted coffee or dessert. Could also extend the patio area and have little tables out there." He points to the kitchen counter where the plans are laid out.

I look over every detail, able to clearly imagine it all. The passion and animation in his face is catching and I eventually find myself telling him the plans I've set in motion at home. We move from the kitchen to the loft upstairs and stretch out on his bed, still talking. He whoops and hollers in all the right places and can't believe I've got everything in place but the location.

"This is huge, Maby! Talk about balls…"

"*Were* we talking about balls?" I tease.

"Well, with you, it's pretty much always on my mind since you told me to get some." He leans over and tickles my side.

"It was just my way of verifying you used them…" My face gets hot as I trail off.

"There are so many things I could say right now," Coen says, laughing. He reaches up and touches my lips and the air shifts.

"Coen, I know we said we weren't talking about Saul tonight, but, I think maybe we should."

"Okay."

"I slept with him."

"I heard."

"I'm sorry."

"We weren't … exclusive."

"I mean I'm sorry about the way you heard."

"Oh yeah, that … it's … okay."

"No, it's not."

"Look, Maby. I'm not gonna lie. It hurt like hell, and

I still would very much like to punch Saul right in the scrotum sack." He leans his forehead against mine. "But you're here and I hope that it means you're choosing me. Even if you don't fully realize it yet, that's what I'm hoping."

I move closer and kiss him. "I think I chose you that first night we went out. The word *love* isn't something I throw around lightly. And neither is *scrotum sack...*"

We laugh and he pulls me on top of him.

"Will you just sleep right here? All night long?" He closes his eyes. "God, you feel so good." He plays with my hair and moans. "Too good." His hands move down my back. "I don't want to wreck anything with you, Maby. Talk to me—tell me what you want."

"I don't think you could wreck anything." My head feels perfect on his chest. I close my eyes and take a deep breath. "It's late. Let's sleep tonight. That way I won't be blushing in front of your family all day tomorrow."

"Oh, that would have been fun. But probably a good idea. It's already gonna be hard for me to ever let you out of my bed." He kisses my head. "I can't promise that I'll stop saying creepy things like that, so ... just know that I mean them in the best possible way."

I giggle and it's the last thing I remember before falling into the sweetest, most peaceful sleep.

❦ ❦ ❦

I WAKE UP when the sun is barely rising, in the same spot as I fell asleep, except Coen's hands are cupping my ass instead of my back. I grin and go back to sleep. A couple hours later, I hear quiet rapping on the door. I jump.

"Coen!" I whisper.

He lifts his head and gives me a huge smile before closing his eyes. There's another tap on the door.

"Someone's at the door." I crawl off of him and he turns on his side, pulling my back into his chest.

"It's just Jade seeing if I wanna go running. I don't." He kisses my neck and runs his hand down my side. "I can't believe we slept in our clothes all night. What a waste of bare skin," he mumbles.

"My dress isn't as bad as your jeans. You should take them off, let your skin breathe."

He starts unbuttoning right away, taking everything off, down to his boxer briefs, while I laugh at him.

"Oh man, that's so much better. Here, let's let your skin breathe too," he says and pulls my dress over my head. "I won't even look." He pulls my body back into him. "Mmm, *skin*."

"Weirdo," I giggle.

"Only room for one, you said," he says.

"For a guy, you sure listen well."

"*Thank* you. Now, hush, or I'm gonna be responsible for you blushing all day."

I laugh again and nestle back into his chest.

35

Flaccid Never Looked So Good

IT'S 9:30 BEFORE I crack my eyes open again. I hear
Coen in the shower and hop up to put a T-shirt on before
he catches me in just my underwear. I remember the bathroom downstairs also had a shower, so I hurry down there
to get mine. I can't wipe the smile off my face. Looking in
the steamed over mirror, I even grin at myself.

"Remember this feeling," I whisper. I poke the apples
of my cheeks, sitting so high up with all the smiling going
on.

I put on a short yellow sundress. Swirly skirt. The
weather is supposed to be warmer and I hope so. I make
my hair as haphazard as possible and go for the red lipstick
even though it's early. Vivid blue flats. Even my outfit is
happy.

Coen's whistling around the *barn*. Feels weird to call
it that, but it's what they all call it, so it must be catching

on. When I open the door to the bathroom and step out, Coen looks up from what he's reading and his eyes light up. He stands up and twirls me around, laughing as I try to keep everything covered.

"You're working against me here," he says as he leans down. "Will I have red lips too?"

"No, this doesn't go anywhere, I promise."

His lips are intoxicating, full and soft—I love to look at them—but when they make even the slightest contact with mine it's perfection. Every cell in my body wakes up with just the barest touch of a kiss. And then his tongue … God, the things he can do with it. And he always *tastes* good. While my body feels like electricity, I also feel limp.

I pull back and try to focus on his face. Pathetic. I know my eyes are completely glazed over. I blink until I can see his features again.

"You okay?" He pulls me back in and kisses down my neck.

"Mmm."

"I am insanely proud of myself for not having my way with you last night with you *laying on top of me*," he grips my face and grits his teeth, "but make that sound again and we won't leave this room for the rest of the day."

"*Mmm*, you're getting all primal, I like it." I bite his shoulder and then sneak under it, picking up my purse by the door. "You comin'?"

He groans and laughs, holding up a hand. "Aunt Eeny…" He gives a slight shudder. "Okay, yes, ready."

"What?"

"She's who got me through last night. Aunt Eeny." He puts a hand on my back and then takes my hand when we get outside. "Full head of hair … on her face."

"I don't believe you!" I laugh. "When can I meet this woman?"

"Tonight, if you'll stay another night with me. She comes over on Saturday nights for my mom's spaghetti."

"This just gets better." We walk up the steps to the house and I look at him. "I can stay as long as you were planning to stay. I'm along for the ride. Throwing out the schedule." My heart palpitates a little when I say that, but it reminds me I need to take my meds this morning.

"You don't need to talk to Saul on Monday?"

"I can postpone it to whenever we get back."

"Think you'd be up to staying until Monday night? That's when I have to get back."

He opens the door while I agree to stay. It's a huge step for me, committing to nearly four days in someone else's space. After being alone so much, it feels almost as significant as telling him I'd marry him. Almost.

Big band music is playing in the kitchen and they're all in there. Janie is flipping an omelet, Scott pushes the button on the toaster, and Jade is setting the table. They yell their greetings and keep working. A new bouquet of hydrangeas and roses sits on the kitchen island and peonies are in a pretty pitcher on the table. I sigh, fully content, and feel tears sneaking up on me again.

Coen notices, but he grins and pulls me to him. "Sweet thing," he whispers, giving me a quick kiss.

Jade does a cat call and I jump back like I've been burned.

"Let's get some coffee in the jumpy one," Coen says, tapping my bum.

Again, I back away, checking to see if his parents are

213

watching. They are. I give Coen dagger eyes and he laughs.

"They're just so happy he's finally got a girlfriend, you guys could totally *do it* right here and they'd be like, 'Woohoo!'" Jade says, pointing at her parents.

Janie smacks Jade with a towel and Scott laughs. My mouth hangs open and I turn bright red.

"Aw. I'm getting my wish … without the benefits," Coen says, his eyes crinkling up as he bites his lip. Louder, he says, "Come on, guys, go easy. We can't show all our craziness in her first visit."

I shake my head. "No, it's good. It helps balance out all the weeping I want to do over how perfect your family is."

Jade comes over and puts her arm around my shoulder, tugging me away from Coen. "I'll let you in on a few secrets. Baby brother here is at his wittiest in the morning. He can fall asleep anywhere at 8:30, so if you're wanting to keep him up, better ply him with caffeine or run around the block around 8. I'm better at night: lippy in the morning, much sweeter with wine. Mom really is perfect all the time, and don't even try to talk to my dad until he's had two cups of coffee. Anything else she should know?" She looks around at everyone.

"I do not go to sleep at 8:30!" Coen argues.

Everyone starts talking at once.

"You totally do."

"If you're still for even five minutes…"

"You have since you were a baby."

I tweak his chin. "Awww. Precious. I can see I'm gonna have to introduce you guys to some real issues."

"We like a little excitement. Bring it." Coen hands me

coffee. "It's not as good as mine, but don't tell my dad."

"That's why you need to hurry up and get here," Scott says, putting the omelets on the table.

"Sit down. Let's eat while it's hot," Janie says.

"Mom, you've gotta hear what Maby is doing. First tell her about the nightmare that is Anna…" Coen nudges me.

"Are you sure? It's such an unpleasant breakfast conversation."

"Tell us!" Janie urges.

"Where to start?" I take a sip of juice. "Well, we were good friends when we opened the shop—I thought. The first uh-oh moment I had was when I found out she would 'forget' to tell me about important meetings with clients. Lunches or meetings that I'd put together and she'd change the time and forget to tell me, so I'd look dumb in front of the vendor. Fortunately, she usually wrecked her relationships with them on her own and they would contact me directly anyway, so it all usually worked out."

"That's awful!" Janie cries. "What's she like now?"

I fill them in on what happened my last week of work and what I've been plotting this week.

They stare at me wide-eyed.

"Brilliant," Scott speaks first.

"You've got some cojones," Jade says.

"I wanna see these vendors you're talking to!" Janie says. "Tell me about their stuff."

"Oh you'd love it. Your shop is like a dream, Janie. It's spectacular, it really is."

"Thanks," she waves me off, "after we eat, will you show me their things online?"

"Sure."

215

They ask more questions about Anna and the location of the shops. I'm able to talk about it without feeling the pang in my gut I've had about Anna since the day I started working with her.

When we're done eating and have cleaned up the kitchen, I sit at the computer with Janie and show her the different websites. She loves all the merchandise, just like I knew she would. We lose track of time, talking in her office, until Coen comes in.

"I've hogged your girl. She's just so fun!" Janie tells Coen.

"I've been called a bombshell, sweet, and fun since I got here. You are all clearly delusional. Not that I'm complaining..." I add, smiling up at Coen.

"We tell it like we see it." Coen smirks. "Hey, would you like to go into town? Maybe by the river?"

"I'd love it!" I stand up and stretch. "Thanks for indulging me, Janie. I could pick your brain all day about all this."

"Oh, you indulged *me*. You've got my wheels spinning about all your plans..." she says. "Should I expect you tonight for spaghetti or do you have something else in the works?" she asks Coen.

"Maby has to meet Aunt Eeny or all my credibility will be shot to hell."

"Fair enough. I'll see you both at 6."

Chest Pillow

WE SPEND THE afternoon in the shops. People greet Coen wherever he goes. It's evident that he's really respected in this busy little tourist town. He seems older than he does in the City, more comfortable in his skin, while I feel more and more like a little kid the longer I'm here.

Giddy. Lighthearted. And so happy I don't even know what to do with myself.

When I've had my fill of shopping, we grab a drink at an old-fashioned tavern and then walk toward the river. A gazebo faces the water and we stop and sit down inside.

"I can see now why you're so special," I tell him. "You've been adored your whole life, but also challenged to do something with yourself … no time for being spoiled, except with love."

He laces his fingers with mine. Slowly slides them out. Laces them back together.

"Not everyone appreciates my upbringing," he says. "Most of my exes have been intimidated by it."

"It's intimidating, in some ways, for sure. But I want to get back to the exes."

"I'll tell you all you want to know, but it's not very exciting. I'd rather talk about you. How about we save the exes conversation for sometime when I don't want to kiss your face off … which will be never." He leans over and kisses the cleavage showing just above my neckline.

I squeak.

"I've been dying to do that all day."

"Hmm, or avoiding something, maybe?" I try to act nonchalant, but it's really hard.

I can't stop thinking about how he made me feel that night that feels like forever ago now. I cross my legs and try to stay focused. I keep hearing him say, "You look … drunk" over and over again. I shift in my seat again.

"Not at all. Okay, exes. Katy, Ashleigh, Sara, Jennifer, and Jess. Oh … and Laura."

"Wow, that's … a lot." I lift an eyebrow.

"You think?" He frowns and sticks out his lips. "I was only serious about one of them. Katy…"

"Were they all tall?"

"Tall? Why do you ask?"

"Your whole family is tall. I'm like the little troll under the bridge. Like the lecher who continuously hugs the women and rests his head on their bosom."

He squeezes his eyes shut and gives his head a shake, like he's clearing it out. "What? *What*?"

"So what happened to Katy?" I attempt to rein in the loony.

He looks at me like I've lost it and chuckles. "I dated

her through college. We broke up soon after we got home. I think she wanted someone more Wall Street than me. And I wanted someone more carefree ... easygoing."

I grip the bench under me. "I'm not carefree, you know."

"You sure about that?"

I nod. "I'm very ... uptight."

He cocks his head and studies me. "Really? I've not seen that side of you yet. I bet it's cute though."

I snort and then laugh at myself. "Did she snort? Ha! I bet I have that on her."

Coen laughs and pulls me closer. "No, she didn't. Do it again," he says, poking me in the side.

I roll my eyes and don't give in to the tickle. "I take medicine to help me not be so ... insane."

He looks to see if I'm joking and when he realizes I'm not, he nods. "Okay. I don't really like using that word about you, but ... what's it like when you're *insane*?"

"I stay awake all night organizing. I wash until I bleed. I count while I'm running until I sometimes pass out. I feel like I'm losing my mind..."

"Wow. I ... didn't realize. I mean, you've mentioned little things and I've noticed you counting under your breath sometimes, and being very *clean*, but ... I didn't know it was quite like that. Must be really difficult." He looks at me and waits for me to say more.

I take a deep breath. "It is, but I've been going to therapy, which has helped a lot. And the medication helps too. Staying in a routine is best for me, but lately I've been able to shake that a little. Maybe *because* of the therapy and medication? I don't know..."

"Will you let me know if you feel it's coming—like a

bad stretch of it?"

"I'll try."

"Is this what you meant before when you said Saul knows what he's getting into?"

"Yes."

Coen nods. "It's all making more sense to me now. I'm glad you told me, Maby. Thank you."

And just like that, I've spilled my worst secret to him and there's no pity or disgust, just kindness and concern.

"Are you okay if I look into this? I don't know much about it, but my mom knows a lot about different herbal remedies and which foods help certain things. We can see what else might also help…"

I stare at him and my eyes fill. Again. It's embarrassing.

"I'm making you cry way too much," he whispers. "That can't be good."

"You are the best thing that's ever happened to me," I tell him.

SPAGHETTI DINNER IS a hilarious affair. Aunt Eeny is exactly how Coen described her, only even slightly more unkempt than I expected. But for all her hairs and odd lumps, she is sweetness personified. And sassy as hell. They are all clearly crazy about her. Eeny, short for Enid, is Janie's grandmother's sister, and is proudly in her 90s. Abraham, her gentleman friend, is the only one she's snippy with, but he seems to eat it up.

"Get me by the girl, Abraham," she snaps.

He promptly scuttles over to help her into the seat next to me at the table.

"So you're trying to steal our young Coen from us," she starts right in.

I stutter around until I notice that her shoulders are shaking just like Janie's did earlier.

"Ahh, the teasing runs in the family, I see." I laugh.

"What do you mean, dear? Who's teasing?" She pokes out her lips and looks around the table. When she sees the look on my face, the shoulders start moving again.

I shake my head. "It's a conspiracy."

"I'm just happy he finally brought you home. Thought we were just gonna have to hear tall tales about you forever." She beams at Coen. "She's a lovely one, dear. Much nicer than that tall one you tried out last." She shakes her head in what appears to be disgust, although she might just be joking again. "For a while there he liked *gold diggers*." She stage whispers *gold diggers*.

"Tall, huh," I say, staring pointedly at Coen.

He clears his throat and has the grace to look contrite. "I didn't know trolls could be soul mates?" he tries, but backs up when I glare at him. "*Kidding*." He peers around me. "I learned my lesson, Aunt Eeny. And I think you scared them all off too."

She throws her head back and laughs at that. "Well, I should hope so!"

"Abraham!" she barks. "Quit dozing. You're missing Mabel. Such a fine name too," she says to the whole table. "They just don't name young folks fine names like that any more."

"Sure don't," Abraham perks up long enough to agree.

The spaghetti is delicious and the wine is hitting us all right. Throughout the night I laugh more than I ever remember laughing. We move from the kitchen to the living room and I cuddle into Coen's side as we all talk. I'm wiping my eyes from laughing, not crying, when I catch Coen staring at me.

"What?"

He gets close so only I can hear him. "I can't believe you're in my life. Being with you is even better than I imagined," he says.

I gulp and turn to face him. "I never dreamed I would find someone like you. Are you sure, Coen? Are you sure you want *me*?"

He leans his forehead against mine. "You've taken possession of my heart little by little, and now you own it, Maby. Completely."

He puts his hand on my cheek and whispers against my lips. "I love you."

"Oh my God, you guys are so hot together. This is so weird!" Jade shrieks. "And gross!"

"Jade!" Janie swats her with a throw pillow.

"Well, it is," she says between her teeth. "I mean, I love it, but … it's … ew."

Coen stands up and pulls me up with him. "Thanks for dinner. I think we're gonna head out. As always, Aunt Eeny…" He kisses her hand and gives everyone else a wave.

I still haven't found my voice after all that just happened, so I wave too, and we get out of there.

37

Burst

WE RUN ACROSS the grass to the barn and when the door shuts behind us, I try to look away, but my gaze keeps shifting to him. He hasn't stopped staring at me.

"I never wanted to carry a tall girl anywhere. With you, I just want to hoist you over my shoulder and carry you around all day like a pet," he says, leaning against the door. "Just something to consider." He shrugs and looks upstairs.

I try to stay serious, but can't keep a straight face. I also can't keep my hands off of him for another second.

"Coen?" I walk toward him and put my hands on his chest before backing away slowly. "Race you to bed?"

I take off running with him not far behind. When we reach the stairs, he swoops me up, takes the stairs two at a time, and tosses me on the bed. He stares down at me.

"Now what?" he asks.

"Let's not sleep with our clothes on tonight."

His shirt is over his head with one yank from the back. I lean up on my elbows to watch.

"Your turn," he says.

"Your pants are still on."

He unbuttons them slowly and takes his sweet time pulling them down. His thumb loops under the waistband of his boxer briefs and my mouth waters waiting for him to take them off. He says something, but I don't hear any of it.

"What?" I ask.

"I said—are *you* sure?" He puts his hand over his mouth and looks at me, his eyes narrowing. After a long pause, he says, without conceit: "When we make love, it's gonna change things. I want to know if you're ready for that before we do."

I move until I'm on my knees in front of him. "Things have already changed for me, Coen. I'm ready … if you are."

He grins and pulls my dress over my head. "Haven't you been hearing me? I've been ready for you for a long time, Maby Armstrong."

His hands travel down my chest and he unhooks my bra, sucking in a breath when it falls to the ground. He smiles at my yellow thong with black skulls.

"You're so edgy," he smirks, getting on his knees while he pulls them off. He looks up at me. "I plan to spend a lot of time in this general vicinity." He waves his hand over the area from my lips to my thighs. "And especially here," he whispers, pulling me into his mouth.

I hold onto his hair for dear life. I nearly fall back on the bed, but his hands are gripped on both cheeks, keeping my buns of nothing close to steel in place.

His tongue. Ohhh. It works miracles. He licks side to side in deliberate strokes and then in and out, screwing me with his mouth. I can't take it. I fall off the edge within minutes and he stands up and lays me back, just barely giving me a break before coming back for more.

I'm not a screamer, but I give it a good go when he gets both his fingers and tongue involved. My whole body feels like lead when he peeks up at me. I lift my head up and smile dreamily at him.

"How do you do that?" I ask groggily. "You're like a professional…"

He laughs and gives me one more lick before kissing his way up my body.

"You're delicious," he says.

I groan, still not entirely comfortable with the thought that I'd be delicious. I tug on his briefs and pull them down. He's kissing my neck so I don't even get to look yet, but when he presses against my stomach, my eyes close in anticipation.

We haven't talked about birth control and all that, but we can work all that out later, I think, as he slides on a condom. I've been meaning to get on the Pill anyway. I put it on my mental checklist, patting myself on the back with how calmly I'm handling everything.

When he presses inside me, my breath hitches. We stare at each other as he inches in all the way.

I gasp.

"Too soon?" he asks, leaning his forehead on mine.

"Noooo," I moan. "*Fuck*." I arch my back and then just stay still for a minute, loving the way I feel completely full.

He twitches inside me when I say that and his eyes squeeze shut. He's still for another minute and then takes a breath.

"Turns out you saying 'fuck' is directly linked with my dick. Don't say it again unless you're ready for this to be over."

I giggle, tempted to say it again just in case he's right. He starts to move then and at first I just take it in, wanting this feeling to last forever. He's barely in me and I come again, which is just shameful, but honestly, it's that good.

Now he's cocky, grinning and thrusting and watching me writhe.

I shift my legs so they're on his shoulders and his eyebrows go up.

"Flexible," he whispers.

Maybe the running and yoga are paying off. I match him thrust for thrust and his eyes glaze over.

"I—knew—it—would be—fucking intense—with you," he says, moving just a little faster. His eyes never leave mine.

"Oh, so you can say it and I can't…"

"You're talking—too well. I must not—be—doing—something—right."

He pulls out and I try to clutch him back to me, but he takes his time going in slowly again. He does it over and over, in and out, going a little further in each time, until my whole body is shaking for him. When he finally goes in as far as he can go, we both moan. I wrap my legs around him and try to inhale him in even more.

When we move now, it's frenzied. I can't stop and neither can he. His hands go underneath me to pull me up even tighter to him and I lose it.

"Coen," I whimper. "Please … ohhh…"

Bliss.

❦ ❦ ❦

AN HOUR LATER, I'm on top. I'm 28 and I've never been on top. It's a whole new world up here. His hands are on my breasts and he looks like an angel smiling up at me. I rotate my hips on him and he groans.

"This—*this* is the best night of my life."

I lean down and kiss him. "You always say that."

"I always mean it."

❦ ❦ ❦

IT'S MIDNIGHT AND we decide to take a shower. It's a little small in there, so we hurry and get back to bed. I'm getting drowsy, but he runs his hands down my legs and my insides liquify.

We face each other and he tentatively pushes inside me. I think we're both a little sore from the last vigorous session, but it just feels too wonderful to stop.

"I want to live in you," he says, touching my lips with his fingers.

"Okay."

"That was easy. I thought it'd take some convincing."

"I'm realizing you have some pretty great ideas." I kiss him and he flips me onto my back.

We go at it long and hard. Until I can't move. He

stays on top of me for a long time and when he finally crawls off, we both fall asleep. Later I get up to go to the bathroom and something falls down my leg. And then drips, actually. I bend down and it's the condom.

"*Shit!*" I run to the bathroom and it's not good. I'm a mess. "Shit, shit, shit."

"What?" Coen asks from the bedroom, groggy.

"The *condom*!"

"*What*? Oh *fuck*! I fell asleep…"

I clean up and he's standing outside the bathroom door when I walk out.

"I'm so sorry, Maby. I … I can't believe I did that."

I stare at him, panicked.

"It's gonna be fine. Come on, let's get some sleep." He takes my hand and leads me back to bed.

I feel shaky and he strokes my back softly until I fall asleep.

Fan the Flames

I'M AWAKE WHEN Coen stirs the next morning. I've slept some, but I've also been worrying throughout the night.

"You okay?" he asks, pulling me close.

"I'm trying not to think about it. I'm gonna get on the Pill this week," I tell him. "I should have done that a long time ago."

"Please don't worry. I'm so sorry I fell asleep. I promise I'll be more—"

"I can't get pregnant, Coen. I can't. It just…"

"It's highly unlikely that you'd get pregnant from this … don't you think?"

"It's totally possible. I Googled it."

He smooths the crease between my eyebrows. "Listen. It will all be okay. Besides, I wouldn't mind having a baby with you," he says with a grin.

229

I push him away.

"Too soon to joke about it?" he asks, patting my hip and pulling me back against him. "Come on, put it out of your mind. I'll be more careful. You'll get on the Pill. I'll convince you to have my baby later…"

"Coen!" I swat him, but I'm laughing now.

"Come here. I'll put on two this time, so I can screw you senseless and have backup."

"How can you even think of sex when we're talking about this?" I scowl at him.

"Oh, I can." He goes under the covers and proves it.

LATER I WATCH him getting dressed and am shocked at the heat that sweeps through my body. I can't seem to get enough of him and am not used to that feeling. Even though I've had the urge to do every obsessive thing I can think of, after our last couple of rounds and my shower, I feel an inexplicable calm. My neuroticism seems to be quelled for the time being by the best sex I've ever had. It wasn't just a one time fluke either; every time has been better than the last, which doesn't even seem possible. The first time was life changing in itself. In my old life, thinking about that one time would have kept me going for a solid week and a half.

I look at him and wonder why in the world he wants to be with someone like me. He could have anyone and there is no question in my mind that any girl he's ever kissed or had sex with is now lost without him.

And if I were to ever, ever in my life, EVER have a

baby, I can't imagine anyone better to be my child's father. The possibility of making a family with him makes my heart twitch in ways I can't let myself think about, and well, I'm jumping ahead of myself.

He buttons his shirt last and I sigh when his chest is fully covered.

"What are you thinking about over there? Are you still stressed?" he asks.

"I feel really lucky," I tell him, "and like I want to keep the blinders over your eyes for as long as I possibly can."

He scrunches his eyebrows together. "What do you mean?"

"I—oh, nothing." I stop the crazy talk and smile. "Do you think everyone *knows*?"

We've missed breakfast and lunch and are trying to make it to dinner on time.

"For all they know we went hiking all day."

I snort. "Yeah, right."

He walks over to me and kisses my neck. "You look beautiful. Not nearly as good as you look naked, but really close."

"You're just changing the subject."

THEY'RE JUST PUTTING everything on the table when we walk in. Scott does a double take when he sees Coen and gives him a hearty slap on the back. We both turn red.

"Co-en is glow-in," Jade sings as she walks by.

He flicks her.

"Oh shoot, I forgot the peppers. Coen, could you slice some really quick? Everyone else has their hands full." Janie smiles at me and then *she* turns pink.

Jade smirks and lifts an eyebrow.

Yep, everyone knows.

There's a little pile of all kinds of peppers. I grab a knife alongside Coen and we start chopping.

"What are these?" I show Coen a pepper.

"Habanero. And these are serrano … both really hot."

"Can't wait to try some. You eat it on everything or just the tacos?"

"I like it on everything," he says, carrying the bowl of peppers to the table.

Conversation is a little awkward in the beginning, but it gets easier as we start eating. I pile the peppers on and dig in like I haven't eaten in weeks. Janie is such a great cook.

Three bites in and I start coughing. I gulp down my water and look around to see if the peppers are killing anyone else. They're all acting like it's nothing.

"Can't handle the heat?" Coen teases.

"Oh, I can handle it." I take another bite and quickly swallow more water.

We hang out for a little bit on the front porch and then Jade convinces all of us to take a walk. I've never been around a family who seems to genuinely enjoy being together so much. It's refreshing. And I'm grateful they seem to have accepted me so quickly. When we come back up to the house, Coen and I say goodnight to everyone. As soon as the door shuts behind us, he's pulling off my clothes. I take off his pants and briefs in one fell swoop and get my hands on him.

He yanks off my panties and slides his fingers in me within minutes.

It's feeling so good and then all of a sudden, something feels a little off. I ignore it and we lay back on the couch. I wrap both hands around him, loving the satiny hardness of him. He moans and leans over me. I'm feeling really weird down below. Worse and worse. I keep ignoring it.

"I've missed being in you," he whispers, grabbing a condom.

I slide it on him and he gets inside me. We move together for a minute and suddenly I feel like I'm on fire. I yelp and he jumps up.

"Something is *wrong*," he says, wide-eyed.

"It's burning. I'm burning!" I jump up.

"Oh God. Me too!" He pulls off the condom. His whole crotch area is red and getting welts. "Ahhh, you too." He points at me and everywhere he has touched is red.

"What's going on?" I yell.

His eyes get huge. "The *peppers*!"

"We washed our hands!"

"Ahhh," he yells. "The shower." He's holding his hands out like they're poison. "Come on."

We get in the shower and scrub our hands and everything else with soap and rinse in cool water. It doesn't stop burning. Our bodies have giant splotches all over now. Even my breasts have welts.

"I can't believe this," he says, looking at me in horror. "Oh babe, I'm so sorry. Here..." He wraps a towel around me. "We need ice."

We go downstairs and he fills two plastic bags with

ice. We sit on the couch with the ice packs on our privates, miserable. Our hands are stuck in small bowls of ice. When I'm not getting enough relief, I slip an ice cube inside me. As soon as it dissolves, I stick in another. It helps a little, but still hurts like crazy.

"When this stops hurting so bad, it will be really, really funny," he says.

I shift in my seat and wince. "It's already kinda funny," I say, looking at his penis poking out of the ice.

He grins and we start laughing until we cry. He reaches up to wipe his eyes and I shout at him to stop before he spreads it there too. I startle him and he jumps, which makes us laugh all the harder.

Later, after we've watched a movie and changed out the ice a few times, we head back upstairs.

"This was not my finest moment," he admits when we crawl into bed.

I laugh again until I'm wheezing. "Your face when you jumped up … I'll never forget that look!"

He shakes his head, chuckling. "At least we learned something…"

"What?"

"Always wear gloves when cutting peppers," he says.

"Like I'll ever eat peppers again…"

39

I is the New Black

THE NEXT DAY we're feeling much better. The welts are gone. We have sex in the shower and thankfully, our lower regions are fully functioning.

I go to the nursery to watch Janie and Scott in action. When I stop in the shop, I'm shocked to see that half of Coen's terrariums sold over the weekend. He blows it off like it's no big deal but then says selling the terrariums has given him more of an income than his full time job at La Colombe.

A tall girl with long black hair is working in the shop. She seems very happy to see Coen. Not so happy to see me. He introduces us. Jess.

He's less touchy-feely in the shop than he has been all weekend and seems relieved when we get back to the nursery. I get a sinking feeling in the pit of my stomach. I ask him later if that's the Jess he dated. He says yes and doesn't elaborate.

I thought if I had to worry about anyone it was Katy, the one he was more serious about, but … Jess. We see her one more time as we're getting ready to leave. Scott, Janie and Jade are hugging us goodbye and Jess comes and stands by Jade, putting her arm around Jade's waist. They seem a little surprised that she's hanging around, but are obviously comfortable around her. Even her name fits right in. J, J, J—jealous, jerk-off, jackal.

I thank the Bradys for a great weekend. They tell me to hurry back—come back every time Coen does if I want, I'm always welcome. Jess doesn't say a word. She just gives me this little mysterious smirk that makes my stomach gnaw itself inside out.

I'm quiet when we leave. Coen is chatting about his schedule this week and I can't stay focused on what he's saying. My stomach is queasy and for the first time since we left for the weekend, I'm anxious to get home.

Traffic isn't as bad going home as it was getting out of town, so we get to my apartment in less than an hour.

Coen pulls up and says, "What do you feel like? You ready to get rid of me yet?"

I look at him and kiss his cheek. "Thank you for the most remarkable weekend I've ever had. I'll never forget it."

He scrunches up his face as he grins. "I plan to have many, *many* more with you, Maby Armstrong."

I hop out and grab my bag. It's then that Coen looks unsure of himself. I hate that I'm making him feel that way, but I know that I'm shutting down fast.

"I'll talk to you tomorrow?" I ask.

"Uh, sure. Okay," he says.

He looks wounded and it makes my heart hurt.

My phone is still sitting between our seats and it buzzes when I reach across to hug him one more time. He sees my phone before I do. I can tell who it is by the way Coen's arms drop. He bites his lip and starts nodding his head awkwardly. He taps the steering wheel with his fist.

"Okay," he says. "Oh-kay."

"Coen ... don't be weird."

"*You* don't be weird, Maby. I'm not ... I don't want to..." He leans his head against the back of his seat and closes his eyes. "*Please* don't ... disappear on me again after the weekend we've just had together. We ... just ... please don't." He looks at me and the intensity in his eyes guts me. "Figure out who you want, Maby. If you want Saul, tell me now. If you want me, I'm right here."

I turn around before I lose it, but then mumble over my shoulder. "What about Jess?" I get louder when he doesn't say anything. "There's something going on there. I can feel it."

He gets out and slams the door. "Don't turn it around on me. If you wanna know something about Jess, just ask and I'll be straight up with you."

"Okay. What's going on with Jess? Why was she so smug when she looked at me?"

His cheeks flush and I can't tell if he's mad or embarrassed.

"I've slept with Jess since she and I broke up," he says quietly. "She knows I've liked you for a long time, but we've still had sex a few times ... not recently, but..."

"Great. That's really great, Coen." I shift my bag and walk toward the door to my building. "When was it?"

He gulps. "It was before you and I ... I haven't slept

with her since the night I first kissed you. But … we nearly did once since then."

"When?"

"The last weekend I asked you to come home with me and you said no." He walks over and holds onto my arm.

"Let me *go*."

He lets go. "Please don't pick a fight with me, Maby. I *didn't* sleep with her that weekend. I promise you I didn't. I felt hopeful about you—even after you said you were seeing Saul too. I told her I was going to pursue you and I meant it. I *don't* like Jess. I only want to be with you."

"Thanks for a great weekend, Coen. I loved meeting your family." I go inside and run up the stairs as fast as I can. The tears are blinding me, but I make it to my apartment without stumbling.

He buzzes, but I don't pick up.

The text from Saul says:

Saul: It's Monday and I do want to talk soon. Sorry I left mad the other night. I just want to say this … I might not have fought for you like I should have, but I'm the one who has always been there. And when this phase with coffee guy is over, I still will be. Call me.

After a steaming shower, I crawl into bed and cry. Fortunately, I'm exhausted, so it doesn't last very long. *It was time for a breakdown anyway*, is the last thing I think before I crash. *This was inevitable.*

❧ ❧ ❧

I WAKE UP from a nightmare. I sit up and peel the gown off of my sweaty chest. I can't remember what the dream was even about, but I know I won't be going back to sleep anytime soon.

I get up and rinse my face with cold water. The look on Coen's face rolls over me and I stagger across the room, stopping only long enough to catch my balance. I pace the living room, kitchen, bedrooms. Steps. Numbers. Pinch, pinch, pinch my skin. Repeat. When the clock says 2:22, I let myself stop pacing. I take another shower and then decide to go through a box I've been avoiding. I may as well yank off the mental Band-Aid while I'm already a mess.

My mom had put all our pictures in a box and kept them in chronological order. I haven't looked at them since she died and I shake when I pull the first picture out. The picture wobbles in my hand until it comes into focus. It's my mom, hugely pregnant. Her hair is long and wild and she looks beautiful. I flip through the ones of me and get to another one of her, holding me. I'm two years old, looking at the camera and my mom is looking at me.

It reminds me of how our life was together. I did my thing and she watched in adoration. She propelled me forward from the sidelines, loving me. I didn't realize how much I relied on her simply holding me and thinking that everything I did was special. It actually made all the difference in the world to have that kind of love. I kept it together for her, because of her, thanks to her ... and now that she's gone, I know I'm not going to get better or any more sane.

The past weekend is the closest I've ever felt to having that, besides with my mother. Coen and his family accepted me without question, and without even having the benefit of time and a history together. I will always be grateful to them for showing me that kind of unconditional acceptance, but they already have the right prospective in the wings—Jess—just waiting to swoop in and show Coen all he's been missing.

Double Barrel Betrayal

MY PHONE IS glaringly silent over the next few days. It's *brutal*. I check it every few minutes to see if Coen has called or if I have a text, but nothing.

I tell myself it's for the best, and that it was going to end up like this anyway, but it's still excruciating. Now that I know exactly what I'm missing, I don't think I'll ever be the same.

I don't usually allow myself to think about the time I spent in the hospital, but it's been going over and over my mind since I got back from Coen's house. If I told him, maybe he'd understand better why he should move on. I know what I'm capable of.

During my appointment with Dr. Still, I tell her I need to up the dosage of both medications and she tells me to just continue to exercise when I'm feeling an overwhelming urge to do a compulsion. I tell her I've run at least 12 miles over the last 3 days and she pauses momentarily, but then congratulates me on finally getting physically fit.

I fight the urge to do my standard—the double bird—but sit on my hands. I still manage to get the two fingers up, but at least I'm the only one who knows.

My apartment has never been cleaner and I've made three photo albums with all the pictures in the photo box. I've gotten a few more vendors to come with me and still haven't returned Anna's calls. I know I'm going to have to come up with a solid course of action for work soon, but so far I still don't know exactly what to do.

"Please call him," Paschal moans.

We're at a bar by the salon on Friday night. I keep re-living minute by minute what Coen and I were doing this time last week.

"He's probably in the barn screwing Jess right now." I lay my head on the bar. I may or may not already be thoroughly trashed.

"Can we call it his *apartment*? I just don't like how dirty 'barn' sounds." Paschal pushes my hair back and looks in my eyes. "Come on. Call him. Now. Please." He hands me my cell phone.

"I missed a text!" I sit up.

"From him?"

"Ew. No. Dalton." I go off on a tangent of fuck, making the older couple next to me glare.

Paschal starts laughing. "Let me see it. Is there a picture?"

I hand him my phone and he reads it out loud.

Dalton: Dreamed about you last night. You will always be hot to me, no matter how bitchy you are.

"Who the hell does he think he is?" I slur.

Paschal is a little bit trashed too and starts laughing harder.

"I'll be right back," he says.

"Hey, leave my phone here."

He holds it up. "I'll be careful with it, promise."

My eyes narrow. "What…"

He does the slow glide to the bathroom—the walk where you try *really* hard not to look drunk.

When he comes back, his face is red and he's laughing so hard he can barely breathe.

"What is so funny? Did he say something else?"

Paschal gives me wide eyes and shrugs. "I might have sent him a little something. Or a *huge* something…"

My mouth drops. "You didn't!"

He nods and I grab the phone.

"Well, the evidence is gone *now*," he says, like I'm slow, "but maybe it will take care of Mini Legs for a little while."

"You're brilliant!" I hug him.

"Yes, I am. Now call Coen!" He taps my phone and nudges it closer to me.

"I can't interrupt the afterglow," I say, my voice hitching at the end. My eyes go blurry at the thought of Jess's long legs wrapped around Coen's back.

"He is not having sex with her."

"You didn't see her. She's beautiful. I bet you anything he is. Right now."

"No. He's not."

I raise my head to shoot daggers at Paschal and he's grinning like an idiot at someone behind me. I turn around and Coen is walking toward us.

"What did you do?" I hit Paschal in the shoulder.

"You can thank me later," he whispers. And then he hops off the bar stool and disappears.

Creep.

I give what I hope is a cool look to Coen.

"Hey," he says.

"Hey."

"So you wanted to talk?" He clears his throat and signals to the bartender.

"What?"

"You're ready to talk?" He sounds agitated.

"Uh … I … okay."

"You texted and I came running."

There's a bitter tone in his voice that I haven't heard before and I don't like it. At all.

"Oh. I … okay."

We sit there for a few minutes. The bartender brings him a beer and gives me another vodka tonic.

"Is that all you're gonna say? Okay?"

"You're mad." I state the obvious.

He nods; his eyebrows shooting up.

My skin goes fiery. "Why? Why are you mad?"

He takes a long swig of his drink and stands up. "This probably wasn't a good idea. I should have known you were drunk to have texted me. Let's talk when you're sober."

I stand up. "No, let's talk now. Why are you mad?"

He gets in my face. "I'm mad that I keep pouring my heart out to you and you keep stomping on it. I'm mad that I had the best weekend of my life and I thought you were feeling it right along with me and then you throw it all

244

away. I'm mad that…"

I hold up my hand. "Okay. Okay! You're mad. Fine."

He shakes his head and laughs. "What do you want from me, Maby? Spell it out for me because I sure as hell can't read you."

I pick up my purse and stand on my tiptoes to reach his ear. "I want you to go to Jess, be happy, live a nice, normal life. I can't give you that. I thought I could, but I can't."

I'm halfway to the door when he grabs my arm.

"If I wanted nice and normal I would have already done that by now, but here I am, wanting *you*."

"If that's supposed to give me warm fuzzies, it's not working." I shake his arm off, look into his miserable brown eyes and before I can be sucked in, I walk out.

He doesn't follow me.

❧ ❧ ❧

JUSTIN CALLS THE next week to tell me they have a few more questions regarding my business loan. I go and spend a few hours and walk out of there with a loan. I call Linda, the real estate agent we used when we found Whatnot Alley and ask her if she has any other shop possibilities.

"I do have one. It's not far from where you are now and quite a bit larger. I thought you were opening another location, though. Did that fall through?"

"No, I'm looking for myself, not Anna."

"Oh. *Oh*, I see."

"Can I see the space soon?"

"You can see it today at 5 if you'd like. They're anxious to get it filled."

We agree to meet and I'm a bundle of nerves in the meantime. I can't even eat. I need to run, but I don't want to have to take another shower.

The space needs some work but has a lot of potential. It's really too much room for me, but I still talk over the numbers with Linda. I stay up late doing my crude version of a blueprint, imagining the way it would look. I keep remembering things I loved about Janie's shop and jot down a few notes to look into different lighting options. The chandeliers really added to her store. I fall asleep with a pile of notes on my chest.

❤ ❤ ❤

I SHOW UP at Whatnot Alley the next morning, ready to confront Anna. Saul is just leaving when I reach the door.

"Maby! What are you doing here?"

"Here to see Anna," I tell him.

"Does she know you're coming?"

"Nope."

He nods. "You look tired. You okay?"

"I've been better."

He nods again. "I miss you, Maby. Did you get my last text? I asked you to call me."

"Yeah. Sorry. I've been … I haven't known what to say."

"When did we get like this? What happened to us?"

He doesn't seem to expect an answer. We both shift our feet and I finally speak up.

"I'm sorry I bailed on you, Saul. You've been a good friend to me and I just … I guess I'm trying to figure everything out. I did get upset with you for taking Anna's side, but I get it. You need the work too."

"I wasn't taking her side, really."

"Yeah, you kinda were. But anyway, the rest … the us part. You know I'm a mess. Doesn't seem to be changing…"

He sticks his hands in his pockets and is about to say something when the door opens.

"I thought that was you," Anna says. "What are you doing here, Mabel?"

"Came to talk to you."

"Oh."

She's caught off guard and I get a sudden heavy dose of guilt. Not just about Anna but about Saul too. I look at him and wish I'd prepared him. He'll never forgive me.

Making the Rounds

NO ONE IS in the shop. I'm momentarily sad by this fact until I remind myself that I don't care anymore. I can't afford to care about Anna or this shop anymore.

I push down any and all feelings and remind myself of how rotten she was to me for so long. It helps.

She goes behind the counter and seems to regain some of her footing back there. I put my elbow on the counter and stare at her for a long moment before speaking. She shuffles from foot to foot.

I'm making her nervous.

Good.

Something comes back to me while I'm standing there. A memory—a conversation with my mom.

"Do you remember talking to my mom about me?" I ask her.

She frowns and shakes her head. "What?"

"You told her in great detail what a mess I was. She asked me then if I was sure we were really friends. I defended you to her."

She widens her eyes and motions with her hand for me to get on with it.

"I wish I'd listened to her."

I open my folder and hand her a piece of paper with a list of vendors on it.

"What's this?" Her brows move into a huge V and stay there.

"It's a list of the vendors who are coming with me."

"*Coming* with you?" she sneers.

"Yes. You are going to be losing vendors once the new merchandise comes out. I know they've let you know they don't want to work with you, so this isn't news to you. I don't know if you realize how that will affect *this* shop—I'm sure you know it will mean no Soho shop, but … it also means this one will be bare come time for the Fall merchandise. Now, here's what I'm proposing. You get your act together with Whatnot Alley, learn the business, etc., and I can either take over the shop in Soho or I will be opening one twice the size three blocks over from you."

The expression on her face is fierce, but as she sets down the list, I see her hand tremble.

I smile and keep talking. "If I were you, I'd sign both stores over to me. We both know that I've done the work here and you've financed it, which isn't *nothing*, but … you don't have the experience. I'm in the position to finance it now and I do have the experience. You're about to have a baby. It's a win-win for us both."

She scowls at me and puts a hand on her hips. Her

baby bump juts out proudly.

"I'm not signing anything over to you."

"Okay. But think about it for a moment. This doesn't just affect me, Anna. It affects you, Joey, the baby, Saul, Peggy…"

"I'm not giving you my businesses, Mabel. I've always known you were missing a screw somewhere and this just proves it if you think you can…"

I hold up my hand and crinkle up my nose, laughing. "Now is not the time for digs, Anna. You don't like me—fine. I really don't like you either." I take a deep breath. It feels so good to say that. "I don't know why we were *ever* friends. Oh wait—we weren't really. But, I'm giving you one more chance to make a good business decision. Let me take over the Soho store and you still have a chance to make something of this one."

"No. I won't be blackmailed. I will do whatever I have to do to make both stores work for me."

I bite my lip and nod. "Okay. Fair enough. I'm done playing nice."

She scoffs. "This was playing nice?"

"You fired me, Anna. I'm still not quite sure why you did it the way you did. No warning, no asking me to improve, no chance to fix anything. Just pure drama, I guess. For you to treat me that way, after all I've done for you—you deserve to lose everything. Don't come crawling back later. You've made your decision."

I close my folder and walk out of the store. The sun is hot on my skin and I lift my face up to feel it.

"You look happier than I expected."

Saul is leaning against the building and stands up straight when I open my eyes to look at him.

"Saul, I have to tell you something and you're not going to like it."

He groans. "Why was I afraid of this?"

❦ ❦ ❦

I SWEETEN THE burn with Saul by asking him to help get my store ready for opening. If Anna does what she says, she'll try to still open the shop in Soho, which means Saul should still get paid. He agrees to it and isn't too angry with me. I think he's in shock that I'm doing all this. He says he'll make sure Anna pays before everything goes to shit. I won't be able to pay him much, but at least he won't be out of work.

After I've gotten home and had a mini-breakdown, I call Linda and tell her I'm ready to move forward. The next morning I sign papers and by the afternoon, I'm standing in an empty shop, looking at the potential.

It's really close to Paschal's salon and La Colombe, which is something I've tried to not think about since seeing it. But now that I'm in here, all I can think about is how much I want to stop in the coffee shop and tell Coen everything. I decide to call Paschal instead. He's still feeling bad about texting Coen, so he picks up all cheery on the first ring.

"Hi, sweetheart. What's up?"

"I'm in my new shop."

"No way!" he yells. It gets muffled, but I hear him saying, "Maby got her store, guys!"

"You need to help me come up with a name."

"Done!" he says. "Shall we go celebrate tonight?"

"I wish, but I have an appointment … maybe this weekend. If you don't STEAL MY PHONE AGAIN!" I yell.

"I deserved that, I did," he says meekly.

"I know you meant well," I concede.

❖ ❖ ❖

I FILL DR. STILL in on everything. She looks mildly alarmed and hugely amused.

"This could either be really therapeutic or a really bad trigger for you," she says.

I hold up both hands and snort. "What is that supposed to mean?"

"Well, you're taking on a lot of stress," she smiles her peaceful smile, "but you're also finally taking control, which is a very, *very* good thing."

"Do you think I can pull this off?" I ask, terrified of what she'll say.

She studies me as the clock ticks loudly beside her. "I do," she nods, "yes, I do."

I let out the breath I've been holding and look at the ceiling. "Thank you," I whisper.

When I leave her office, I get a text that surprises me.

Jade: Can we meet and talk?

I text her right back.

Sure.

Jade: Tomorrow morning? You name the place.

I have an inspector coming to the shop in the morning. I give her the address to meet me there, so I don't have to reschedule with him.

❦ ❦ ❦

JADE SHOWS UP right after the inspector does and looks around while I'm talking to him. When he gets started with his job, I go stand with her by the front window.

"So this is pretty great," she says.

"Yeah. It's a big deal for me. I hope I can pull it off."

"It's huge and you can totally pull it off," she says.

"Is Coen okay?" I cut to the real reason she's here.

"No, Maby, he's not, and he won't be without you."

She puts her hand on my arm as she says it and I try to subtly move away. Her words feel like an anchor pulling me to the bottom of the ocean.

"He'll be okay," I whisper.

"Why do you say that? You don't have the right to say that!" she cries.

I look at her, panicking. "He's young. He could have anyone in the entire world. I'm not good for him, Jade. I'm not!"

"How can you even think that? You're perfect together." Her eyes fill with tears and she turns away. "Sorry, I don't know why I'm so emotional. I just feel really strongly about this. I love my brother, and what I know of you I love too. Already. That's saying a lot! I haven't liked *any-one* he's dated!"

I look at her then, wanting to remind her of Jess with her arm looped around Jade's waist, but she's on a roll, so I just listen.

"And he's not that young. He's old enough to know who he wants and he wants you. He doesn't give up either, so I doubt it's over. I know it isn't for him, anyway. I don't know why you think you're not good for him, but from what I see when you're together … it's magical." She frowns at my snort. "Don't—it's true. My family talked about it the whole week after you left—the two of you have this … light around you…" She clears her throat. "He would *kill* me if he knew I was here. Please, just … I don't know what's going on. He mentioned Jess—she is wrong for him on *so* many levels…"

She puts her hands on my cheeks and my eyes get huge. No girl has ever done this to me and it's unsettling, but kind of nice.

"I never thought I would meet someone that I thought was worthy of my brother. I mean, think about it, he really is the sweetest person you'll ever meet. Not just a good looking guy … so much more. I thought you saw that and appreciated it." Her hands drop and she takes a deep breath. "I've said too much. *Please* don't tell him I came, but do think about what I've said."

She hugs me and is gone before I can say a word.

42

Best Served Crazy

SAUL COMES TO the shop every day for the next week, tearing down a wall and replacing the floor. He goes to buy paint and I strip the wallpaper in the back bathroom. It's been surprisingly easy to be around him. We've settled into our old comfortable camaraderie.

He hasn't asked about Coen and I haven't offered any information. He seems to just know that it didn't work out. I try not to read into that. Things happen. It doesn't necessarily mean I'm crazy. Even though I am, I still have a hard time knowing that everyone else thinks so.

I work hard and barely sleep. The exhaustion helps me not think about Coen so much. I start my period and weep for half of a day, sad that my condom mishap with Coen didn't result in a baby. Eventually I push that to the back of my mind for the insanity that it is, but it doesn't mean I don't think about how that would have tied him to me forever.

I *ache* ... for things I shouldn't. I'm not ready for a baby and don't know if I ever will be, but the thought of Coen as a father is enough to make me wish I could be. Really any thought I have of Coen at all is enough to make me wish I could crawl out of my skin and be *anyone* else. Someone happy and together and sane and ... *not* me.

I have a store name pow-wow with Paschal. It's the easiest part of this whole adventure. I tell him what I've been thinking and he yells his approval for five minutes straight.

"That's perfect!" He laughs. "Corny, and perfect. People can't help but love going to a shop called that."

My Happy Place.

Saul makes progress painting, while I go around the neighborhood shops and introduce myself. I make up my own business cards and fliers, just like I did with Paschal's salon, only people are even more inclined to chat when they find out it's my shop.

NEARLY TWO MONTHS later, deliveries come in and it starts feeling *real*. Saul stops by one day while I'm moving furniture around and helps me get it right. The day the chandeliers arrive, I cry as I'm opening each crate. I wish Janie could see the things I've found; she'd love it. In fact, I can hardly look at anything in the shop without thinking of Coen and his family. They made an imprint on me that doesn't seem to be fading.

The night before I'm supposed to open is a hot July

evening. I'm at the store doing my customary checks and re-checks. I've begun a bad habit of doing everything 13 times. My thought is that the number 13 is so unlucky that maybe if I intentionally do everything 13 times, it will un-do whatever bad luck the number carries with it.

It's ridiculous, I know, but hopefully this particular phase will pass. That's what I tell myself these days when I'm driving myself insane. *This will pass and then I'll start another equally annoying habit…*

I hear a little tap on the window and I look up to see Saul. He holds up a bottle of champagne and I go unlock the door and let him in.

"Hey!" I give him a hug. "How'd you know I was here?"

"I knew you'd still be here making sure everything is ready. It looks spectacular, Maby. You should go home and get some sleep. The week is gonna be nuts."

"You really think it looks spectacular?" I look around and agree that it does, but it's good to hear it from some-one else. I trust his opinion, too.

"You know I do." His voice is husky and sweet.

I smile at him. "You've helped *make* it, Saul. I can't thank you enough for all the work you've put into this place. Really—thank you."

"I'd do anything for you, Maby."

He hands me a glass of champagne and I feel a little awkward under his intense gaze. He hasn't done much to let me know whether he's still interested or not over the last couple of months, which I've *appreciated*, but the look in his eyes now is clear.

"Anna keeps trying to dig information out of me about this place," he says. "I told her yesterday that I'm not talking about it with her."

"How was her opening week?"

She opened a couple weeks ago and this is the first time I've allowed myself to ask Saul about it.

"It was less than stellar," he admits.

I can't help it—I grin. It grows until it reaches full cheese ball status.

He pats my cheek. "You're so cute. Rotten, but cute."

I take a sip of the champagne. "Mmm, this is good." I lift my glass and clink his. He moves closer to me and I back up. "I'm just gonna turn the lights off and head out."

"Walk you home?"

"Sure."

Saul is quiet the first few minutes on our walk. When he clears his throat, I'm almost certain I know what's coming. I open my mouth to stop him, but he's talking before I can.

"Look, Maby, the last couple of months have been great. It's felt like old times, and yet, I feel like we've gotten even closer."

I put my hand on his arm. "It really has been great. Listen, I'm happy with how things are now. Just like this…"

His mouth opens and closes. He tilts his head. "But, I'm ready to see where things can go with us … we already know we're good together. I'm ready for us to…"

"Saul, I know we could probably be happy together." I take a deep breath. "But I know now that what I feel for you … I don't want to be … *more*."

He stops walking. "I don't believe that. I *love* how we are together."

I nod. "I do too." He starts to say something, so I dive

258

in all the way. "But I'm in love with someone else."

He leans over and puts his hands on his knees, with his head down.

"Say something, Saul."

"You've relegated me to friend status." His voice sounds strangled.

"It's what we've always been, right? And I think it's probably best that it stays like that," I tell him.

He stands back up and stares at me. "I like you better when you're mental."

I whack him on the head.

"Ow!" he yelps.

"You deserved that! Now get me home so I can go to bed."

"Can we at least go back to being the kind of friends we were before? The kind that makes out and has occasional hot sex?" He trails behind me.

"Quit looking at my ass, Saul. And no. It's too confusing. We're finally working again and I don't want to wreck it."

He grumbles and starts walking beside me. "Does coffee guy know you're in love with him?"

"Yeah, pretty sure he does. But it doesn't matter. I have the shop to focus on. I'm healthier right now, but we both know it won't last…"

He scowls. "You should at least be with me until he comes back around."

I snort. "That's the stupidest thing I've ever heard."

"You're gonna regret it when I find someone else," he says as we get to my building.

"The fact that you're looking ahead to someone else lets me know you're gonna be just fine." I smile up at him

259

and kiss his chin. "Night, Saul. I love you. Don't waste any more time on me, okay?"

"You could never be a waste of time, Maby." He wraps his arms around me and kisses me on the mouth.

My eyes are blurry when we pull apart. "Night, Saul."

"Night. I'll stop by the shop to see how it's going tomorrow."

"I'd like that." I hold my hand up and then walk inside, feeling so grateful that I still have my friend.

43

Puff

I HAVE A new dress for each day of opening week. Doesn't it just sound delightful to say, *I'm going to My Happy Place*? I think so. I arrive three hours before opening and pace the floor. When it's finally time for me to unlock the door and flip around the open sign, I step outside to get fresh air before being inside all day. I nearly trip over something and look down. It's a square terrarium and sitting next to that is a to-go cup of coffee. I pick it up and look around everywhere to see if he's around, but he isn't. There's a card under the terrarium.

I've peeked in the window a few times.
Once a creeper, always a creeper, I guess.
Your Happy Place will be a huge success.
You deserve it. Congratulations, Maby.
~Coen

The tears drop on the card and I take it inside, placing the terrarium on the counter by the cash register. People from the surrounding businesses start dropping by to congratulate me, and then before I know it, actual customers are coming through. The terrarium gets a lot of comments as people make their purchases and I tell them about this great shop I know of about an hour outside of the City...

Saul and Paschal stop by at different times and are excited about the steady stream of people that come in while they're there. I have a permanent smile on my face all day and when I lock and unlock and lock and unlock and lock the door at closing time, I feel almost content. Or at least as content as I'll probably ever feel.

❦ ❦ ❦

SOMETIMES WHEN I miss him really bad, I go to the cafe across the street from La Colombe. I usually wear a hat or sunglasses and have a book or newspaper to cover me in a hurry if I need it. I've seen him 13 times. Once Jade was with him, but usually he's rushing into work or leaving for the day. The last time, the 13th time, he was with a girl. I haven't gone back.

❦ ❦ ❦

THE WEEKS FLOW from one to the next with little variation. Business is good—nothing fabulous, but somewhat better than I'd hoped. I try to keep a steady routine, so I can keep it together. Still on my medication, still going to therapy, and still alone. I get tempted to call Coen sometimes and have been asked out a couple times—by guys who could never live up to him—but now that I've seen how much it hurts to lose someone I love, I'm okay with being on my own. It's just better this way.

A couple of months after opening, a girl from a reality TV show I've never seen comes in the shop. She buys a ton and says she'll tell everyone she knows about the store. I thank her and throw a few extra business cards in her bags. A few days later, I get a phone call asking if a TV crew can come film her at My Happy Place.

I agree to it and after the show airs, the store blows up. I hire two employees, Melody and Kara, work long

263

hours, and seem to be handling it all fairly well. There are still issues. Sometimes Melody and Kara come in the shop and it's all completely redecorated, and then two days later, it's back the way it was before, but they just shake their heads and go about their work.

It's early October and I walk into the shop later than usual. I didn't sleep last night and woke up crying about my mom. It's been a while, but I feel the unsteady winds flapping around my brain and it's got me shaken up. I walk in the store and there he stands. He's saying something and Kara is laughing like it's the funniest thing she's ever heard.

He turns around and my heart stops.

"There she is," he says.

"Coen … *hi*!" I walk over to him and don't know whether to hug him or not.

He takes care of the issue for me and gives me a big hug.

"The place looks great. The terrarium looks right at home," he whispers into my ear.

I shiver and smile up at him. "Thank you. I love it. I should have texted or called to thank you…"

He shrugs it off.

"It's good to see you. What's … going on with you?" I stutter.

He motions outside. "Could we step outside for a minute?"

"Sure." I look at Kara, who nods encouragingly. We walk outside and lean against the glass in front.

"So, how are you?" he asks.

"I'm good. How about you?"

"This has gone on long enough, Maby." He stands up

straight and moves in front of me.

I stand up straight and shield my eyes from the sun. "What has?"

"This," he points back and forth between us, "*us* not talking. Don't you miss me? Don't you at least want to *see* me? Don't you miss your *coffee*?" His voice rises with each word.

I put my hand down and squint at him.

"I miss *you*," he continues. "And I've been too proud to come crawling back to you after the way things ended with us. But enough is enough, dammit. I can't keep doing this. I thought I'd give you time and you'd realize you couldn't live without me, but fuck it to shit, you're taking *forever*." He's red now. Both hands are on his hips and he's glaring at me.

My mouth is hanging open and he's waiting on me to say something. I can't.

"Maby!" he yells.

I jump.

That seems to soften him and he puts his hands on my shoulders. "Sorry. I shouldn't … no, I'm *not* sorry. You need to hear how miserable I've been! You can't just come into my life and twist things all up into a fucking rainbow and then leave me hanging out there, *alone*. That's just not right. Not when I *know* you were happy too."

My lip trembles and I start blinking really fast, trying not to cry.

"You told me you loved me," he whispers. He stares at me and when I don't say anything, his hands drop. He yanks on his hair and turns away from me.

"I can't believe you're not saying anything. What was this to you, Maby? A shitty experiment? What do you fucking expect from me?" His voice is hoarse and for a minute, I think he's going to cry. He doesn't. He revs up for more. He turns around and I notice his bloodshot eyes. They narrow in on me. "Are you sleeping with Saul? Did you go back to him? That's it, isn't it?"

"It's not like that," I stutter, but he doesn't seem to hear me. I'm stunned and afraid and so unbelievably sad.

He puts his head in his hands and then slides his hands back in his hair. "Well, this has not gone as I planned. Silly me, I thought we could have an adult conversation here."

He looks at me and the resignation in his eyes severs deep into my guts.

"Have a nice life, Maby."

He walks away and doesn't look back.

I'm not sure how long I stand outside. I go around the corner, so customers don't see me weeping in front of the shop. A guy is leaning against the side of the building and when he sees me crying, he offers me a cigarette. I take it. I had a brief stint with smoking in college and it's like riding a bike, you can always pick it right back up.

I replay the conversation, or rather all the things Coen said, over and over in my mind and feel so incredibly sorry for everything I've put him through. I feel terrible about it. But maybe if he thinks I'm with Saul, he can move forward with his life and get over me

44

Up and Down and Back Again

ANNA'S SOHO LOCATION doesn't make it, and I can't even feel happy about it shutting down. Business is going great for me and I can't even fully enjoy it. I feel lost and empty. About everything. And then to make matters worse, Saul won't leave me alone.

The changes are subtle and at first I think it's my imagination, but he starts hanging around all the time and getting a little more touchy feely—like he used to be. We were that way with each other for so long that it's easy to fall back into. And I'm gaping hole lonely.

I try to distance myself from him, but he just keeps coming back for more. Instead of confronting him, I shut down. I stop sleeping, my hair grows out and I start yanking it out. Paschal is horrified. He doesn't know that's what's happening—and it's not enough that *everyone* can tell—but he thinks I need to go to the doctor because I might have a disease that's making my hair fall out.

I miss appointments with Dr. Still. I don't want to disappoint her and this new hair thing is embarrassing. I'll have to see her soon to get a refill on my prescriptions. Haven't been running. Or doing yoga. But I'm smoking now, so at least I'm skinny.

I don't know what I'd do without Melody and Kara. They keep the store going. I still do the purchasing, but I can do most of that from my apartment.

I know I'm losing it, but I can't seem to stop it from happening this time.

❖ ❖ ❖

PASCHAL COMES OVER one night and begs me to let him chop my hair off again. I agree to it, hoping it will help me stop pulling.

"What is this?" He holds up the cigarettes that are sitting on my kitchen counter. His whole face is one big scowl.

I scowl right back at him. "What does it look like?"

"You're smoking? Ew. No wonder your apartment smells like a freaking ashtray. Come on, Maby. I'm worried about you. I wish you'd *call Coen*. You were so much happier with him."

I light a cigarette and blow in his face. You'd think I'd set his body on fire, the way he leaps around the house, waving his arms wildly. I start laughing and can't stop. And then I cry.

"I'm gonna be 29 next month," I wail. "And look at me. I'm more of a mess than ever."

He snuffs out my cigarette and pulls me to the couch,

laying my head on his shoulder carefully, so I don't mess up the hairdo he just gave me.

"You are a mess, but you've got lots of wonderful going on too. Your store! What about that?"

I shake my head. "It's only a matter of time before I mess that up too," I whisper.

He props me up and dries my face. "Who are you? You might be a mess, but you always pull yourself together. I don't know what to do with this poor-me person in front of me right now." He holds my chin in place. "I'm putting makeup on you and we're getting out tonight. You've been working too hard and alone in this smelly apartment too long. Go shave your legs."

"I don't want to go out. Let's just stay here." I sniffle and force myself to smile so he doesn't make me leave the house.

He pulls me off the couch. "GO."

I obey and when we leave my apartment, I don't even try to argue when he dumps my cigarettes down the garbage chute. I can always buy more.

We get in a taxi and go to a club not far from my place. I've only been there one other time. There's a line to get in and the music is pumping every time the door opens.

"Are you sure we should go here? I'm not in the mood and besides, this place is too cool for me," I mutter between my teeth.

"You look fabulous and we are gonna show off my skills." Paschal's eyes scale me like I'm his specimen. "I did damn good. Just smile."

I'm midway through an eye roll when he grips my arm.

"What?" I ask, looking at him.

269

He's looking in the door just before it closes and the bouncer stamps our hands.

"Nothing," he smiles at me, "come on. Let's do this."

The bass pulses through my veins the minute we get inside. I feel it in my chest and have to move in spite of myself. Paschal starts dancing and pulls me out on the floor. He grinds against me while eyeing the guy next to us. I'm pretty sure if I stepped aside, they would be making out within minutes. When I try to do just that, he pulls me back to him.

"Nuh-uh, you're not going anywhere," he yells, shimmying down my body. "*Dance!*"

So I do. And Paschal is so lost in it that I get lost in it too. Paschal's hands slide down the side of my body and he turns me this way and that, doing something between the salsa and dirty dancing. He turns me around, so my back is against his chest and holds my stomach into his waist, slowly circling his hips. I laugh and finally let go. It feels so good. I'm about to tell him how right he was to bring me here when his hands sweep over my boobs. My eyes get wide. He tilts me backwards and upright, flings me out and back to him, and then all of a sudden, he lets go.

"Getting drinks," he tosses over his shoulder.

I stare after him, confused and then someone pulls me back against their chest.

"Uh, hang on a minute," I say, trying to turn around. I'm swirled around and face to face with Coen.

He doesn't smile. The word *smolder* comes to mind when I see his eyes and I don't bother thinking anymore, I just move. Paschal's little show makes sense now.

I dance with complete recklessness, every ounce of

inhibition falling away. His intensity seeps into my pores and I can't help but be caught up in it. The friction between us only serves to make every touch more compelling. One song goes into the next without stopping and I don't want it to ever end.

He pulls me into him, our bodies sleek with sweat and desire, so that I feel every contour. I close my eyes and remember exactly how it felt to be with him. It's so real and with the way his leg is grinding between my legs, a shudder runs through me right there. I gasp and hang onto him as a wave goes through me. When I open my eyes, the tiniest of smiles plays around his lips. He knows. He sees right through me.

Embarrassed, I pull away and the moment is broken. He lets go, turns around, and walks into the crowd of people.

I stand on my tiptoes, trying to see him, but too many people are in the way. Paschal seems to appear from thin air.

"Where were you?" I give him a light push in the chest.

"That was the hottest thing I've ever seen in my entire life," he says. "You guys made a baby right here in front of everyone."

I give him a harder push this time.

"Where did he go? Do you see him now?"

"Oh, he left," he answers. "Wanna see if he's outside?"

I grab his hand and drag him outside. Coen is gone.

"Did you tell him we were here?" I ask.

Paschal shakes his head. "I learned my lesson after the last time. No. It was destiny."

I groan. "I need a cigarette."

"No, you don't. You need to call Coen right now and finish what you guys started in there."

Exposed Nerve

OF COURSE I don't call him.

I disintegrate. We get to the apartment and I'm frantic. The worse I feel, the more I talk myself out of ever calling Coen again. I'm right to stay away from him. Any time I think about how intense our chemistry is, I have 6 more thoughts to counteract it. I'm doing the right thing.

I start pacing and then move to washing fanatically.

Paschal finally sees the reality of my mess. He hangs in there pretty well, but I scare him when I won't stop. Normally I can wait until I'm alone, but seeing Coen shook me up too much. I cannot talk myself out of washing my hands and I don't care enough to want to.

"You've gotta stop, Maby. Please. Your hands are raw," he says, putting his hands on the back of my arms. "They're bleeding. *Maby!*"

I shake him off and keep going. He leaves the room

and I lose track of time. I just have to wash it all off. It won't be okay unless I can wash it away.

I hear talking in the other room and panic, but ignore it. Coen walks into the bathroom and pulls me back from the sink. I push him away and keep washing.

I'm fine. I'm fine. I'm fine. I'm fine. I'm fine. I'm fine," I say. It has to be 6 times or I won't be fine.

"You're going to be fine, but you need to stop washing your hands. Please, Maby. Stop. Paschal said you've been washing for an hour."

"No," I shake my head, "that's not true. We haven't even been home that long. I'm just gonna wash a few more times and then I'll stop." It's all coming out very fast.

He picks me up and carries me away from the sink and I lose it. I flail around and he doesn't let go. He carries me out of the apartment and holds me down in a cab. The cab driver says something, but I can't hear it.

I'm mortified. I feel like my insides are eating away at me. I can't breathe. I still can't stop the dark from closing in.

I pass out.

I come to with a bright light. I get excited until I realize I'm alive. A doctor has a small flashlight and is peering into my eyes. My hands are bandaged and sting. I'm in a small ER room and a nurse is standing next to the doctor. Dr. Kerry, his name tag says.

"I'm fine. I just panicked. I'm fine now," I tell him.

He ignores me and keeps looking me over, while the nurse has the blood pressure cuff on my arm. They go in and out a few times over the next couple of hours. I suppose they're checking to see if I'm stable or not. When they decide I might be, the doctor comes back in and asks

274

a series of questions.

"Have you had alcohol tonight?" he asks.

"No."

"Any medication?"

I tell him the medication I'm on. "For OCD," I add.

"Have you been taking it regularly?"

"I haven't taken it in a week … or maybe two or three…"

"Do you frequently pass out?"

"Not very often, sometimes."

"And do you know what caused it tonight?"

"I panicked when my friend stopped me from … washing my hands." I feel so stupid when I say it, but there it is.

When I tell him I haven't slept in a long time, he asks even more questions. He pauses and stares at me when I tell him how long I've actually gone without sleep. This seems to concern him as much as my raw hands and makes him think I'm suffering from severe depression. I snort.

"So you're aware that you're depressed?"

"Uh, yeah. Who *isn't* aware that I'm depressed is the question."

"Well, it sounds like a *serious* stretch of depression, nothing to take lightly," he says with a frown. "Oftentimes depression and OCD go hand in hand."

I glaze over a little. I want to act like a child and say, "No duh." But I don't.

"I want you to see your therapist on Monday. We can recommend another if you don't feel like she's helping. I'd also like you to see your family doctor. For now, I'll give you something to help you sleep, but I want you to promise you'll do these other things I've suggested."

"Okay, I will."

"It's possible that your medication needs to be changed. Sometimes it takes a while to get that right." He leans forward. "Now hear me when I say this: I know it can be very tempting to stop therapy, but try to fight that urge. Medication doesn't always work for everyone, but it sounds like it has been successful with you ... when you take it regularly. So stay on top of both of those things. Especially if you're not sleeping—think of that as a huge red glowing indicator that you need to get back on track."

He pats my arm and smiles kindly. His kindness makes my eyes water.

"I looked like an idiot in front of the guy I like." I sniff.

"We've all done that at some point or another," he says gently. He stands up. "Do whatever you have to do to get some sleep. You're overdue a good long rest."

"I can't afford a good long rest," I mumble, but not loud enough for him to hear me.

While I'm waiting for the nurse to come back in and give me discharge papers, Coen steps in the doorway. I can hardly look at him. He comes over and sits on the bed. I'm glad he doesn't hesitate to be near me. When we finally make eye contact, he looks exhausted and afraid. I start to cry. He pulls me into his arms and holds me tight.

"I'm sorry," I tell him.

"I should have never walked away from you," he says. "Not months ago. Not tonight. I've just been *so angry*. I haven't known what to do with all the anger. I'm the one who should be sorry."

I lean away from him. "This isn't your fault, Coen. This is *me*. I haven't wanted you to see this, but this is me and I don't know how to change it. I…"

The nurse walks in and has me sign the forms. She gives me a prescription and instructs me how to take it. When she walks out, Dr. Kerry walks back in.

He stops when he sees Coen and asks for another moment with me alone. Coen steps out and the doctor steps closer.

"I don't typically do what I'm about to do, but … I've struggled with OCD myself and so I feel sympathetic to what you're going through." He takes off his glasses and rubs his nose. "I want to recommend a holistic doctor to you. He has more leeway with certain things than I do here at the hospital." He steps even closer and talks softly. "I've found a certain … *herb* … to be more helpful than medication. For me, anyway." He looks at me pointedly and my eyes get wide.

He nods when he knows that I understand what he's saying.

"He's located in New Jersey, is the only catch. Things aren't legal here yet … that will hopefully change soon, but … for now, New Jersey is manageable. Yes?"

I'm too speechless to answer.

He taps his clipboard and walks to the door. "*Please* go through him and not elsewhere. He'll give you the correct dosage, tell you the best ways to ingest … he can be reached on Saturdays." He gives me a big smile and walks out.

Paschal and Coen both walk in once the doctor leaves. Paschal looks guilty.

"Please don't be mad at me for calling him," he whispers when he hugs me. "I didn't know what to do."

"It's okay. I'm sorry I flipped," I say sheepishly.

He waves his hand. "Don't apologize. You do keep things exciting," he teases, giving me a wobbly smile.

"Do you have someone who can watch the store for you this weekend?" Coen asks, stepping up beside Paschal.

"Melody works Saturdays and I'm not open as long on Sundays. Melody might be able to cover it too."

"Would you be willing to come home with me for a couple days?" he asks. "I'll make everyone leave you alone so you can just rest, but I really ... please? I'd love it if you did."

I look at him and am so torn. Everything in me is screaming to go with him, but my heart is wrestling with exposing myself even more. I know after the night I've had, I'm going to shut down. I can feel the exhaustion already and I haven't even taken the medicine yet.

"You don't have to decide anything about ... anything," he says. "Just please let me take care of you this weekend."

I nod and he lets out a huge exhale.

Spoon

WE STOP BY my place and get a bag together. I text Saul so he doesn't worry if he comes over during the weekend. I feel bad for telling him I'm going to Coen's via text, but it's the middle of the night.

He answers back right away.

Saul: You're back with coffee guy??? When were you gonna tell me?

I had a rough night. Paschal called him. I'm gonna stay at his parents' for a couple days.

I don't offer any more than that. I don't *know* any more than that.

Saul: You should have called *me*.

I don't answer. I already feel guilty enough about Saul. Even though I haven't slept with him again, we've been together so much, it felt inevitable. I've been avoiding it with everything, but ... too many more nights of loneliness and I can't say I wouldn't eventually cave.

I hate how weak I am.

Coen and I don't talk much on the drive out of town. He asks if I'm hot or cold. I have my blanket wrapped around me and tell him I'm fine.

"Please don't ever tell me you're fine again." He stares at me before turning back to the road. "Unless you really mean it..."

"Fair enough," I answer.

It's 3 in the morning when we pull into the long driveway. I breathe in deeply through my nose and lean my head back against the seat while we pass the nursery and the house and then pull up to the barn. I'm terrified with how good it feels to be back.

We go inside and I can't look at him. I think he's avoiding looking at me too. He carries my bag upstairs and then turns around to go back down.

"I'll be on the couch if you need me," he says. "Do you need anything? Oh, I'll grab water for you..."

"Thank you."

I put on my favorite black tank top and hot pink shorts. Coen comes back up with a water bottle and sets it on the table beside the bed.

"Night..." he says as he's going downstairs.

"Night..."

I take the medicine and lean back. Ahh, Coen's pillow. I pull his blankets up around my chin and close my eyes. The exhaustion is thick and suffocating, taking me under. I keep drifting off and jumping awake, feeling like I'm falling.

He's chasing me. The whites of his eyes flash in the dark and I nearly trip over my mom's body. I slip in the blood and think I'm gonna fall, but have to keep running. I choke. So tired. I can't let him catch me. He's on my heels and when he puts his hands on my back, I scream.

"Shhh, it's okay. You're dreaming. It's just a dream…"

I look around wildly and can barely make out Coen. He wraps his arms around me and we lay back down. My whole body is trembling and I try to catch my breath. I fall back to sleep with Coen holding me.

Several times I groggily come to, and Coen is spooned tight up against me. I keep falling back to sleep, so content with him next to me. When I wake up and he's gone, I sit up. I have no grasp on what time it could be. Everything feels foggy. I stand up and look out the window. It's dark.

I pick up my phone and look at the time. I've slept the whole day away. Unbelievable.

Before I even see what Coen is doing, I take a shower. I think about Coen's arms wrapped around me all night and know that it was him, more than the medicine, that helped me sleep better than I have in months. When I'm dressed, I venture downstairs and he's nowhere to be found. I get a water bottle out of the fridge and he comes in the door.

"Sleeping Beauty is awake!" He's holding two heaping plates of spaghetti. "I wasn't sure if you'd want to see everyone just yet, so I brought it over. Spaghetti night, you know."

"I'm so hungry." I smile shyly at him and take a plate. "Thank you."

We sit down at the bar side by side.

"How are you feeling?"

"I don't think I've slept so well in … well, I can't remember when."

"You needed it," he says softly.

I nod.

We focus on eating, but it's not uncomfortable, just quiet. I clean my plate and he smiles.

"I can go get more, if you want."

I hold up my hand. "Oh no. I'm good."

He takes our plates and rinses them off. When he turns around to look at me, he looks serious. I swallow.

"You were crying in your sleep. That's why I came in. Do you remember what you were dreaming about?"

I flush. "I dream about him a lot…"

"Who?"

"The man who … killed my mother. I-I keep dreaming that he's chasing me."

He steps closer and takes my hand. "Is that why you're not sleeping?"

"Yes."

"You're going to therapy?"

"I was. I haven't been lately."

"Why not?"

"I haven't been doing well. It's embarrassing to keep failing."

He doesn't say anything.

"Last night the doctor implied that I should try marijuana…"

Coen's eyes widen and I laugh.

"I know! I couldn't believe it! Wasn't expecting that. He told me where to get it in New Jersey."

"I can get some right here," he says.

"I didn't know you were into that!"

"I'm not really, but I will be if you need some…" He bumps his shoulder into mine. "Give me an hour and I'll have some for you—my buddy James will hook us up."

I shake my head and laugh. "I don't want to get anyone in trouble."

"My parents do it sometimes," Coen laughs.

"No way!"

"Maybe I'll just ask them to get it."

"Don't you dare!" I put my hand on his arm and snatch it back.

He looks at me for a long moment but doesn't say anything. His expression is suddenly guarded and I have no idea what he's thinking. It's unsettling. He's always been an open book with me.

Finally, he says, "I'll try James first. If I don't get through to him, I'll *subtly* ask my parents if they have any around. Okay?"

"I should have just gone to New Jersey," I moan.

"Oh quit. We are not driving to New Jersey for pot."

I chuckle and bite my thumbnail. He goes outside with his phone and I resist the urge to pace. He comes back in within five minutes.

"Wanna go for a little drive?"

"That was fast."

We get in the car and as we're pulling out, I ask him if his parents think I'm rude for not coming over.

"I told them you haven't been sleeping and were getting sick from the stress. They want you to stay as long as you want. I think they'd move me out if it meant you'd stay," he admits. "Shit, forget I said that."

"Why? It's sweet."

He shakes his head and doesn't answer.

"What, Coen?"

He looks over. "This is hard. I don't know how to not … I just—I don't want to scare you off, okay?" He runs his hand through his hair and I wish I could do the same thing. "Just … keep talking to me. Okay? Whatever happens with us, Maby—I don't want to completely lose you again. Even if it means we're friends who only see each other once in a while. I swear … that would be better than what it's been."

My eyes get blurry and I look out the window and nod. "Okay."

He pulls into a parking lot. "Ready to get high?"

He looks at me then and his dimple goes in so deep with his grin that I sigh.

47

And Then There Was Awkward

"HOW LONG HAS it been since you've done this?" he asks when we get back to his place.

"I've never done pot," I admit.

"*Never?*"

"No! I don't typically break the law!"

"Oh, this is gonna be fun."

We get out of the car and go inside. He hands me the bag. I sit down on the couch and try to get my nerve.

"My mom would kill me if she knew I was doing this," I tell him. "She was the one who could always get me out of the bad stretches. I haven't worked out how to cope without her."

He puts his arm around my waist. "You've been through so much. It's understandable that you're having a hard time without her."

I look at him and then open the bag, take a joint out,

and hand him one.

"No, it's okay. I'll just watch."

"What? You have to do it with me."

"It doesn't usually affect me. I don't wanna waste it…"

"Well, you're no fun."

"Already she's pressuring me," he laughs. "Okay, how about we share one to start with? That will probably be plenty anyway. Maybe I just haven't had the good stuff. James swears this is good. Look, he even included a lighter. What a nice drug dealer."

We both laugh and he lights one and hands it to me.

I take a puff, cough, and hold it out for him.

"Take another puff or two," he says.

So I do.

"You're kinda doing it like a pro, Maby. Sure you haven't done this before?"

"I have occasional dalliances with cigarettes. Paschal dumped my stash, though, so maybe I'll just have to do this instead."

"It's definitely healthier," he says, taking a pull. "Feel anything yet?"

It's a few more minutes before I feel anything. When I do, I try to keep from laughing, so I don't do the stereotypical weird laugh that goes along with weed. All of a sudden, I get a feeling throughout my body that takes me by surprise. I stretch my arms out and moan.

"Ohhhh!"

"What?" Coen laughs. "Are you—what's going on?"

"It's like my *skin* is having an orgasm!" I moan. "Mmmm…"

"Shut up. You're turning me on. Not allowed this

weekend." He laughs again. "I … yeah … I think I'm feel-ing this a little bit. Not the orgasm thing, but … a little bit *happy*."

I lean back on the couch and stare at Coen. He looks so cute I just want to eat him, I think, and then I die laugh-ing.

"What?" He laughs again. "I'm not high. I'm just laughing because you're laughing."

"Mmm-hmm," I sputter and start laughing again.

"Lightweight," he says.

We take our time finishing the joint and when I take the last drag, he raises his eyebrow. "Need more?"

I shake my head. "No, I'm feeling pretty good. Kinda … sleepy," I trail off.

"All those orgasms can do that to you," he says. "Come here, sleepyhead." He picks me up and carries me upstairs.

I unbutton my jeans and he helps me pull them off, and then puts the covers over me. He's getting ready to leave when I call out.

"Coen? Stay with me? Please?"

"Yeah, I'll come right back."

I've already dozed off when he lays down beside me. I nestle into his chest and go back to sleep.

I FEEL COEN moving and crack an eye open. My head is on his chest and my leg is wrapped around his. He lifts his head, looking at the clock.

"Wow," he says with a groggy voice. "Noon."

"No way," I say, closing my eyes.

"How do you feel?" he asks.

"Like I've had the best sleep ever."

He puts his hand in my hair and rubs my head. "Good."

"How about you?" I ask him.

"Same."

His heart suddenly thumps harder underneath my ear and he shifts his leg out from under mine. He mumbles something and moves the pillow under my head while he gets up.

"Close your eyes," he says, when he stands up.

I smile as I close them. He's hurrying off to the bathroom and the shower starts running. He's in there a long time. When he comes back out, I lean on both elbows and watch him.

"Would you like me to go get some food?" he asks. "There's food at the house or I could go pick up something in town…"

"I could come with you after my shower, if that's okay."

"Of course." He smiles at me.

"Your dimple is dangerous," I say quietly.

"Oh yeah?"

It dents in deeper as he tries to stop smiling.

I fall back on my pillow and he laughs. As soon as he leaves the room, I get out of bed and shower. I throw on a long sweater and leggings. He's not inside, so I step out and walk toward the house. And then I see him by the porch with Jess. It's too far to hear anything, but I can tell they're having words. She's getting in his face and he turns away from her. He looks mad.

I try to back up, but he sees me and starts walking toward me. Jess gives me a look and storms off toward the shop.

"Lover's quarrel?" I say with a side of snark. I feel bad immediately when his face drops.

"Don't start, Maby."

I lift an eyebrow.

"I mean it. Don't. I don't want Jess. Period." He rubs his face with one hand and looks at me out of the corner of his eye. "I can't help it if she wants *me*," he says and then presses his lips together.

My eyes get huge. "Coen Brady!"

He cringes. "I know. I know that was a jerk thing to say. It's just … I've tried everything. She's not getting the message!"

"Well, sex usually makes people think you want to be with them," I say snottily.

He charges at me and before I know it, I'm over his shoulder. He's smacking my butt and tickling me all at once.

"Put me down!" I yell between hysterics.

"Take it back!" he yells back.

"What I said was true!"

"I am not having sex with Jess!" he yells and then curses. "I am not having sex with Jess," he says quietly when he puts me down. He leans down in my face. "And you know it."

I put my hands on my hips. "I have no rights over who you do or do not have sex with."

He pushes both hands off my hips and says, "No, you don't."

I glare at him and he jumps toward me like he's going

to haul me over his shoulder again. I start laughing and double over.

The door slams off of the front porch and Scott comes out and leans over the railing.

"Hey, Maby," he waves, "good to see you. When you guys get done discussing the lack of sex with Jess, wanna come get some food?"

I go red and give Coen one more glare.

He avoids looking at me, poking me in the side instead. "Yeah, we'll be right in. Or we might go by the river and get something there … what do you think, Maby?" He finally turns to look at me.

"We'll be right in!" I tell Scott and hurry toward the house.

Coen is on my heels all the way up the stairs of the porch, tickling me and laughing when I jump. I stop abruptly and he runs into me. He wraps his arms around me and gives me a hug, leaning his head down on my shoulder.

"That's more like it," he says in my ear. "I'm not sleeping with anyone, Maby, just in case you wanted to know."

I let myself lean back into his hug for a moment and then we go inside.

48

Sacred Sacredness

JANIE AND SCOTT give me huge hugs when I come in the house. Janie puts two more place settings on the table.

"Jade's not home?" I ask.

"No, she had gigs all weekend," Janie says.

We sit down and pass dishes around. Janie looks at me and smiles.

"It is *so* good to see you," she says.

I feel Coen shift next to me and look at him. He's nervous.

"You too," I tell her with a smile.

"Are you feeling any better? Coen says you've been exhausted."

He clears his throat and she looks at him. "Mom…" He gives a subtle shake with his head.

"What? I'm just concerned. I'm not probing…"

There's a pregnant pause where the clank of the utensils against the dishes sounds extra loud. I get everything on my plate and then look around the table.

"It's okay," I jump in. "I don't know if Coen told you, but … he took me to the ER Friday night." I take a dinner roll, my hand shaking as I slather butter on it. I plunge in anyway. "The thing is … I've been diagnosed with severe depression on top of OCD, and I've wanted to avoid having Coen, or any of you for that matter, deal with my mess. I'm taking medication and going to therapy, but I still have really bad bouts with it. Friday was the first time Coen's ever really seen it. It's so humiliating and I just … feel like I'm better off on my own because of it." I look down at my plate and take a breath. "The doctor recommended that I do marijuana, which I've never tried, so Coen and I did some last night. I hope that's okay to say." Coen is staring at me with his mouth open. "And I've slept better the last two nights than I have since my mom died." I look around the table and they're hanging on my every word. "I really have enjoyed being here, every time I come, but I wouldn't blame any of you for never wanting to see me again! I'm the first to admit that I'm crazy." I pause and look at Coen. "Coen is really special to me—you all are—and I have wished I could just… protect him from … me."

Coen takes my hand and squeezes it.

I dig into my food then. "Mmm, this roast is delicious."

Scott sets down his glass. "Thank you for being so honest, Maby. I think I can speak for all of us when I say that we really love it when you visit. You're refreshing and … easy and pleasant to be around. As for crazy, that remains to be seen. I haven't experienced your crazy side yet," he laughs, "and whether you come back, that's up to you. You know, I've always wished I could protect my kids from certain things and particular people, but … they make up their own minds. He's an adult. What are you gonna do?" He holds his hands up. "I do know that Coen sure is happier when you're here. Speaking of crazy … he seemed to lose a little touch of sanity when you disappeared on him."

I start laughing then and we all lose it. The nervous energy is high and we all laugh a little longer than normal.

"Unbelievable," Coen says when we've stopped. "Nothing is sacred with you people."

The conversation finally shifts to other topics and everyone breathes easier.

Janie asks me all about the store and is excited with how well everything is going.

"Running a store is highly stressful," she says. "Don't be too hard on yourself. And make sure you have plenty of help."

I nod. "I've got two employees who have helped so much," I tell her.

"I heard a little mention of Jess earlier," Janie says with a smile. "I'm probably going to have to find someone else." She shakes her head. "Her obsession with Coen is getting in the way of her work."

I look at Coen and he shrugs.

"I tried to tell you," he mouths.

I roll my eyes and everyone laughs.

We sit around the table for a long time and then clean the kitchen. I look at the clock and am surprised to see it's almost time for dinner.

"You ready to head back pretty soon?" Coen asks.

"Not really, but … yeah." I say. I feel heavy just

thinking about going back to my apartment.

❧ ❧ ❧

ON THE RIDE home, I get quieter and quieter.

"You okay?" Coen asks. He puts his hand on my shoulders and keeps watching the road.

"Not ready to go back," I tell him.

"No? Why don't you come stay with me for a while?"

"Mmm, that probably wouldn't be a good idea," I say.

"Why not?"

I don't answer. I look out the window and try to think of a reason. I can't think of any, except the fact that I'm unpredictable and that should be enough.

"What's going on with you and Saul these days?"

I look at him and he glances over at me, trying to read my face.

"I told him I couldn't be with him, but ... we've been spending a lot of time together and ... I don't know. I'm trying to not let anything happen."

"What does that mean? Do you *want* something to happen?"

I scrape the chipped polish off my nail. "I'm lonely."

"You're lonely? What the hell do you mean, you're *lonely*?" He sounds mad.

"Don't get angry with me. Yes, I'm lonely."

"So you're gonna be with him because of that? Why can't you be with me?"

I huff. "I'm trying to be honest here, Coen. I don't want to hurt you or Saul. It's just ... with Saul, I feel like he won't..." I look at him and he's glaring at me.

"*What*?"

"I feel like he won't take it as hard if I hurt him."

He rears his head back and hits the steering wheel. Definitely mad.

"For someone so intelligent, sometimes you say really ignorant things, Maby! Sometimes I can't believe that I'm the younger one in this relationship."

"Hey! Don't be mean."

"I'm not trying to be mean. I'm trying to be honest here too," he snaps.

He pulls the car to the side of the road and looks at me. I stare straight ahead.

"Look at me!" he says.

I look at him and he takes my hand.

"Do you know why he wouldn't take it as hard?"

I don't say anything.

"You do, right? It's because he doesn't love you like I do." His thumb rubs my hand and he moves his hand up to cup my cheek. "I love you so much, Maby. I love you and I'm not gonna let you run from me anymore."

"I can't hurt you, Coen. I won't do it." I bite down on the inside of my cheek.

"I hurt every second I'm not with you." He leans over until his face is an inch from mine. "The longer we're apart, the emptier I feel inside. The times you let me in … it's like the sun finally coming out after a week of clouds. I *need* you, Maby. And I think you need me too."

I blink and look away. He holds my chin and turns me back to face him. We stare each other down and he eventually sighs and leans back into his seat. He looks over his shoulder and pulls the car back onto the highway.

"I'm not giving up on you," he says.

Rotten

WE'RE QUIET THE rest of the drive and when we get to my apartment, Coen parks. He hops out with me and gets my bag out of the car. I try to grab it from him, but he says he's got it and walks up with me.

When we get inside my place, he sets down the bag and says, "I'll wait for you while you get your things."

"What?" I crinkle my face at him.

"Why don't you pack for the week and anything else you need, we can just buy..." He smiles a huge smile and I look at him like he's loony.

"I'm not staying with you."

"Would you rather I stay here? I'll need new clothes and will be smelling up the place by tomorrow morning if I have to keep wearing this..."

"You're crazy."

"Yep, you're not the only one." He plops down on the

couch and puts his hands behind his head.

"I'm not going home with you," I repeat.

He starts pulling off his shirt. "I guess I'll just take this off, so I can wear it again tomorrow…" He stands up and starts unbuttoning his jeans.

"What are you *doing*?"

"So I can wear them tomorrow too…" he says, pulling them off.

His boxer briefs are white and I can see through them a little bit. I shake myself.

"Hey, I'm up here," he teases.

"You've lost your mind," I say.

"Yes, I have." He nods.

He moves toward me and I back up.

"Listen. You said it yourself—you're lonely. You weren't ready to come back. And I don't want to leave you alone right now. I'm lonely without you too. So, come home with me." He holds his hand up. "I know, you can give me a sample run. See how I hold up after a week's time."

"Sample run of what?" I ask.

"A live-in boyfriend," he says.

"Oh no. No, no, no. I might be immoral, but I'm not living with a boyfriend."

"You just want to move straight to marriage?" he asks, nodding his head. "It's a bit fast, but I'm okay with that. We can go to the justice of the peace tomorrow first thing, get this squared away."

"No!"

He pulls me to him and I have to fight to keep my eyes from rolling back in my head with how good he feels. I try to squirm away, but he holds me in place.

"I won't make you marry me tomorrow, but I am making you come with me tonight. And pretty soon you're gonna be begging me to never let you go. Mark my words." He kisses my cheek. "Now, go get your things and come home with me."

I don't know what I'm thinking, but I do what he says. Mostly because I don't trust myself around those underwear any longer, but also, because it feels really good to be wanted. And if I'm being completely honest with myself, because I find it an incredible turn on to be told what to do.

❦ ❦ ❦

JUST BECAUSE I go with him doesn't mean I make it easy on him. I gripe and complain the whole way to his apartment. But when we get inside his place and I see the terrariums he's working on, I forget to be miffed.

"This is amazing!" I pick up one that has tiny flowers inside. "It's so delicate!"

He stands behind me and puts his arms around my waist. "I thought you'd like that one," he says. "I actually made it with you in mind."

"Do you always say the perfect thing?" I move away from him and go to another one.

"I'm not trying to say the perfect thing," he says. "Part of what I love about you is the fact that I don't feel like I *have* to say the perfect thing…"

He walks into the kitchen. "Want a glass of wine? Beer?"

I shake my head. "I better not."

"What's with all this 'better not' and 'that's probably not a good idea' business?" He grabs a beer out of the refrigerator.

"I don't need to be seduced, thank you very much."

His head falls back as he laughs. He raises his beer to me and mischief twinkles out of his eyes. He looks like he's going to say something and stops. He laughs again.

"What?" I ask.

"The only seduction around here will be *you* seducing *me*," he says. "It's going to be fun."

He gives me another cocky grin and I toss one of his throw pillows at him, knocking him in the head. He doesn't seem fazed.

"I don't seduce arrogant little shits," I tell him.

He lifts an eyebrow and shrugs. "We'll see," he says softly.

He looks so damn delicious I have to turn away. His laugh fills the apartment.

"Are you hungry?"

"I'm just gonna go to bed," I tell him.

"Oh, okay. I'll be in there soon. Have to water everything."

"No need to come anytime soon," I tell him and he laughs again. "Quit being so pleased with yourself."

"I can't help it," he says. He walks over to me and kisses my shoulder. "Sleep well, Maby. I can't wait to spoon with you tonight."

❧ ❧ ❧

THE ONLY THING better than having sex with Coen is sleeping with him. I fall asleep before he comes to bed and immediately am being chased. It's that sleep where I feel like I'm awake, but not enough to be more than heavy lead. I gasp and try to get away, but am too thick to move. I cry out and feel myself being pulled up out of the water.

"Baby, it's okay. I'm here. I'm sorry. I should have come to bed with you," he whispers. "Shh. It's just a dream. Sleep, Maby. I've got you."

I lean back and let myself be lulled back to sleep. I love him. It scares me to death how much I love him.

HE HAS COFFEE ready for me before I get out of the shower. I thought he was perky every other time I was around him, but this morning I catch him singing in the kitchen.

"You're a morning person," I groan. "You're too much!"

"Morning, Maby! You look pretty." He kisses my cheek. He hands me a mug and doesn't say another word.

I finish getting ready and we figure out how we're going to get to work. He decides to drop me off and says he'll pick me up whenever I need. I agree to it to avoid another argument, and also, I really like sleeping with him.

Before we get to the store, he says, "How long have you been having these dreams, Maby?"

"Off and on since my mom died," I tell him.

We pull up to the shop and he puts his hand on my shoulder before I get out. "Maby?"

I look at him and he pushes his lips out, thinking.

"Never mind. Have a good day, okay?"

"You too." I hop out and wave once more before going inside.

I have one of the best days I've had in a long time.

❦ ❦ ❦

HE TEXTS ME about a half hour before the shop closes to see when I want to be picked up. I tell him to get me in an hour. Right before I lock the door, Saul walks up.

"Hey, you're back," he says.

"Yeah. How's it going?" I ask, letting him inside.

I start turning off lights and doing my nightly routine, while Saul leans against the counter, watching me.

"You're awfully perky," he says.

"I am?"

"*Yes*, you are. What's going on with coffee guy?"

"Well, he's on his way to pick me up pretty soon."

"*Really.*"

He stares at me, but I keep working. I start the vacuum and Saul takes it from me and vacuums while I count the money. When he shuts it off, there's a knock on the door and it's Coen. Great.

"Hi," he says to both of us.

We both say hello and then it's quiet.

"I'll call you later," Saul says to me and starts to walk out.

"She's at my place right now," Coen says. He looks at me and puts his fist over his mouth. "Sorry, Maby."

I narrow my eyes at him.

301

"Is that right?" Saul says. "Were you going to tell me, Maby?"

"Yes, of course. I didn't think it was necessary right this *minute*," I glare at both of them, "but yes, I would have told you. It's not what you think. Not that it matters, but it's not. He's helping me," I finish lamely.

"I see. Well, good luck with that," he says. "I wish you'd have called me Friday." He leans in and talks so only I can hear. "I know how you get, Maby. I know you don't want him to see that, so let me…"

"Too late, he already has," I tell him.

Saul stands up straight again and is about to walk out, when I touch his arm.

"I do want to talk soon. I don't want there to be any weirdness between us."

He nods and puts his hand in his pocket. "Well, you know where to find me. See ya, coffee guy."

"See ya," Coen echoes.

When he leaves I get in Coen's face. "That was low, Coen. You didn't need to say anything right then."

"I'm sorry. It just came out! I'm sorry! You're right, I shouldn't have said anything at all … but would you have if I hadn't?"

"It's not really your business whether I would have or not."

"Right. Okay." He backs up and looks down at the floor.

"Let's go eat. I'm starving," I say.

He perks up and I point at him. "Act like that again and I'm going home. And if you won't leave, you can live in your own stink for all I care!"

"Point taken," he says.

50

Twister

"I MADE AN appointment to see my therapist tomorrow afternoon," I tell Coen at dinner.

We're at a little Italian restaurant by work. I've been wanting to come for a while, but never wanted to come in by myself. It looked too romantic from the windows. Now that I'm inside, I'm really glad I didn't—it's very romantic. Or maybe it's just how good-looking Coen is. I can't take my eyes off of him, so I have to balance it out with therapist talk.

"Good. What time? Do you want me to pick you up?"

"No, it's okay. I can take the subway."

He studies my face. "Okay. Meet for dinner at home?"

I flush and am glad there's only candlelight in the restaurant. "I can meet you at your place, if you want, yes."

He grins. "Are you gonna tell her about the weed?"

he asks.

"I might ask her about it. Or I might just give that doctor in New Jersey a call … see how often I should do it."

"That's smart."

We have wine and before I know it, we're laughing, flirting, and I'm coming up with excuses to touch him every few minutes. His sleeves are pushed up, so I feel skin whenever I touch his arm, and it's enough to send a thrill through me every time. The next time I do it, his fingers grasp mine and he pulls my fingers to his lips.

"I love you, Maby Armstrong," he whispers.

I get flustered and he doesn't seem to mind. He smiles and puts my hand back where it was resting on his arm.

"For the life of me, I can't figure out why," I whisper back.

"You just haven't realized yet how great you are," he says. "Everyone else sees it."

WHEN WE GET back to the apartment, we end up in the bathroom at the same time, brushing our teeth.

"Look at us, living together," he says with his mouth full of toothpaste.

"We are *not* living together."

"Feels like it to me." He spits in the sink, wipes his mouth and whistles on his way out of the bathroom.

"Ew. No, we're not."

"Okay, Maby," he calls from the other room.

This time, when I get up to go to bed, he turns off the TV and follows me into the bedroom.

"Are you really gonna sleep in all that?" he asks, pointing at my pajamas.

I've put on the flannel ones, just because I'm starting not to trust myself.

"What's wrong with these?" I grumble.

"You're gonna be hot." He shrugs. "You look cute as hell, but I think you'd sleep better in your tank top and shorts."

"Oh really," I snap at him, "since when do you know what I'll sleep better in?"

"Since we started living together…"

I whack him over the head with my pillow.

"Oh, you don't want to do that," he says, picking up his pillow.

I run to the other side of the room, dodging it. He's across the bed in two seconds, picking me up and throwing me on the bed. His legs hold me down as I try to squirm out from under him. He raises his eyebrows.

"Are you gonna behave?" he asks.

"No," I yell.

He tickles me until I squeak.

"Now are you?"

"No?" I whisper, laughing hard.

He tickles me until I can't breathe.

"Now?"

I nod, unable to stop laughing.

He grabs one of his T-shirts out of the drawer, still holding me down. "How 'bout this?" he asks.

I roll my eyes. His eyes get wide and he comes at me like he's going to tickle me again.

"Yessss!" I yell.

"That's more like it." He laughs. "Here," he pulls off my top and I try to hurriedly cover my breasts, "let's just get this on ya."

"Coen!" I yelp.

He tries to keep a straight face. He pulls his shirt over my head. "There, much better."

He stands up and turns around. I have a feeling he's trying to be subtle about the sudden development in his pants, but it's too late, I already felt it. I can't look at him. Even though we've already been together, all of this skirting around each other makes it feel brand new. And magnified, if that's even possible.

He doesn't look at me but points behind him. "I won't look while you take off the pants."

"I'm not…"

"Just take them off, Maby. Be comfortable." He pulls his shirt over his head and leaves his pants on. "See? I'll leave mine on."

I take them off and get under the blankets quickly. He's right. I do sleep better.

I TELL DR. STILL everything and she's so understanding and sympathetic that I feel bad for doubting she'd be anything less. She reiterates that I need to continue with therapy and medication. We skirt around the marijuana topic and she's surprisingly onboard, even though she can't 'technically' say a lot about it. I can tell she thinks it will help, if I don't do too much at a time.

She listens intently about Coen and says I seem happier than she's ever seen me, which is strange, given that I was in the hospital not even a week ago.

"I'd like you to allow times for the anxiety. Let yourself fully worry about whatever you want for an hour each day. You can do two hour blocks to start with, if you need to, but we can work our way to one hour block. I want to see you next week and make sure you've worried an hour each day. I mean, *really* go there. Do that and we'll discuss what happens next week."

I know my uncertainty shows.

"Trust me," she says.

"Okay."

❖ ❖ ❖

THE NEXT DAY I choose to worry the hour before work. I get up before Coen does and pace his apartment. I make coffee and open one of his cabinets 27 times before I can let it go. When he comes into the kitchen, I've worried about my apartment, work, him, Saul, the feeling in my chest when I think of going home, the thought of staying here, and it's only been thirty minutes.

He stops and notices me pacing, but doesn't say anything. He pours a cup of coffee and watches me. I don't look at him. I take a shower and shave my legs 7 times before I can get out. My 'worry time' goes a little over an hour, but when I notice the time I take a deep breath and tell myself if I feel the need, I can do another hour when I get home from work.

I finally look at Coen right before we walk to his car.

"Hi," I say.

"Hi, love," he says.

And that's that.

❖ ❖ ❖

I CALL SAUL when I get to work and ask if he'll meet me for lunch.

"I have to help Anna with some things. Whatnot Alley is closing. She just told me last night," he says.

"You're kidding!" I'm shocked she's closing so soon. I can't say I'm surprised it's happening, but I did expect her to give it more of a run than this.

"Now that she's had the baby, I think she realizes she just can't do it. It was pretty obvious as soon as you left, but she kept trying for a while. Would tonight work to meet?"

I hesitate for a moment. "Sure."

We agree to meet at a cafe a few blocks over after I get off.

I text Coen to let him know I'll be home late and that I'm meeting Saul.

He's quiet for a long time and then eventually he sends back a cryptic: **K.**

Saul is in the cafe when I get there. I blow on my hands when I get inside.

"Chilly?" he asks.

"Yeah." I hug him and sit down. We order and it takes a while before the conversation starts flowing.

"So … you're living with him?" he asks.

"I've been staying there a few days," I say.

"So, living with him."

"Not exactly." What is it with everyone and 'living together'?

"Things going well?" He stops eating and looks at me.

"It's too soon to tell, but … I really like him, Saul. I've been fighting a relationship for so long, but … he makes me think it could work. Maybe."

Saul leans back in his seat and then looks down at his food.

"I can't believe it," he finally says. "I just … I thought it would be me. All this time. Even after you said you loved him before … I still thought it would be me."

"For a long time, I used to think so too," I tell him.

"I still wish it *was* me," he says quietly. He looks at me and his eyes crinkle in a soft smile.

I lean toward him. "You've been my best friend and you always will be," I tell him. "I'll always love you, Saul."

"It will be different though," he says, taking my hand. "And if he hurts you, I will scalp him."

"Gross! Don't get ahead of yourself. He doesn't even know yet how I'm thinking."

"How could he not? You're staying with him!" He scrunches his face at me.

"We're being friends. It's all very high brow," I tell him.

He looks up at the ceiling. "Maybe it *will* be good to have a 'normal' girlfriend."

I reach over and twist his nipple until he yelps.

51

Gardenia Wishes

COEN DOESN'T SAY much when I get to the apartment. I can't tell if he's upset or just quiet. He doesn't ask me about my dinner with Saul and I don't say anything about it.

We're getting ready for bed and I put on a tank top and shorts before we have a knock-down, drag-out as my grandma used to say. It doesn't even get a reaction out of him. He crawls in bed beside me and turns out the light. I turn on my side and he curls into my back like he has the other nights. I close my eyes and realize that I didn't feel the need for another worry hour. I thought for sure I would.

"Maby?" he whispers.

"What?"

"I'm glad you came home tonight, that's all."

My heart breaks a little that I hurt him. "You weren't

sure if I would?"

"No, I wasn't."

"I'm sorry."

"We can talk about it tomorrow. It's late. I just … had to say that."

"I wish I weren't so complicated, Coen."

"Don't say that. I don't wish you were any different than you are. I love everything about you."

"I spent time in a mental hospital. Not much to love there." Somehow it's easier to say it in the dark.

"You did? When?"

His fingers lightly tickle my arm and I shiver. He hugs me tighter to him.

"After my mom died."

"Were you close to Saul then?"

"Yeah, but I had a boyfriend. He was cheating on me with one of my friends and when I got out of the hospital, he broke up with me."

"Asshole," he mutters.

"I hated him, but I also didn't blame him for that. I was madder at him for cheating on me."

"How long were you in there?"

"A week. But I get terrified that I'll have to go back. I lost it in there."

"I'm surprised you don't hate me for taking you to the ER."

"I know it was the right thing to do. I don't blame you for that. It was scary, though."

"Can you tell when you're getting bad?"

"Most of the time."

He leans up on his elbow and runs his hand along my cheek. I look at him and in the moonlight, he looks like an angel. I think he might really be one sometimes.

"Maby, promise me something." He traces the outline of my face.

I nod.

"Promise me you'll tell me when you feel even a hint of it coming on strong. Let me try to help. I'll do whatever I can to keep you out of there."

A tear falls down my cheek. "Okay. I will."

"Thank you for telling me that." He lays back down and continues stroking my arm until I fall asleep.

I don't remember having any bad dreams when I wake up the next morning.

HE GETS UP early with me the next morning.

"I'm going for a run. Wanna come?" he asks.

I pause for a moment. "That sounds good…"

He smiles. "You don't sound very sure…"

"Well, Dr. Still told me to allow an hour—or two if I need it—to worry as hard as I can. She wants me to do it all week."

"That seems … the opposite of what I'd think they'd be telling you. Oh! So is *that* what you were doing yesterday?"

"Yeah."

"I didn't start worrying about it until you were out with Saul last night. Thought maybe I should have paid more attention to that."

"No. Unrelated. I needed to let Saul know where things stood with us."

He nods. "Us, me and you? Or us, you and him?"

"Us, me and him."

He keeps nodding. "Okay…"

"We're friends and we'll always be friends," I tell him.

He grins and his eyebrows crease in the middle. "Yeah, of course," he says, nonchalantly, but his grin gets bigger. "So, do you need to worry now or do you want to run now, worry later?"

"I'll run now, worry later."

"Good plan."

❧ ❧ ❧

I WORRY DURING my lunch hour. It actually works out great. I walk the neighborhood and get all the worrying out of the way, and the rest of the afternoon goes by so fast. When Coen picks me up from work, we stop by the store and get groceries.

"Look at us, living together," he says as we're checking out.

"We are not living together," I say, but I have to turn away so he doesn't see me smiling.

"Mmm-hmm."

I try to pay and he won't let me. He looks at the cashier and points at me.

"Finally got her to move in with me," he says proudly.

"Aw, congratulations," she says, smiling at us.

"Thanks." He smiles at her and then looks at me and laughs.

I roll my eyes and he swats me on the rear end when we walk outside.

♦ ♦ ♦

I WAKE UP one morning the next week and he comes in carrying a breakfast tray. There's a little dish with gardenias in it and a plate of pancakes and coffee.

"Happy Birthday, Maby Armstrong."

"How did you know?" I sit up and try to smooth down my hair.

He cringes. "Sorry ... I had to look at your driver's license when I took you to the hospital that night. And I kept thinking you'd bring up your birthday, but you never did. Had to take measures into my own hands..." he trails off.

I look down at the beautiful tray he's put together and up in his kind brown eyes. I lean my head back against the bed frame and the tears gush out.

He picks up the tray and moves it to the end of the bed. He pulls me to him and I hold onto him for dear life.

"I did the wrong thing," he whispers. "I should have realized this was a hard day for you."

"You couldn't have known it. You're so good to me. I don't deserve it." I sniffle against his shirt. "I just ... I miss my mom. She always made my birthday special." I wipe my face and lean back. "Don't feel bad, please."

He looks out the window. "I can't imagine, Maby. I'm so sorry." He puts his hand on my arm. "I sorta asked Kara to work for you today. I know that was out of line, but ... she was really glad to do something for you. I'm off work too. We could spend the day together … or you could have some time alone … whatever you need."

"No! I don't need to be alone. I know that."

"Well, good thing you're living with me, so you don't have to be…" he whispers.

I snort. "You never quit, do you?"

"Nope."

"It's Friday. Could we—what if we went to the barn?" I ask shyly.

His eyes light up. "Does that sound good? Sure. Let's do it."

We go by my apartment, so I can get a few sweaters and I end up getting enough clothes for the next month. I try to subtly pack it in a suitcase, so he doesn't realize what I'm doing, but when I have two suitcases full and am still piling clothes on top of those, he quirks an eyebrow.

"You realize we can move you in when we get back, right?"

I flick him and he jogs away from me, his laughter echoing in the stairwell.

Impromptu

WE STOP AND eat a leisurely lunch and he drives around the river for a while before we go to his house. He shows me where he went to school and points out some of his favorite places to hike. I'm starting to think he's avoiding going home, when he finally starts heading down the familiar street to his house. There are extra cars parked outside the house when we get there.

"It's like there's a party going on or something," Coen says, parking behind a Ford Fusion.

"Is that Jade's car?"

He smiles. "She is supposed to be here later."

We walk inside and a roomful of people yells, "Happy Birthday!"

"What? I didn't think—you didn't have *time* to plan a party! How in the world?" I laugh. "I saw all the cars and it still didn't register."

Paschal, Melissa, Melody, Jade, Scott and Janie. Katie and Todd are even there—I haven't seen them since the night I met them, but they're as sweet as ever.

I hug everyone and Coen subtly hands me wet wipes as he pulls me aside to meet the one guy I don't recognize. He seriously doesn't miss a thing.

"And this is James," Coen says, sweeping his arm out to introduce us. "Kara will be here a little later, after she closes up."

"I can't believe you did this!"

"Well, it was convenient that you wanted to come here today, since I'd already planned on bringing you. We just showed up a little earlier than they thought we would."

"We didn't get to decorate," Jade pouts, "but this way we get more time with you." She squeezes me.

Melissa and Melody come stand by us.

"It's so fun to have everyone all in one place."

"You gonna cut the peppers tonight?" I hear Todd teasing Coen.

My mouth drops and Coen's head whips around to see if I heard. He looks apologetic and I laugh.

Later, when we sit down to eat, he leans over and says, "Sorry 'bout the peppers. It was too crazy—I had to warn someone of the dangers."

"Mmm-hmm," I giggle, "I was just afraid your parents would hear Todd and somehow know. Nothing seems to get past them. Kinda like you with the wet wipes. How did you know I was desperate for them?"

"I'd have to be blind not to notice the dozen times you used them on our first date."

"I've thought *you* were really into them, at your place and everything—which was really hot."

"I can be, if that does something for you." Dimple. He kisses my hand and smiles. "Hey, I … should have invited Saul. It was selfish of me not to and … I'm sorry."

I shake my head and take a drink of the wine he sets in front of me. "Truthfully, it's probably easier right now that he's not. We're gonna be fine, but it might be an adjustment with him for a while. And … I'm kinda glad to see you're human for once, you selfish bastard."

He does a mock gasp and holds his hand up to his chest, wounded. Janie asks him to help her for a minute and he gets up. I look at Paschal, on the other side of me, and he mouths, *"I'm in love with this family."*

"I know. They're perfect, aren't they? I can't even believe…"

"You deserve to be right here in the big fat middle of this, Maby," he says in my ear.

I reach over and hug him.

Coen comes out carrying carrot cake with candles, singing. Janie stands next to him and when everyone stops singing, my eyes blur over.

"I'm gonna cry—what else is new?" I laugh.

"Make a wish," Janie says.

"If this is a dream, I don't want to wake up," I look at Coen when I say it and his eyes shine like sparklers in the candlelight.

"You're beautiful," he whispers. "Blow out your candles, love."

I blow them out and everyone cheers.

❤ ❤ ❤

THERE ARE A few presents, which I very awkwardly open. I'm loving having friends, but still not quite sure what to do with all the attention. I have a few places on my hands still from my manic washing/ER episode that I'm hoping are only conspicuous to me and not everyone else. There's one bad cut that keeps getting reopened and I'm keeping it covered with a Hello Kitty Band-Aid. I thank everyone a million times, until Jade starts sticking the bows on me every time I say it.

"I've saved your presents for later," Coen says, handing me the last bag.

Paschal jumps up. "Oh, that's for you to open later too," he says, through gritted teeth. He shakes his head, embarrassed. "I didn't mean for that to get ... mixed up with the rest." He sits down and turns pink.

"Well, that makes me want to know what's in it really bad," Coen says.

Paschal waves. "Later," he laughs.

We hang out for a few hours in the living room. Jade pulls out her guitar after a while and sings. She talks Coen into singing with her on one and I'm shocked by his voice.

"Tell him he needs to do a gig with me sometime, Maby!" she says.

"You really do," I tell him. "You sound so good together."

Later I try to hide a yawn and Coen notices.

"You sleepy, birthday girl?"

"I'm fine," I say.

He smiles at my choice of words.

"I really am."

And I mean it.

❦ ❦ ❦

"SO THERE ARE more presents?" I tease when we get back to the barn.

"Oh, here I thought you were too sleepy." He puts his arms around my waist.

"Nope."

"Okay, wait here." He scoots me to the couch and I sit down. He comes back with two packages and something behind his back. "Which do you want to open first?"

I point behind his back.

He pulls it out and it's a small Christmas star terrarium.

"Coen, it's beautiful," I say in awe as he holds it up in the light. "How did you get that in inside?"

"I had to work with toothpicks. It's my first one. Sample run," he kisses my cheek, "just like me."

I swallow and feel my insides mush together even more. *I love him. I love him. I love him.*

He sets the star on the counter and then sits down on the coffee table in front of me and hands me the packages.

"Just little somethings," he says.

"Thank you," I whisper.

"You've already thanked me plenty," he whispers back. "Open!"

The first package has a tiny glass pipe.

"Ha!" I choke. "Pretty! You crack me up."

"James brought over a new batch too, if you want to try it out." He motions over his shoulder.

"I'm feeling too happy right now. I don't even need it."

"Oh! Good to know." He smiles. "And this is just …
so you can stay out of my T-shirts," he rolls his eyes, "you
know how I hate that."

"Psh, yeah, okay," I say sarcastically. "You only
force me into them at least twice a week."

"Hey, it's the only way I can *kind of* see you naked,
so I'll take it," he says. "Shit. Why am I giving you this?"

"Give me that." I snatch the bag out of his hands. Inside is a pair of satiny pajamas. Long sleeves, full cover-
age. I frown.

"These are for a couple reasons. One is, it's getting
cold outside." He points out the door. "I think it might
snow early this year. Can't have you chilled."

"And the other reason?"

"You're *killing* me with the shorts and tank tops."

I snicker and he leans up and kisses my forehead.

"Happy Birthday, Maby. Why don't you go put those
on … right now?" He stands up and goes into the kitchen.

I pick up my presents and see the bag from Paschal as
I'm walking upstairs. I take my time putting things away. I
think I hear Coen in the downstairs bathroom, maybe even
in the shower. He's constantly showering. I go brush my
teeth and open the bag from Paschal while I'm still in the
bathroom.

The card inside says: *For your inner vixen. XO, Paschal. P.S. Don't make the poor guy wait any longer.*

It's a black nightie. I put it on and good lord have
mercy, vixen is a nice word for it.

I don't let myself think about what I'm about to do. I
just open the door and step out. Coen is at the dresser,
wearing pajama bottoms. His hair is wet and his chest is
bare, drops of water still scattered across his shoulders. I

watch the muscles in his back get taut as he stretches an arm up over his head and then the other, doing neck circles. He gives his hair a good shake and turns around.

"Wha—!" he yells when he sees me standing there.

I laugh and push my hair out of my eyes.

"You … startled me," he says. He moves closer, his eyes taking in every square inch of my body. When he reaches me, he takes my hand, turning me slowly around. "*Maby*," his voice sounds raspy, "the surprise is on me."

I reach out and touch his chest, catching the water drops on my finger and then I stick my finger in my mouth and lick the water off.

"*Damn*."

I step closer and he keeps staring at me, completely still.

"Coen?"

"Yeah?"

"This is me seducing you."

That seems to put fire in his blood. His mouth curves up and he pulls me against him. His head bends down until our lips barely touch and he says, "This is the best birthday of my life."

Everything Is Better With You

TO SAY THE night is euphoric would be an understatement. It's an awakening. Talk about a harmonic convergence—that has never felt more true than now. Something inside me has broken, *let go*, and I don't have anything holding me back as I love him.

I tell him that, over and over, as I cover his body with kisses. *I love you, Coen Brady.* As we make love again when the sun comes up. When he stirs in his sleep and reaches for me once more. I can't tell him enough.

He's shown me in so many ways, every day that we're together, what love is. And if he'll have me, I want to show him every day for as long as I live, how much I love him and how grateful I am for his love.

Before going back to the City Sunday night, we eat dinner with the family. I can tell that they're taking note of the way we are with each other today versus last night. I see a few secretive grins and winks between Scott and

323

Janie and I'm too happy to be embarrassed.

On the way home, I stare at him. He keeps looking over at me and smiling.

"Last night was ... I can't stop thinking about it." He shakes his head. "I think you might really love me. Can't believe it."

"I do," I say softly. I can't stop smiling either. I press my lips together and look out the window.

"What's on your mind, love?"

"Well ... I was thinking maybe we could get the rest of my things sometime soon? I'm hardly at my place—I could get out of there."

"Ahhh! You want to LIVE TOGETHER?" he yells, banging the steering wheel. His nose scrunches up and he leans forward, yelling, "Yes! Ahahaha!"

I laugh and clear my throat. "There was actually something else I wondered. Instead of me moving into your apartment—I mean, I could for a while, but—what if we moved into the barn together? You start your coffee shop. Melody and Kara want more hours. I could still do the purchasing and go in a day or two a week. Help out at your mom's shop if she wanted ... or help at the coffee shop."

His eyes get huge. He pretends his hand is shaking as he lifts it up to his mouth.

I nudge his arm. "You are a *nut*."

He pulls my hand up and kisses it. "I love this idea. What has you thinking this way? Not that I'm complaining at *all*, but you've been hesitant and now you seem all in."

"I'm still afraid. I don't know if I'll be able to keep it together. I don't even know for sure how long you'll *want* to have me around, once we're actually LIVING TO-

GETHER," I tuck my chin and raise my eyebrows with those words, "but every time I'm with you is wonderful. You've seen me at some of my worst times and keep sticking around. I've felt like I didn't deserve you. I admit, I *still* don't think I do, but I want to hang onto you as long as possible."

"Stop saying you don't deserve me. Nothing is further from the truth." His tone is no-nonsense. He looks away long enough to maneuver around traffic. "Hey, do you mind if we get your things tomorrow night? I want to take my girlfriend home and make love to her." He grins.

"Take me home."

❧ ❧ ❧

I TRY TO grab my suitcases from the trunk, but he hauls me over his shoulder.

"I'll come back for them. I've got something to take care of first," he says, kissing my side and running up the stairs.

We pass a couple coming downstairs and Coen greets them.

"Maby," he says, pointing at me. "Doug and Sarah."

I wave. "Hi."

I hear them chuckling as they move away.

He goes up another flight. When we get to his door, he fumbles with the keys and takes a deep breath.

"Put me down. I know I'm heavy."

"You are not. I am a little … winded from the stairs, though." He swats my bum. "You're light."

He finally gets the door open and kicks it closed behind him.

"Quit trying to sweet talk me, you've already got me." I reach down and pinch his butt.

He groans. "When will you start believing what I say?"

He gets to his room and lowers me gently on the bed. "I have imagined doing this to you a thousand times since the first night you stayed here," he says, looking down at me.

We start pulling all our clothes off. He tosses his on the floor and I lay mine carefully on the bed beside us.

"Does it bother you that I toss my clothes on the floor?"

"Not now. But it will if you leave them there." I grin.

"Noted."

"Stop talking now," I whisper and pull him down to kiss me.

THE NEXT DAY I make an appointment to get on the Pill. I'm able to get in around 4:00, so Kara covers the store while I go. On the subway, I text Coen to let him know that he doesn't need to pick me up.

Coen: Don't forget we have an apartment to pack up!

I'm trying to make sure we don't have a baby living with us too!

Coen: :) You know how I feel about that.

Who ARE you?

Coen: Your studly lovahhh

O.O

Coen: ^^^ Is that your pregnant boobs? I like!

It's googly eyeballs. Remember when I said there was only room for one weirdo? You've officially taken over the role.

Coen: It took you long enough to realize...

I'm almost there. Meet me at my apartment at 6?

Coen: I'll probably beat you there.

XO

Coen: Now, what's happening with those boobs?!

I laugh out loud and the lady next to me snickers too. I look over and she quickly looks away from my phone.

My appointment goes well, but I'm running a little behind by the time I get my prescription and walk the last few blocks home. I go ahead and stick a pill in and swallow it without water. I'm a little hungry and forgot to see what we were doing for dinner, so I text Coen to see if I should grab something or if he wants to get food delivered. He doesn't answer, so I keep walking. It's 6:13 when I walk up my 36 stairs.

I won't even miss this place, I think before reaching the last flight. Too many sad times. The thought of Coen's living, breathing, *alive* apartment with all his beloved plants and comfortable furniture makes me nearly giddy. I give a tap, tap to the door to warn Coen I'm coming in and unlock the door. It's still dark.

"Coen?" I call.

No answer. I check my phone. No texts from him. He must have gotten stuck at La C. I flip on the lights and get started on my bedroom. I grab garbage bags, since all my suitcases are already at his place. While I'm packing, I go ahead and do my sorting process, with a pile for Goodwill, a pile to throw, and a pile to keep. I lose track of time. Damn, it feels good to get organized. I've been feeling better, but it will always feel good to pare down even more.

I'm stunned when I pick up my phone and it says 7:26. I call him and it goes straight to voicemail. I don't leave a message, but call La Colombe and ask if Coen is still there.

"No, he left at 5," they answer.

I hang up and sit down. *I'm not gonna worry. Not gonna worry. Not gonna. Not...*

I clutch the phone and am trying to figure out who I could try next, when my phone rings. It's a number I don't recognize.

"Hello?"

"Maby? It's Scott. Coen's okay, but he's been in an accident. He's hurt pretty bad, but he's asking for you. At

328

Presbyterian." I hear someone talking in the background. "Maby? You there?"

I immediately shake so hard I can barely hold the phone. "I'll be right there," I choke out.

Please

I CANNOT LOSE Coen Brady.

I chew my nails the whole subway ride. When I get to the hospital, I stare at the door and try to still the shakes.

I hate hospitals. Everything fades into each other in shades of brown and grey and fluorescent. I stopped noticing the cheery scrubs the minute I had to go to the lowest level of the hospital and identify my mother's body two years ago.

I haven't said it out loud or told anyone, but it's raging in my head like a loud gong. Two years ago tomorrow. I had to come to *this* hospital and confirm that the lifeless, bloody body in the morgue was my mother. I promised myself I'd never come back here.

Two fucking years and here I am again.

Two years without her.

I've been happily packing my apartment to move in

with Coen, pushing down the fact that it's been two years, not realizing that the love of my life was in danger. I don't know why I thought my life could go uphill and stay there.

The sadness of this being the anniversary of my mom's death would have caught up with me. I've known this for at least a week and have been trying to work out a plan for not losing my mind over it. I thought I would schedule at least 3 blocks of 'worry hour' sometime when Coen wasn't looking, but the rest of the time, I'd hoped we'd have crazy amounts of sex to make up for all the time I'd spent pushing him away. In my head, it had seemed like a wonderful, promising distraction.

This does not fit into my plan.

I can't wrap my mind around an accident. And this, coming back here now, is like a sick joke.

47, 48, 49, 50 ... back to 48, 49, 50. You don't have time for this, Maby! I yell inside my head. I'm stuck in front of the hospital, counting steps.

This is the way things go in my world. They don't go this way in Coen's world, though, so this is a surprise. One that has twisted everything upside down.

He has to be okay. I can't afford to lose my mind right now. I have to get to him. *This is not about you, Maby,* I say out loud and it helps me get in the door.

I run into the ER and realize I'm not even sure where he is. Fuck. I didn't even ask. I wipe my face and move from foot to foot while I wait for the person in front of me to get done at the information desk. The minute they step aside I move forward.

"I'm here to see Coen Brady?"

"One moment," she says, tap, tap, tapping on her computer.

331

I want to run around and look over her shoulder and do some tap, tap, tapping myself.

"I believe he's having tests done. He hasn't been admitted into a regular room yet." She tells me how to get to the waiting room that's near the room he'll eventually be in. "You'll want to go up that elevator and down the hall to the right." She points over my shoulder and I nod. She tells me more turns and I walk away with her still saying something.

I get on the elevator and can't remember the first turn she said, much less the rest. I do know the floor and push the number. When I get off, Jade is in the hall, looking as lost as I feel.

"Maby!" She hugs me. "Have you seen him yet?"

"No. I just got here. Have you?" I mentally kick myself for wasting so much time outside.

"No. I think my parents are down here."

She puts her arm around my waist and we walk hurriedly down the hall. We pass a nurses' station and she points us in the right direction. Janie is in the corner of the room, blowing her nose. She stands up when she sees us.

"Hey." She sniffles. "A car ran a red light and barreled right into him. He's lucky to be alive, the police said. He's having lots of tests done. They think he's got some broken ribs, and maybe his pelvis? He looks awful, but they said most of that is just cosmetic. Dad's with him." She puts her arms around both of us and we huddle together, crying. "I think he'll be out in about an hour. He was so worried about you waiting for him, Maby."

We move to the chairs and I sit down, putting my head in my hands. The tears don't stop. We don't talk, but just sit there, nervously waiting.

I sit as long as I can and then start pacing. When I feel like I'm making them too nervous, I step out of the room and walk up and down the hall.

Finally, Janie comes out and says, "Scott just texted that he's in his room."

We walk to the room and I stand back to let Janie and Jade go in first, but Janie holds onto our arms and we all go in. Coen's eyes are closed, but when he hears us, he opens his eyes and gives a faint smile. He reaches his hand out and we all take turns hugging him.

"You okay?" he whispers to me.

"I want to know if *you* are okay," I whisper.

He closes his eyes. "I think I look worse than I am," he says. "I'm *fine*." He cracks open an eye and smiles at that. "They've got me drugged up."

One of my tears drops onto his hand.

"Please, don't worry, Maby. I think I've got some broken ribs. I'm just sore. You go home and try out that new pipe and try to relax." He grins. "I've already asked Dad to help move your stuff to my apartment."

"Stop worrying about me. I can't believe you're thinking about that right now."

"Are you kidding? I finally got you to agree to live with me." He chuckles and grimaces.

I lay my head on his chest and start my inner plea bargaining with God and my mother and grandmother and anyone else up there who might help.

He strokes my head. "Listen to me. I feel good," he says. "Look at me, Maby."

I lift my head up. "And you listen to me. I can't lose you, Coen."

"Lose me? I just got you. I'm not going anywhere. Do

333

you hear me?"

"I hear you," I tell him.

Coen lifts my head off of his chest. "You're *not* hearing me. You're going to the worst possible scenario. Car accidents happen. I made it out of a crunched up SUV and here I am talking to you." He closes his eyes for a second and blinks them open. "Life is pretty great. You need a little bit of this medicine they gave me." He chuckles and pulls my head closer, talking so only I can hear him. "I'm ticked that I'm not packing up your place tonight and wasting all this time in *here*. I had *plans* for tonight. They involved not sleeping nearly so much as I'm about to." The dimples come out. "I'm not going anywhere. It's been my mantra since I met you. In my head mostly, but…" His voice fades off.

We all watch him like a hawk until he falls asleep and then we still stand over him. The doctor comes in after what seems like forever. He wakes Coen up and checks his eyes and a few of the deeper cuts.

"A couple broken ribs, but everything else seems okay. I think you're really fortunate to be in such good shape, from what I hear about your vehicle."

Coen nods. "Yep. I had one of those 'life flashes before me' moments…"

My eyes get huge and the tears just won't stop. I go back and forth between tissues and wet wipes, my skin is raw and I know I'm all kinds of hot mess.

"These things tend to offer clarity," the doctor says while he writes on the chart. "You're too young for your life to flash before you, so be careful out there. I can call in your prescription to your pharmacy. You're going to be sore for a while with the ribs, but … like I said, you're young."

He smiles at Coen and gives me a slight wink. His face falls a little when he sees I'm bawling. I shake my head and give a wobbly smile. Janie puts her arm around my waist.

He turns back to Coen. "I'd like you to see your physician in the next couple of weeks, see how you're healing up. But, I don't see a reason to hold you down any longer."

"Thanks for everything," Coen says.

When the doctor leaves the room, there's a collective sigh around the room.

"See? I'm all set." He holds his side as he moves his feet off the bed. "Can we move your things later this week?" he asks.

I put my head in my hands and weep. Coen stands up and puts his arms around me. Everyone gathers around us and we have a huge group hug. I've never had one of those and I have to say, it is the best.

"I'm sorry I'm freaking out. I'm just so relieved. And I love all of you."

They laugh at me and Jade kisses my cheek before backing away.

"You're stuck with us," she says. "We love you too. Leave us again and you're dead meat."

Scott jumps in. "What she said! Hey, I'll go get the car. We can drive you guys home, get you settled in…"

"Thanks, Dad," Coen says.

They walk out, the air so much lighter than before. I grin up at him and try to find a place to squeeze. I settle for his nose. "That goes for you too, by the way. The leaving and you're dead meat part!"

"What? I never left!"

"Well, still!" I say, before blowing my nose. "And I'm not going anywhere either," I whisper in his ear.

I feel his ear lift slightly and know he's smiling.

"Take me home," he says.

And Then...

IT'S A HARD week, but we get through it. Coen barely makes a peep about the pain he's in, but I hover over him, making sure he doesn't have to even blink without my help. I don't have to slot in worry time, it's naturally working itself out in my stress about him. In spite of everything, we have one of the best weeks of our relationship. We talk non-stop. I cook for him, and he goes on about my cooking like I am making his whole world complete. We watch every movie we've ever wanted to see. At night, when I can tell he's the most uncomfortable, I read to him.

We don't leave the apartment, except for the day we go to my mom's gravesite. It's something I've never done and once I go, I know why. She isn't there. I feel less of her in the cemetery than anywhere else.

I feel her when Coen and I talk about her—we talk about her a *lot*. I wish with everything in me that they could have met each other. She would have been crazy about him. She would have imagined grandbabies with his dimples and our brown eyes. She would sparkle as much as I do over the way he loves me. And the way I love him.

337

I can just imagine her shaking her head and smiling that sideways smile, the one that looked like she had a secret. Those eyes that knew sadness and sorrow and pain, but that gave so much life and love and heart with every look. She would be ecstatic about this change in my life. I'm pretty sure she would have been fighting for him from the very beginning.

He would love her too. When I tell him the things she'd say, the way she took care of me—the way we took care of each other—he smiles and says, "You're so much like her, aren't you?" And I thank him for caring and for seeing a little bit of her in me. He takes out his favorite picture of us from the photo album and puts it in a frame in his living room.

Our living room. I'm still having a hard time thinking of it as ours. But I'm getting there, and maybe one day I'll actually believe it.

Maybe More Later...

Acknowledgments

I HAVE SO many great people in my life. I love each and every one of you. Thank you for loving me, encouraging me, and for helping me in this writing process. I'm always afraid I'll forget someone, so this makes me nervous, but I have to give some extra love to:

My husband and kids, for being so wonderful, keeping me sane, and for your unbelievable patience with my spacey eyes.

Tosha Khoury, for working tirelessly on my behalf. You are my other half. So happy we're doing this together.

My betas. I am so grateful for your input. Tosha Khoury, Calia Read, Courtney Shutes, Rebecca Espinoza, Melissa Brown, Melissa Sutherland, and Ken. You made this process so fun.

Marie Piquette and Maria Milano, who went above and beyond and were excellent consulting editors for this project. You both made this book better!

Blade. You're a rockstar.

I love you, Savita Naik. Thank you for all you do to encourage me. Your love has made such a difference in my life and I'll never be able to say it enough. Thanks for being gung-ho about whatever new venture I'm on (I'm on this one for good, you'll be pleased to know) and for your unending faith in me. <3

JT Formatting, you're wonderful and so good to me. Thanks for putting up with me long after a book is released!

Christine Brae, thank you for putting my chapter in your book! Means so much to me. Love you.

To the SH, you make this book world (and otherwise) better. XOXO

Thank you to my street team! I'm so grateful for you!

Special thanks to Jennifer Mirabelli, MJ Fryer, Soreonne Spellman, Dawnita Kiefer, Heather Halloran, Laura Wilson, Robin Segnitz, Kelly Moorhouse, Belen Rojas, Jodie Stipetich, Tiffany McQueen, Sara Johns, Amanda Ackerman, Jen Joanisse, Joanne Cowan, Kellie Donaldson, Randi Edwards, Joanne Christenson, Kim Rinaldi, Megan Lavo, Vanessa Proehl, Jennifer Luvstoread, Lyndsay Matteo, Jessica Hurtado, Judy Franks, and Erin Spencer for your extra support.

You made me cry, all of you who wrote a line or two about *Maybe Maby*. Thank you for taking the time to read it and do this for me. The things you had to say ... I'm overwhelmed. A.L. Jackson, Claire Contreras, Melissa Brown, Maggi Myers, M.J. Abraham, Leslie Fear, Andrea Randall, Rebecca Espinoza, Natasha is a Book Junkie, Jessica & Rachel from Bookslapped, Jodie from Lustful Literature Blog, Laura from Word, Randi from Always a Book Lover, Judging Books By Their Covers, Jennifer from Schmexy Girl Book Blog, Amanda from The Novel Tease, Maria Milano from K&M's Book Haven, Dawnita

Kiefer, Belen Rojas, and Robin Segnitz, thank you.

Thank you so much, Christine from Shh Mom's Reading, for all your hard work coordinating my book blitz and release. Such a huge help! Xo

A huge thank you to all the blogs who have reviewed my work and share things without me even knowing half of the time! I couldn't do this without you! Special thanks in particular to The Rock Stars of Romance, Natasha is a Book Junkie, The Sub Club Books, Aestas Book Blog, Reality Bites! Let's Get Lost!, Biblio Belles, Judging Books By Their Covers, Three Chicks and Their Books, Southern Belle Book Blog, True Story Book Blog, Bridger Bitches Book Blog, Scandalous Book Blog, Kindle Crack, Madison Says, Addicted2Heroines, Book Reader Chronicles, Still Seeking Allies, Book Babes Unite, The Little Black Book Blog, Nose Stuck in a Book Blog, Jessica's Book Review, Always a Book Lover, The Book Avenue, Hesperia Loves Books, Reading Books Like a Boss, Best-Sellers & BestStellars, Stick Girl Book Reviews, Swept Away By Romance, Up All Night Book Blog, Word, Lustful Literature, Love Between the Sheets, The Autumn Review, Have Book Will Read, A.K.A. The Book Harlots Review, Booze, Bookz, and Bad Boyz, Tissues and Tomes Book Blog, The Book Hookers, Lost in a Book Blog, Spoils of Wear, The Novel Tease, Angie & Jessica's Dream Reads, K&M's Book Haven, Sweet Spot Book Blog, Talk Books to Me, Sassy Divas Book Blog, Flirty & Dirty Book Blog and Smut Book Junkie for being part of *Maybe Maby's* book blitz festivities. And so many more blogs—I wish I could see each and every thing you write and thank you personally. Special thank you to Natasha for singing far and wide about *True Love Story* and already,

Maybe Maby. Thank you to Maryse for helping *True Love Story* grow, and Aestas for putting *In the Fields* on people's radar. I really appreciate it.

To every reader who has taken the time to review or write me a message about one of my books, thank you.

Courtney, Staci, Jill, Ashleigh, Nadine, Melissa, Jeanie, Halima, Geneva, Jonathan…just because I love you and always will. Come home, Ashley T! Any day we can be together is a good day for me.

Tarryn, my little black-winged kindred spirit. I love you so.

About the Author

FOR INFORMATION ABOUT WILLOW ASTER AND
HER BOOKS VISIT:

http://www.willowaster.com/

Facebook
https://www.facebook.com/willowasterauthor

Goodreads
http://www.goodreads.com/author/show/6863360.Willow_Aster

OTHER TITLES BY WILLOW ASTER

True ~~Love~~ Story

In the Fields